A novel by...

BEATRICE BRADSHAW

Love in the Scottish Christmas Village

Part 5 in the 'Escape to Scotland'-series

Join for a free story:
beatricebradshaw.com/sign-up

One night. No strings. That was the deal.

A castle party. A linen closet. One unforgettable hook-up.

Photographer Trish thought her fling with Jack, the rugged single dad, was a one-off.

Now back in the Scottish Highlands for a Christmas shoot, avoiding the sexy postie in Kilcranach is near impossible. And also not what Trish wants…

She's a nerdy perfectionist with big dreams. He's a commitment-phobic small-town postman. As December's festivities push them together, their one-night deal is quickly becoming the worst-kept secret in Scotland. And they're falling faster than the snowflakes.

But can they risk their hearts and friendships on a love that was never supposed to happen?

Content Note

This romance is written in British English ('realise' instead of 'realize'). There's also a bit of a Scottish accent here and there – the story is set in Scotland, after all.

Please be aware: this book contains several explicit and rather smutty open-door sex scenes and quite a bit of profanity. It also touches on topics that could trigger certain audiences, such as parental abandonment and neglect, alcoholism, grief, and divorce. It's best to be prepared.

Your mental health matters. <3

You are enough.

1

rish felt about as merry as a deflated PVC snowman. The Edinburgh Christmas Market sprawled across East Princes Street Gardens, a kaleidoscope that begged to be captured through her lens.

Not the glitz, but the grit.

Couples sipped from Santa-boot mugs, their faces glowing from the booze. Groups of friends squeezed into a giant plastic snow globe, trying to look happy for social media. A Santa Claus with a stained beard and bloodshot eyes was pocketing loose change from his donation bucket. In a corner, a hunched figure rifled through a bin, searching for food scraps amidst the gaudy excess of the market.

Above it all, Edinburgh Castle loomed majestically, floodlit against the inky sky like something out of a fairy tale. It was magical. It was tragic. All a question of perspective, of what you chose to focus on – as was everything in life.

From where Trish stood, it was also brutally boring.

Amidst the bustling crowd, she pulled her scarf tighter and glanced at her date. Sebastian was tall, handsome, and endlessly droning on about interest rates or golf handicaps – she'd lost track ages ago. His plummy English accent and the tinny sound of *Feliz Navidad* from the speakers grated on her nerves.

Why did I decide to go out with a banker again?

A group of tourists jostled past, nearly knocking over her mug of overpriced seasonal beverage. Sebastian didn't even notice. '...and that's when I realised the true potential of hedge fund arbitrage,' he explained, oblivious to her glazed expression. His voice was as bland as unseasoned porridge.

Right now, Trish would rather be stuck in a darkroom with faulty equipment than endure another moment of this financial lecture masquerading as a date.

December is the worst time for dates, everybody is so desperate not to be alone for Christmas.

She took a generous swig of her lukewarm 'original German Glühwein'. It did little to thaw her growing irritation.

'Tell me, Sebastian,' she interrupted, unable to contain herself any longer, 'do you ever talk about anything besides money and golf?'

He blinked, caught off guard. 'I suppose one can always discuss the Scottish weather.'

'Jesus Christ,' Trish muttered under her breath. He'd seemed a tad more interesting in the messages they'd exchanged on the app.

But then again, that bar was devastatingly low to begin with.

She despised dating apps. It was like diving in a pool of poo to search for a tiny gold coin that might or might not exist. Too many dick pics, too few brain flexes, zero heart.

Where's the magic in that?

Then again, she'd been half a bottle of wine deep when she'd swiped right, still stinging from that Instagram engagement post of Marc with his fiancée. She couldn't even be mad. A gorgeous Polish molecular biologist, of all things. Part of her wanted to congratulate him. The other part...

Trish and Marc's break up after ten years had been a long

time coming and more or less mutual. But his moving on so completely only five months later not.

It seemed…unjust.

Trish thought back to that rainy day eight weeks ago when she'd packed up her camera equipment and her tired heart and moved from London to Edinburgh. Scotland's capital was stunning, gothic spires and hidden histories underneath its streets, winding alleyways, and closes. The way the morning mist clung to Arthur's Seat, how the entire city seemed to glow golden in the late afternoon sun. When it wasn't raining. But even then, a photographer's dream. And Edinburgh was the perfect escape – close enough to visit Marla in the Highlands now and then, far enough to avoid bumping into Marc and his soon-to-be-wife – or worse Trish's parents – down in London.

'…the weather is hardly a problem if you're properly kitted out, and a good shoot is worth it. Just last month, Jonesy and I…'

Ugh.

Trish faded Sebastian out again. She looked around, searching for an exit route among the throngs of people pushing through the rows of wooden chalets. She blinked against the sting of her contact lenses, wondering what the hell had possessed her to swap out her glasses today, of all days. Vanity? Or maybe some misguided attempt to seem more put-together for this date? Whatever the reason, it was biting her in the eyes now, a constant scratchy reminder. Her breath formed little clouds in the frosty air as her gaze drifted over the sea of bobbing Santa hats and reindeer antlers, her eye habitually framing potential shots. A nearby stall hawked tacky tartan trinkets. Perhaps she could fake a sudden, over-whelming desire for a bagpipe-shaped bottle opener and ram it into her ears?

Just as she was contemplating the merits of accidentally dumping her drink on Sebastian's impeccably creased trousers and making a run for it, her phone buzzed. Trish nearly wept with relief.

'Pardon me,' she said, not sorry at all. 'I have to take this.'

Sebastian nodded magnanimously, as if granting a royal pardon. Trish resisted the urge to curtsy mockingly as she stepped away.

'Marla, you beautiful, brilliant lifesaver,' Trish breathed into the phone. 'I could kiss your stinky bum right now.'

Her best friend's warm laugh crackled through the line. 'That bad, huh?'

'Worse. I'm on a date with the human equivalent of a spreadsheet. He's handsome, think blonde Henry Cavill, but he's about as interesting as watching paint dry.'

'Ouch. Well, consider this your get-out-of-jail-free card then. I need a favour.'

Trish perked up. 'Name it. I'll do anything to escape Mister Hedge Fund.'

'How do you feel about a Highland adventure?' A hint of mischief tinged Marla's voice. 'I need some professional winter shots of Hazelbrae for the website. Plus, I'm putting on a small event for Christmas. A village fair of sorts. Could use your professional eye for both.'

Trish's heart leapt. Hazelbrae. The gorgeous eighteenth-century castle her best friend had inherited a year ago, nestled in the Scottish Highlands. It was the perfect excuse to flee Edinburgh and her disastrous, half-hearted, pathetic attempts at dating.

'Marl, you had me at "Highland adventure." When do you need me?'

'As soon as you can get your arse up here. Lots of snow's about to fall, which rarely ever happens, and it's going to be magical. Or so Niall says.'

Trish glanced back at Sebastian, who was now engrossed in his phone, probably checking stock prices. 'I'll start packing tonight and leave first thing tomorrow. Got to sort out my gear.'

'Brilliant! See you soon, love.'

Trish ended the call, a genuine smile on her cold cheeks. She turned back to her date, summoning her most neutral expression. 'Listen, Sebastian. I've just had an urgent work call for a last-minute photo shoot in the Highlands and I have to bugger off. Okay?'

Sebastian nodded and had the decency to pretend to look slightly crestfallen. 'Of course. Fine. Don't worry. Have a safe trip.'

If he cared at all, it was only by a hair more than she did.

Trish was already backing away. 'Thanks. I really must dash. Lots of packing to do, lenses to clean, that sort of thing.' She turned and fled before he could respond, weaving through the crowds with desperate determination.

As she reached Princes Street, Trish slowed her pace, exhaling a long breath. The relief of escape mingled with a familiar melancholy that seemed to creep in whenever she thought about the holidays.

Five months since Marc. Five months of trying to outrun disappointment and alienation and a severe identity crisis. At thirty-six, Trish should have figured things out by now.

Nada.

She'd hoped Edinburgh would be a fresh start, a chance to reinvent herself away from London's memories and her parents' crushing expectations. And maybe it would be. She'd only moved here in early October, determined to concentrate on her career and nothing else. To make it as a photographer. She'd always been behind the camera, but she'd only jumped into the profession two-and-a-half years ago, leaving her job in marketing behind. It was…tough.

Trish pulled her down coat tighter, her thoughts drifting to Hazelbrae and the promise of escape it offered. A week or two with Marla in Kilcranach was exactly what she needed. A chance to lose herself behind the lens, to capture some of that wild Scottish beauty in a way that made her soul sing.

And also…a chance to see that Scot again.

Trish's cheeks burned brighter than Rudolph's nose as the memory hit her. She hadn't intended to pounce on Jack MacGregor when she'd first clapped eyes on the man at Hazelbrae's opening party three months ago, but… There was something about him. That cocky grin, those smouldering eyes had peeled back layers she hadn't even known she was hiding. He'd made her feel as exposed as a raw negative. Jack had lit a fire in her Trish thought had long since died out.

Well, it hadn't.

Like…not at all.

Maybe it had been the champagne fizzing through her veins. Maybe it had been the ache of her recent breakup, the raw need to feel wanted again after years of emotional drought. Of rejection. Failure.

But yeah, that day in September, Trish had thrown caution to the wind faster than she'd ever ditched a bad composition. First, their eyes had locked across the room. Then they'd had a chat. Jack had listened, he'd been kind and fun. He'd made her laugh when she hadn't in ages, melting her like the first warmth after winter. Trish had never felt such an easy, instant connection to anyone. Jack had seen her as someone fun, rather than as the 'nerdy perfectionist', an 'unrealistic dreamer', or 'an obsessed camera weirdo'.

Marc's fucking words when he'd told her she'd had to move out.

Being with Jack had been about feeling something – anything – after years of numbness. Trish had needed to feel alive, to stop caring what everyone thought for once. And for those stolen moments, she had. She'd been so bloody tired of being careful, of overthinking everything. She'd wanted to be reckless, to let her body lead instead of her overactive brain.

He'd taken her hand, tangling his fingers with hers. 'Come with me.'

And like a moth drawn to a flame, she had.

Oh, boy.

For once, she hadn't been Trish the perfectionist, Trish the overachiever, Trish the optimistic people-pleaser, the dumped nerd. She'd just been…Trish, the happy slut in the closet. Fucking with a stranger. Purely, uninhibitedly, gloriously alive.

In that moment, pushed against the shelves, a dam had broken. All the pent-up frustration from decades of trying to be the perfect daughter, the ideal girlfriend, the professional, the aspiring artist – it had all come rushing out in a flood of desire.

Jack had hitched her leg around his waist, grinding against her core like he owned that joint. He'd coaxed sounds from her she hadn't even known she was capable of.

'Shh,' he'd murmured against her skin, his breath hot on her ear. 'Don't want the whole party hearing what a horny girl you are, do we?'

It had been like he was speaking directly to that hidden, hungry part of herself. The part that craved more than safe, predictable, beige lovemaking in a darkened bedroom. The part that wanted to lose control completely.

And, that was the astonishing part, she'd almost had.

Almost.

Trish had struggled with orgasms during penetrative sex all of her life. They'd been elusive, like trying to capture the perfect shot of a rare bird – always just out of reach. With Marc, and the few others before him, she'd felt unable to focus, unable to click.

But Jack… Jack had known exactly how to touch her, to zoom in on her pleasure centres.

Trish had come close. So damn close.

But then Marla had yanked the door open, and well, that had been the end of it.

Warmth tingled at her toes, spreading in a rush up her thighs, as she remembered how it had felt with him. More than a rebound, their instant connection had almost been scary. Too much too soon too fast.

So when he'd texted her once, she'd ghosted him. She'd had no idea what to say.

A pang of guilt niggled at Trish. Had she used him? Treated him like a human tripod to steady her world after that break-up? They'd both been clear about it being a fun fuck. She didn't owe him anything. She didn't *want* to owe anyone anything. After Marc, the last thing she needed had been to tumble headlong into feelings again.

But…

The other reason she'd never answered his text was the minor inconvenience that Jack was her best friend's boyfriend's friend.

On top of that, he was also a divorced dad of three kids and, according to Marla's occasional anecdotes, a bit of a mad shagger.

In other words: triple trouble.

With a triple-sized gift – and the skill to use it.

Her nipples hardened beneath her woollen jumper. Getting turned on in the middle of a busy Edinburgh street by the mere memory of a phenomenal cock was hardly appropriate, but neither was shagging your best friend's boyfriend's best friend in a linen closet.

After having come so close to coming, Trish was curious if she could repeat that experience with someone else. Anyone.

Hence the app.

And yet, all she found there were lame ducks like Sebastian, whom she'd never even go near any closet with. Trish shook her head forcefully, as if the physical motion could dislodge the thoughts of her first and only one-night-stand.

No. She couldn't afford to meddle with her best friend's found family in Kilcranach. Marla was finally happy, and Trish would rather throw her Leica SL2 off Arthur's Seat than ruin that for her with complicated, hormone-driven entanglements. She also couldn't afford to hang on to a guy, anyway. Not when her career was still on shaky ground. Hazelbrae was a welcome escape and a professional opportunity rolled into one. Work, her best friend, snow – no distractions.

As she hurried down the bustling street, Trish told herself that this trip was strictly about work, about helping Marla. Nothing more.

And absolutely no one else.

2

J ack MacGregor wondered if he'd lost control of his kitchen or his life.

The aroma of burnt toast hung in the air, mingling with the sweet scent of spilt orange juice and the faint, lingering odour of week-old tiny football socks. Jack surveyed the scene of utter carnage that was his kitchen with a weary sigh.

Beth was decorating a slice of toast with bits of cheddar, her seven-year-old creativity in full swing as she turned it into an inedible masterpiece. Jack Jr., two years older and ever the serious one, was glued to a YouTube video about the latest Nerf gun, oblivious to the sticky puddle of juice spreading across the table. And Phil, a whirlwind of energy for a lad of five, was using his spoons to pound out a chaotic rhythm on the battered cereal box.

Let him. Maybe he becomes a Topper Headon one day.

A vintage concert poster for The Clash hung crookedly above a sink full of dishes. Next to it, a novelty apron declaring 'Kiss the Cook' dangled from a nearby hook and collected dust. Jack's eyes flicked to the calendar on the fridge, its surface a jumble of scribbled appointments and custody schedules. Three years, and the sight of Melissa's swirly handwriting still made his stomach clench. One week on, one week off – a rhythm as familiar now as the beat of his favourite songs. And even that had been a battle.

He grabbed a magnet shaped like a guitar pick, pinning a new permission slip next to a photo of the kids at Craig's summer barbecue. Melissa's new bloke, real estate agent, all teeth and charm, with a big house in the next village. Close enough to co-parent, far enough to avoid running into them. And not on his daily route. Small blessings.

'Right, you lot,' Jack announced. 'Two minutes to finish up. Or Santa's bringing you sprouts instead of presents.'

As expected, the threat had zero effect. Jack Jr. had just begun a Nerf gun assault on the living room wall. Beth defiantly took a bite of her toast masterpiece, while Phil's drumming on the kitchen table intensified.

'Oi! Ya wee monsters!' Jack raised his voice, a hint of exasperation creeping in. 'I mean it!'

Jack Jr. fired one last foam dart, narrowly missing a framed family photo. 'Aye, Da, but I'm practising my aim!'

'And I'm not done with my toast,' Beth chimed in, her chin smeared with mayonnaise.

Phil's rhythmic pounding continued unabated.

Jack ran a hand through his short, dishevelled hair. 'That's it. No Christmas presents for the lot of you.'

This finally got their attention. Three pairs of wide eyes locked onto him.

'You wouldn't,' Jack Jr. gasped, lowering his Nerf gun.

'Try me, pal.' Jack crossed his arms and attempted his best stern dad face. It was a bluff, of course, but he needed some semblance of control over the morning chaos.

Beth's lower lip trembled. 'But Da, Santa wouldn't forget us, would he?'

Jack Jr. rolled his eyes. He was in on the truth, but he'd promised not to tell his siblings.

Jack's resolve softened at his daughter's worried expression. He crouched down beside her, wiping the smear of mayonnaise off her face. 'Course not, darlin'. Santa knows you're good weans…most of the time.' He winked, eliciting a giggle from Beth. 'But I'm the postie here, so I'm crucial to the gifts getting delivered – or not. Santa can't do it all on his own. Now, come on.' He stood up and clapped his hands. 'Let's move it!'

Jack adored his kids, but sometimes their boundless energy felt like a small army invading his world of comfortable chaos. And he had little authority over them. Occasionally it worked, though. Like now. The kitchen erupted into a flurry of activity as the three children scrambled to finish breakfast and gather their things. Jack navigated the obstacle course of backpacks and toys.

This was the busiest time of year for him. And Melissa had promised she'd take the menace this week on top of the next to help him. They should've been with her until the thirteenth. But then her plans had gone to pot, so now it was back to the usual ping-pong of schedules. The next handover was in two days, Friday after school. Jack rubbed his temples, a headache brewing.

A quick shag would take the edge off.

Yes, he was a part-time dad. But he wasn't *only* a dad. And he wasn't only Kilcranach's postie. He was also a man.

A free man.

A free man with an appetite.

After breaking free from the shackles of his miserable marriage three years ago, Jack had dived dick-first into a smorgasbord of sexual pleasures. Each romp felt like reclaiming a piece of his soul from the dusty corners of monogamy, filling the void left by years of routine and endless, caustic fights.

Because occasional hate-fucks are a lot less fun than they might sound. Even if they produce adorable mini-mes.

No strings, no expectations, just a parade of consenting partners. He'd become a regular on the dating app, swiping his way through Oban, Fort William, and even Inverness on his days off. The thrill of sneaking out of hotels and bedrooms, the satisfaction of leaving before the post-coital awkwardness set in. No messy feelings, no promises he couldn't keep with his fingers crossed behind his back. Nothing but unadulterated adult fun.

After years of not making Melissa happy, Jack had discovered that he had a bit of a talent when it came to getting women off, leaving a trail of trembling thighs in his wake. He was a proud craftsman.

But lately… something was off. He couldn't muster the energy to gorge on the usual buffet of potential shags. He hadn't so much as looked at the app since…

Hazelbrae's grand opening.

Which wasn't quite accurate. Or at least not the whole truth.

Not since Trish Whitmore.

Aye, he remembered her full name. And that wasn't the only thing he remembered.

Wild curls tickling his chest, breathless laughter when he'd fumbled with her bra in that cramped linen closet, those honey-browns wide and hazy in the dim light as she'd looked up at him over her shoulder, the sight of her bent over…

But not just that.

Something about her had knocked him off-kilter that day. Maybe it was how she'd rambled on about light and apertures with tipsy enthusiasm, or the way she'd snorted mid-laugh when he'd made a terrible pun. She'd been unguarded, passionate about her art, a bit awkward, wearing her insecurities and enthusiasms right there on her sleeve. No games, no performance. And for a guy who'd figured out young that letting people see the real you was an open invitation to getting stomped on – her raw authenticity had hit him so hard he'd been counting constellations for days.

He'd sent her a text after that night, a casual, 'That was fun.'

Massively underplaying it there, son.

No reply. Radio silence. The memory of her ghosting him stung like a thousand paper cuts on his ego, and he didn't know why.

Your loss, lass.

Still, ever since that party, his dick seemed to have developed a discerning palate. Jack tried to shake off thoughts of her. It had just been another hook-up. Casual was safer. Casual was easier. Casual was his thing.

Not to speak of the uncomfortable fact that this was his best friend's girlfriend's best friend. Far too close to home for his taste. Jack scrubbed his chin, still unsure why he'd thrown his 'keep it ootside the village' rule to the wind for her. Could get far too complicated far too fast. So, he'd probably dodged a bullet there.

Yet there was one detail that nagged at him worse than Melissa's constant antics: he hadn't made Trish come.

Him. The man who prided himself on his ability to reduce women to quivering, satisfied puddles. To give them what they yearned for. It was a splinter in his finger, irritating and impossible to ignore. He'd replay their encounter, searching for where he'd gone wrong. Yes, they'd been interrupted. But it shouldn't have taken that long in the first place. Had he been too pished? Perhaps that's why she'd disappeared, didn't give him the chance to…what? Make it right?

Dinnae be daft, man. It was a quickie, not a bloody fairy tale.

But it fucking bothered him. And made him want to pin her against the nearest wall and prove himself all over again.

Part of him wondered what might've happened if they hadn't been interrupted. Jack shook his head. That was a thing of the past. A fun slip-up with an imperfect ending. He had more relevant fish to fry right now – like getting three kids out the door without losing his sanity in the process.

'Right, ya wee terrors. Time to move your bums before I turn into the Grinch and cancel Christmas myself!'

He herded the kids towards the door, dodging stray Lego bricks like landmines. As he manoeuvred Phil's arms into his coat sleeves, Jack caught a glimpse of himself in the hallway mirror. He looked rough. Hair sticking up like he'd been electrocuted, five-day stubble, and bags under his eyes that could carry the weekly messages.

The joys of fatherhood.

Jack grabbed his postie jacket, patting the pockets to make sure he had his keys and phone. No time for a proper shave or even a comb through his disaster of a mop.

Could be worse, I could be working in an office. And still be married.

3

F *ucking Christmas.*

Jack's van rattled down the winding road to Hazel-brae House. The steering wheel juddered under his hands as he was drumming the Beatles' *Tomorrow Never Knows* with his fingers. It was a rare braw day, sunny with a sparkling layer of frost over every surface. But a mountain of parcels and envelopes teetered precariously on the passenger seat, threatening to avalanche with each pothole.

Jack groaned, remembering the upcoming Christmas ceilidh at the Blue Bonnet this Friday. Gwen had roped him and the others into playing with the band again. Not that he minded, really. Music made him forget about his life. But the thought of grinning through another performance in three days felt like one more thing pulling at him right now.

The castle's blonde sandstone walls gleamed through the neatly trimmed ivy. The mullion windows, big and old, stared down like they had stories to tell. The late eighteenth century country house looked impressive – clean, sturdy, and a bit intimidating – but not cold. It felt lived in, like someone cared about every stone and shutter. Hadn't always been the case, but Marla had turned the place around in less than a year.

16

Now it was a bed-and-breakfast and a retreat for healthcare workers.

This was the longest driveway of his route, but worth the trek for the view alone.

As Jack pulled into the sweeping approach of the old manor house, the unusual stillness struck him. No Marla pottering about, no guests milling around the entrance.

He hopped out, snatching up the towering stack of post and parcels that threatened to spill from his arms. The pile reached well above his eye line, he saw fuck all. Still, he'd walked this path hundreds of times. Little bend, three steps up to the front door, piece of cake.

The stack wobbled in his arms as he navigated the frosty gravel. 'Right, let's get this over—' The words died in his throat as his foot connected with something squishy *and* solid.

Time slowed. The parcels launched skyward in a graceful arc. His arms windmilled. The ground rushed up to meet him as letters rained down like confetti.

'FUCK!'

He crashed onto something that definitely wasn't gravel. Something warm and soft that went 'oof'.

'Ouch! What the—' A voice squeaked beneath him.

Jack blinked, finding himself on top of…

Trish.

Holy shit.

He froze, every nerve ending on high alert. Warmth radiated through her joggers, and her lush arse was nestled right against his groin like it was custom made to fit there. Jack's cock twitched at the sensation. And the memory.

'Bloody hell. Trying to give a man a heart attack?'

Trish squirmed beneath him, sending a hungry jolt through his system. '*You* ran *me* over?'

Jesus, he needed to move. It was hard to concentrate on untangling himself when the faint scent of her shampoo was messing with his head. And his dick.

'Right, sorry.' Jack scrambled to his feet, adjusting himself as discreetly as possible. He offered her a hand up, wincing as his scraped knee stung.

Damn shorts.

Her hands flew to her camera, cradled against her chest. 'Shit, please be okay…'

She ran her fingers over the camera's sleek body. The lens cap had popped off. A second later, she let out a sigh of relief. Only then did she yank out her earbuds and look at him, eyes widening behind her glasses. 'Oh, hi. Wow. That was…unexpected.'

She fidgeted with the camera, cheeks crimson. Was she flustered because of their collision, or…? His mind flashed to his unanswered text, then to his semi against her arse just moments ago. He shoved his hands in his pockets, trying to read her expression, but she wouldn't meet his eyes. The morning frost suddenly felt like a blessing against his burning skin.

She flicked bits of gravel from her joggers. 'Didn't hear you coming. When I'm behind the camera, I forget what's going on around me. Especially with the earbuds.'

Jack stood there, gawping like an idiot, self-consciousness creeping up his spine.

'What are you doing here?' they asked in unison.

He cleared his throat. 'You know, uh, delivering the mail. As you can tell by my uniform. And what brings you back to this neck of the woods?'

'Got in last night. Marla needs help with some promo shots.'

'Ah. And how long are you gonna be in town?'

'Just a week or so,' she said.

'I see.'

Her coat was open. Jack's gaze dropped to where her sweatshirt had ridden up, revealing a tempting strip of skin.

Very soft skin. He yanked his eyes away, focusing on the chaos of scattered mail. 'This is gonna take a while to sort.'

'Here, let me help.' Trish crouched down, gathering envelopes.

'No need, I've got it.'

'Nonsense! I was in your way.'

Their hands touched as they reached for the brown paper package. The touch set off tiny sparks, like striking flint against steel, and Jack yanked his hand back. Her fingers were still there, hovering over the parcel. The spot where they'd connected tingled. It was just a brush, so why did his pulse feel like it was trying to escape through his neck?

He gave a lopsided grin to cover the moment. 'Careful, Shutterbug. Don't want to go breaking any fragile post on my watch.'

Jack's focus stayed glued to the letters, desperate to ignore the way her presence seemed to wrap around him. The air between them buzzed with unsaid things, a pressure cooker waiting to pop. His knee started to throb, a little reminder of that humiliating dive he'd taken minutes ago. The sorting dragged on in a silence that wasn't just awkward. It was a brick wall so thick he could've drilled a shelf into it.

Speaking of drilling and shelves...

Stop it, man.

Her thoughts went in the same direction.

'Jack, I—' Trish started, then faltered. 'About that night, why I—'

'Nae bother. Water under the bridge.' He cut her off and plastered on his signature grin. Took some effort. 'No need to make it weird. We had fun once, why make it messy?'

But then there she was, the same woman who'd had him tongue-tied with a single smile the second he'd laid eyes on her. The woman whose realness and fire had thrown him completely off balance.

Trish's face fell slightly, but she nodded. 'Right. Of course. Yeah.'

'Marla in?'

'Yes, she's inside the house.' Trish picked a pine needle off her coat. 'I'm taking some winter shots for the website. You know, all that arty stuff.'

'So you've said.' Jack nodded, trying to keep his eyes from wandering to the sliver of stomach exposed as she moved.

'I have, haven't I? Maybe I have a concussion.'

Jack's throat tightened. Shite, she was cute – like a clumsy kitten trying to act cool and calm. She wasn't, though. Her glasses kept sliding down her nose. He had to fight the urge to reach out and push them back up for her.

'Well, I'd better get a move on… Can't keep the good people of Kilcranach waiting for their Christmas stuff.' He gestured vaguely. 'This week's been mad with the kids, and now I'm getting knocked over by stray photographers.'

'Yes, absolutely. Go on, Postman Pat,' Trish said, her eyes lingering a beat too long. 'Don't let me keep you.'

'See you around, Shutterbug.'

Jack's mind raced as he approached Hazelbrae's front door, his body on autopilot. How she'd felt pressed against him, all soft curves… and how they'd been interrupted before she'd finished. If only… No. Nope. He didn't do repeats, and he certainly didn't do complicated. He'd spent years carefully cultivating his circle. It worked. And Trish? She was Marla's best mate, which made her firmly off-limits.

Christ, just imagine the awkward dinners if things went tits up.

He'd seen enough relationships implode. His own marriage had been a masterclass in how to properly bollock things up.

Plus she lived in Edinburgh or London or wherever. Might as well be on Mars.

But as he knocked on the door, waiting for Marla to answer, his traitorous mind wandered. What if he just…

Bad idea. Fucked-up idea. The kind of idea that led to hurt feelings and disappointed friends. He'd already dipped his wick where he shouldn't have once. Doing it again would be asking for trouble.

But it still royally pissed him off that she hadn't…

Get over it, knobhead.

Marla's voice floated from inside, calling out that she'd be there in a minute. Jack shifted his weight, acutely aware of Trish's presence. He felt her gaze burning into his back. Or maybe that was just his overactive imagination.

The door swung open, revealing a frazzled-looking Marla. 'Jack! Thank God, I've been waiting for these.'

He handed over the stack of mail, forcing a grin. 'Aye, special delivery for the lady of the manor. Though I think your photographer might be more interested in capturing the local wildlife than the house.'

Marla rolled her eyes. 'She's been out there since dawn. I swear, nothing gets between that woman and her camera.'

Jack gave a dry laugh, the sound barely making it past his throat. 'Duty calls. Places to go, post to deliver, you know how it is. Busiest time of year. Ta!'

As he turned to leave, his gaze drifted to Trish. She was crouched by a flower bed, her camera pointed at something he couldn't see. As if she was actively trying to look busy. Jack hurried back to his van. He had a job to do and kids to pick up later. No time for complicated women with eyes that saw too much.

As he drove away, the rough leather of the wheel bit into his palms. Jack gripped tighter, willing his body to behave and his mind to focus on literally anything else.

Fucking Christmas indeed.

4

The joy in the room was real, but Trish felt like she was borrowing it.

The Blue Bonnet pulsed with Christmas cheer, a swirl of belly laughs, and clinking pints. Fiona's fiddle had Trish's foot tapping under the sticky table. The pub sprawled in a straight line, a series of rooms strung together like beads on a thread. Fairy lights blinked above like drunken fireflies. The place reeked of mulled wine, pine twigs, and what Trish could only categorise as unbridled Scottish fun. The air thrummed with it, thick enough to taste, like a shot of something bold that burned all the way down.

The ceilidh in the back room was in full swing. Gwen's parents, visiting from Alicante, whirled across the worn floorboards in the back room. Sylvia Bellbottom's silver hair glinted in the light as she twirled with William Collins. The solicitor had loosened his bow tie and was cutting a nimble figure as he led her through a complicated reel.

And Marla… Oh boy, Marla was *thriving*.

Her skin glowed, and she laughed so hard she could barely keep up with the dance steps. Trish couldn't remember

22

the last time she'd seen her friend this alive, this carefree. Like…ever.

Trish tried to share in the moment, to catch that same spark, but it danced just out of reach. A perfectly timed snapshot of what happiness should look like. Everyone seemed to belong. But her? A passing shadow on someone else's canvas.

Two seats next to her, Kilcranach's retired teacher Janet Bellbottom swayed on her barstool, wrapped in a leopard-print cardigan. Here in the front room, a trio of burly crofters in the corner belted out Robbie Williams' *Angels* for some reason, the lyrics slurring into each other, drinks splashing as their arms waved dramatically and they kept hugging each other.

Trish leaned against the bar, the smooth surface grounding her as she cradled a ginger beer, the bottle slick with condensation. Her camera sat in her room in Hazelbrae. Marla had forced her to leave it behind. 'You need to be *in* the picture tonight, not taking them.'

Inevitably, Trish's gaze latched onto Jack on the makeshift stage, the double bass cradled between his thighs like she wished she was. His fingers danced over the strings, creating a beat that curled around her like smoke.

Jack's roguish grin lit up the stage, his easy charm pulling her in. But she knew better. He'd made her feel things – things she wasn't ready for. Ghosting him had been the shortcut to protecting herself, even if it meant leaving things unfinished.

And awkward AF.

Trish's breath caught as she remembered their collision at Hazelbrae two days ago. Mortification crept up her spine like ivy. God, she'd been sprawled in the dirt on her stomach like she was making the world's worst snow angel.

Real dignified, Patricia Gabriela Lucia Velasco-Whitmore.

She still smelled the scent of his fresh aftershave mingling with frost-tinged air. That's how she'd known it was him within a fraction of a second. That – and the hard, undeniable ridge pressing into her ass. She'd recognised that anywhere.

But the worst part? How her body had melted into his touch like butter on a hot scone. For one breathless moment, she'd wanted nothing more than to grind up on him, to feel that sweet pressure…

Trish took a long sip of her drink, hoping the cool liquid would douse the flames rising within her.

And then she kept staring at him through the door like some kind of creep.

Every laugh Jack shared with Niall on stage – and there were plenty – made his eyes crinkle and shimmer. The lights danced across his hair. Hazel shot through with gold and single threads of silver, gleaming like burnished wood. He was a year younger than Niall, so in his late thirties? They'd never talked age. Hadn't mattered.

Trish bit her lip as she traced the strong line of his jaw. When Jack threw his head back, laughing deeply, the tendons in his neck flexed and he looked like a chiselled statue. She wanted to capture that shape in stark black and white. On analogue film, watch it slowly develop in a dark room. She still did that sometimes, even in this digital age.

As a photographer, Trish had long inhabited the background, a silent observer. She snared moments as they slipped through time, keeping them at arm's length. That was her safe space, her place in life. Always the photographer, never in the photo. Through the lens was how the world made sense to her. But tonight? Tonight, she felt the pull of the present. A taut thread, just waiting to snap.

Nope.

No matter how much she ached to chase the orgasm Jack had almost lured out of her, no matter how she yearned to feel that again, it was a lost cause. Like trying to develop a perfect print from a roll of film exposed to the harsh light of reality.

If she crossed that line with Jack and things fell apart, there would be hell to pay. Her friendship with Marla could take a hit. What if it got so awkward she couldn't face coming back up here? Worse, what if it caused tension between Marla and Niall, forcing them to pick sides? And Kilcranach was a tiny town. Word would spread, and while Trish could brush off gossip, it might stick to Marla, dragging Hazelbrae into the drama and damaging her business. After everything Marla had been through – the grief, the loss, the fight to rebuild her life – she deserved happiness and success. Not complications born of Trish's poor choices and raging hormones.

No. It wasn't worth the risk.

'Awright there, hen?' Gwen appeared in front of Trish, wiping the bar down with a grin that said, *'I've already figured you out'*. Her emerald green hair was festooned with tinsel, making her look like some punk-rock Christmas elf. 'You've been eyeing him like a steak pie since you sat down.'

Trish choked on her drink. 'Um… What? No. I'm just taking it all in.'

'Aye, and I'm the Queen of Sheba.' Gwen snorted. 'Keep telling yourself that.' She winked and sauntered off to serve another patron.

Gwen was right, of course. But Jack was Marla's boyfriend's friend, a divorced dad of three, a serial shagger. And Trish was reeling from her breakup. A lot less so now than three months ago, but still.

The band stopped for a break and Marla came prancing over to the bar in the front room, positively glowing.

'You look so happy, it's gross,' Trish said with a smile.

'I know. And I am. Kilcranach is the greatest thing that has ever happened to me. Other than you, of course. These weirdos… They are my family. Zero doubt.'

Trish flattened her tongue to the roof of her mouth and

made a clicking sound. 'And who knew you were such a light-footed dancer?'

'Jesus, no! More of a motivated moose, making up for skill with enthusiasm. But it works.' She leaned in to Trish's ear. 'Mr Collins gave me a few lessons. What about you? Are you enjoying your first ceilidh?'

Trish nodded. 'Absolutely! Great party.'

Just a little fib.

Just then, Niall appeared behind Marla and snaked his arms around her. 'Finally, I get to kiss my favourite groupie.'

They were so cute together, it was ridiculous.

And then *he* was there, too, and Trish's stomach did a little flip. Jack was close enough that his arm almost touched hers, and the warmth of him seeped into her skin, even though they weren't touching. It made her want to edge closer, just to see if that fire would spread.

Which she very much mustn't.

'Well, well, Shutterbug.' Jack turned his head to face her. 'Didn't expect to see you in the Bonnet.'

'Didn't expect or didn't dare to dream? It's a small town. Where else would I be on a Friday night while I'm here?'

She told herself to focus on the music, on Marla's laugh from across the room, on anything but the magnetic pull of his presence. Yes, they were bound to bump into each other. But did he have to be so…distractingly close?

'Fair point.' He signalled Gwen for a pint. 'Enjoying the show?'

'It's not completely terrible.' Trish fought a smile. 'For a bunch of amateurs.'

Jack clutched his chest in mock offence. 'You wound me. We're basically the Beatles of Kilcranach.'

'More like the Monkees.'

It was easy. Too easy to fall into the banter, the chemistry. She wasn't looking for this. Except every time he smiled at her, certain parts of her seemed to graciously forget all about the repercussions.

Jack cleared his throat. 'So, uh, how's the photography going?'

She blinked, snapping out of her daze. 'Oh, good. Yeah. Lots of…shots.' She focused her eyes on her drink. 'But sometimes I think I'm not cut out for this gig, you know? It feels like every job could be the one that proves I'm not good enough.' She didn't mean to say it – it just slipped out, like a secret she'd been keeping from even herself.

'I'm no expert, but I highly doubt that. Marla mentioned you've been up at the crack of dawn every day.'

'Early bird gets the picture of the worm.' Trish lifted one shoulder. 'The light's best then.'

Jack's eyes twinkled. 'I remember. You were eager to get the right angle that morning.'

Before she was able to respond, a cheer went up from the crowd.

'Awright, ya drunken numpties!' Gwen bellowed, climbing atop the bar. 'Time for a proper Christmas tradition! Kissy times!'

She waved a sprig of mistletoe over Niall and Marla's heads. Not that those two lovebirds would've needed an incentive. Without waiting a split second, Niall kissed his woman. His brooding features softened with an affection so raw it was almost indecent, his hand cupping Marla's cheek like it was the most precious porcelain.

Jesus, those two.

Next were the two Mrs Bellbottoms. 'Dearie, we've been married for ages. We don't need some overpriced greenery for a sneaky snog.'

Gwen wiggled the twig. 'It's tradition. Nae excuse!'

They laughed and then their lips met – not for a chaste smooch, but a proper, full-throttle kiss – before they pulled back. A rosy flush bloomed on Sylvia's cheeks, and Janet Bell-bottom beamed.

'Wooohooo!' Marla cheered.

Then Gwen moved over to…Trish and Jack.

Oh no. No, no, no.

Gwen brandished the sprig like a weapon, her chipped tooth gleaming. 'Pucker up, you lot!'

Trish's hands curled reflexively at her sides. 'Oh, we're not—'

But the crowd was already chanting, egged on by a tipsy Janet Bellbottom. 'Kiss! Kiss! Kiss!'

Jack quirked an eyebrow and grinned. 'What do you say, Shutterbug? For tradition's sake? You don't want to mess with the traditions here. Townsfolk tend to react badly to that.'

Trish's heart hammered against her ribs. 'Okay. If we must.'

'Oh, you definitely must,' Gwen said with a wink.

He leaned in, his lips drifting over hers in a chaste peck. And even that fleeting contact sent sparks skittering across Trish's skin like flaming glitter. She pulled back, breathless, acutely aware of the pub's eyes on them.

'There,' Jack said, his voice a touch husky. 'Tradition preserved. All is well.'

She nodded, not trusting herself to speak. His low chuckle made her toes curl in her boots. He was still too close, radiating heat like a furnace. A measured step back, a casual glance around the pub, as if the raucous crowd held more fascination than the man beside her.

Nothing. It had been nothing. A feather-light dusting of lips, barely a whisper of contact. But a flare of excitement pulsed in her belly and refused to be snuffed out. She swept her fingertips over her lips. Half startled, half hoping to trap the feel of his kiss, to stop it from slipping into memory.

Don't get involved, don't touch him again. Don't, don't, don't.

It was a silent mantra, but it wasn't working. Trish let out a shaky breath. She needed air. Another ginger beer. And possibly a deep-dive into an ice bucket.

29

5

Trish stormed off, craving peace – and crashed straight into trouble.

As she hurried towards the bathroom, she slammed into an immovable force that was Jack's solid frame. 'Ouch!'

His grip was strong enough to stop her mid-stumble, his body like a granite slab she couldn't get around. She didn't need to look up to know it was him. She knew from the way her pulse crashed against her ribs.

'Slow down there, Shutterbug.' His voice rolled out, purring in her bones. 'We wouldn't want you to fall...again.'

She took a step back, attempting to regain control. 'Thanks. I was just...um, heading to the loo.'

His eyes twinkled. 'Want me to tag along?'

A tingle traced the nape of her neck. 'I meant the actual bathroom, not an invitation for a quickie.'

He grinned. 'Aye, I figured as much. But I dare to dream, as you said.'

'You're impossible.' She rolled her eyes but couldn't prevent a smile.

'So I've been told.' Jack leaned casually against the wall,

half-blocking her path. 'But there's something I've been meaning to discuss with you.'

'And what might that be?'

He came closer, his gaze raking over her. 'Unfinished business.'

Trish's lungs forgot how to work for a second. 'I thought we agreed that was a one-time thing.'

'Aye, we did. And it was.' Jack's hand reached up to tuck a stray curl behind her ear. 'But here's the problem...' His fingers trailed down her neck, setting off a flurry of goose-bumps. 'I don't like leaving things unresolved.'

'What do you mean?'

'We were interrupted.'

Trish's mouth went dry. 'Yes, we were.'

'Shame.' Jack's eyes latched onto hers.

'Shame.'

His nose almost touched hers. She could count each of his eyelashes, thick and unfairly long for a bloke. Flecks of gold danced in his cinnamon brown irises, like whisky catching the light.

Trish's lips parted, her breath escaping in a shaky whoosh. Jack's mouth hovered so close she could taste his breath. The pub's chaos faded to white noise, leaving only the throb of her pulse in her ears.

He slid his hand to her cheek, his palm rough against her skin. His thumb skimmed along her jawline, like he was memorising every angle. It made her skin prickle.

'You know what I think? I think you wanted me to kiss you for real under the mistletoe. I *felt* it.'

'Doesn't matter. We shouldn't.'

'Naw, probably not.' But he made no move to let her go.

Her gaze flicked to his mouth, noting the slight upturn at the corner. She ran her tongue across her bottom lip. His eyes dropped to follow the movement. Time slowed as they stood there.

Her chin tilted up. The rational part of her brain screamed about boundaries and complications, urging her to jump off this runaway train before it careened out of control. But it was drowned out by the thundering of her pulse and the tangible charge crackling between them.

Trish's fingers pulsed with the urge to tangle in his hair, to map the strong lines of his shoulders. She craved more than just a snapshot of life. She wanted to plunge into the frame.

The world snapped down to slivers of sensation: the grit of his stubble, the heat rolling off his skin, the wicked curve of his lips that dared her to dive headfirst into disaster.

Fuck it.

With a soft gasp that was half surrender, half defiance, she closed the infinitesimal gap between them.

It was soft at first. Cautious. And she felt his smile – smug, like he'd won a bet. Jack's mouth played with hers, drawing her into a deeper kiss. His scruff rasped against her chin as he angled his head, the sound impossibly loud in the bubble they'd created. A tremor kicked low in her chest as his gentle touch became a firm grip, yanking her closer, like a bass note thrumming through them amid the distant sound of fiddles and laughter.

She sank into it, every nerve ending alight with the heady thrill of his closeness. Her lips moved with fervour, dragging over his with a hunger that surprised even her. Each roll of her tongue one more moment on the edge of a cliff, calling her to leap. Her fingers clutched at the fabric of his shirt.

This was real.

Jack groaned, and Trish's back hit the wall, the impact jolting through her as his body crashed against hers.

He tore his mouth from hers. 'Fuck. Trish. Don't kiss me like that.'

'What... Like what?' She was a lot less experienced than him, but...

'So fucking sweet.'

'Jack…' Her voice carried a warning.

'I know.' He trailed kisses down her throat. 'You're leaving soon. I'm a mess. Our friends… This is a bad idea.'

'The worst.' Her hands still fisted in his shirt, pulling him closer as her brain howled at her to push him away.

'A disaster.' His hand slid down her side, following the arc of her hip before settling on her inner thigh. 'But you want this.'

His hand moved between her legs.

'Do I? And…what makes you so sure?'

'Because I can see it in your eyes.' He pushed his palm against her mound. 'The same hunger that's been eating me alive since that day.'

'Yes… But this is crazy,' she whispered as her hips arched into his touch.

'Aye.'

She felt the warmth of his hand, the weight of his touch through the barrier of her clothing. Her head fell back against the wall, her eyes drifting shut. 'Fuck, Jack…'

'Aye, that would be fun.' He moved his fingers, applying just the right amount of pressure to make her gasp. 'I can feel how hot you are for me, even through these damn jeans.'

Trish's legs went soft at his words. Her hips moved of their own accord, grinding against his hand. The seam of her jeans rubbed against her sensitive nub with each movement of Jack's hand. 'I… We can't…'

'Now is neither the time nor the place. I know.' Jack's hand stilled, his forehead resting against Trish's. 'Fuck.' His breath was hot on her cheek. 'I shouldn't have…'

Her body roared in protest as he withdrew his hand from her.

They stared at each other, chests heaving.

Oh God. Did I seriously just kiss him?

'We can't… I mean, Marla and Niall…' She straightened her clothes, acutely aware of how close they still stood.

'I know.' Jack sighed and leaned against the opposite wall. 'It'd be a right shiteshow if they found out. I lost half of my friends with the divorce already.'

Trish nodded, a taut pull in her stomach. 'Yeah. There's that. And I'm leaving in a week. It's not like we could—'

'What, have a hot Highland fling?' Jack's mouth quirked into a half-smile. 'Fuck our brains out until you bugger off back to the big city?'

She pinned her lower lip between her teeth to suppress a grin. 'You're being silly. And I'm not someone who's good at casual.'

'Part of my charm.' His expression sobered. 'And I'm not good at anything *but* casual. I'm not cut out for a relationship. Three weans, a job that barely pays the bills, and more baggage than Heathrow at Christmas.'

Trish's heart clenched. 'You're making it hard to walk away, you know.'

'Listen,' he rubbed the back of his neck. 'You're worth more than some rushed moment in a closet or a bit of shagging. You deserve something real…and better than what I can offer. Talented, kind, pretty – the triple whammy.'

She snorted. 'Smooth talker.'

'I try.' Jack's eyes met hers, serious now. 'But I'm generally a fuck-up, plain and simple.'

Trish's chest ached at the self-loathing in his voice. 'Bullshit. That's not true. You're—'

'A part-time da who won't keep his dick in his pants?' Jack's laugh was bitter. 'I'm not the bloke you bring home to mummy and daddy.'

Like I'd ever bring anyone home to those tossers, not even myself if I could help it.

'I'm not exactly…well, anything at the moment, really. No career, no stable roots. It's all up in the air,' Trish said, forcing a lightness she didn't feel. 'Guess I'm not the type you'd bring home, either.'

'So, neither of us is looking to complicate life.' He blew out a breath. 'See? Wrong place, wrong time.'

'So… Friends without benefits?' She squeezed her eyes shut, forcing her jittery heartbeat to steady.

'Aye. Friends without benefits.'

The door banged open, shattering their bubble. Hamish McTavish, local sheep farmer and notorious lightweight, stumbled in. 'Oi!' he slurred, squinting at them. 'This isnae the gents!'

Jack stepped in front of Trish. 'Christ, Hamish. You're fuckin' steamin'.'

Hamish swayed, grabbing the doorframe for support. 'Aye, and I need a pish. So if ye dinnae mind…' He waggled his eyebrows at Trish. 'Unless the lassie wants tae hold it for me?'

'Let's get you sorted before I have to deck you for sexual harassment,' Jack said. 'Because steamin' or not, that's not okay.'

Trish grimaced. 'Yeah, I'll pass.'

'Suit yersel'.' Hamish lurched forward, nearly face-planting into Jack's chest.

Jack steadied him with a frown. 'Come on, ya bampot.'

As he steered Hamish towards the proper facilities, he glanced back at Trish. Their eyes locked, the sizzle from moments ago still simmering beneath the surface.

Trish mouthed, 'Later?' before she could stop herself.

Jack's answering grin had tiny fireworks flaring under her skin. He winked, then disappeared around the corner with his inebriated charge.

Trish sagged against the wall, her legs wobbly, and pressed her thighs together, all too aware of the ache between them.

Friends without benefits, like hell.

She fled back to the main room, lips still tingling with that forbidden warmth. The ceilidh after-party was blurry, a series of fleeting impressions rather than a cohesive whole. Only the memory of Jack's kiss remained vividly clear.

Trish spotted Marla by the bar, deep in conversation with Niall. Guilt gnawed at her gut. What kind of friend was she, snogging her best friend's neighbour and postie in a dark corner by the bogs? Her best friend's best friend. That was a no-go in any rule book. And for good reasons. Marla trusted her. Getting mixed up with Jack – for the second time – crossed an unspoken line.

But as Jack re-emerged, looking deliciously rumpled, Trish's traitorous body thrummed with want.

You're here for one more week. Then you go back to Edinburgh, and this…whatever it is…becomes a distant memory.

Nothing but a wildly hot wank fantasy.

6

Jack tugged at the scratchy white beard, wondering for the umpteenth time how he'd let Marla talk him into this Santa gig. One day after the annual Christmas ceilidh no less. He was socially hungover, tired, overworked, and underfucked.

The memory of last night's encounter with Trish struck him like an avalanche, crashing down before he had a chance to brace himself.

Not that he had thought of much else since then.

Christ, the way she'd melted against him. The curve of her hip under his palm, the little gasp she'd made when he'd pushed her against the wall. His mouth went bone-dry like he'd swallowed a handful of sand. It had been reckless, snogging her like that. Stupid. But the way she'd looked at him, all wide-eyed and wanting…

A heavy thud landed just below Jack's sternum, a reminder he wasn't as invincible as he thought. He couldn't shake the feeling that he'd cocked things up somehow.

He groaned inwardly.

At least the kids were still with Melissa now until next week. He missed them – the giggles, the endless questions, and the constant faffin' aboot that made the house feel alive – but it was nice to have some peace. Externally, at least.

Only now, he was the climbing frame for all the children of Kilcranach and the surrounding area.

But Jack simply couldn't say no to Marla. No one could – least of all Niall. That bloke had been a goner for her the second she'd set foot into this tiny town. Jack smiled beneath his fake beard. Niall deserved this happiness. About time that daft bugger found someone who properly appreciated him. He'd been through enough shite with losing his da, his wife, and all that. And seeing his pal so besotted with Marla was brilliant.

The smile faded, and Jack's thoughts turned inward, a familiar heaviness settling in his chest as he confronted the messy reality of his life – a divorced dad pushing forty.

This is it, mate. A washed-up postie's small-town life.

Gwen sidled up, dressed as a Christmas elf. She'd traded her usual black, pointy hat for a red Christmas one and even sported elf ears.

'Och, what's with the face?' She winked at him. 'Cheer up, Santa.'

'Piss off,' Jack grumbled, though there was no edge to it. This was Gwen, after all. Petite, sweet, and only in her mid-twenties, but never to be messed with in any way, shape, or form.

'I look like a twat.'

'Aye, but a jolly twat.' Gwen adjusted his fake belly. 'Now smile and spread some Christmas magic. The children are watching.'

Jack plastered on what he hoped was a convincing 'Ho ho ho' grin. Who was he kidding? He was a part-time dad who could barely keep his own life together, let alone play Santa to a bunch of starry-eyed, sticky-fingered children. What right did he have to promise them anything? Wasn't gonna happen anyway.

Jack surveyed the winter festival sprawling across the Hazelbrae gardens, feeling like he'd walked into a Hallmark movie. The makeshift grotto – a hodgepodge of hay bales, fairy lights, and what looked suspiciously like Niall's old armchair – stood out like a sore thumb against Hazelbrae's elegant facade. Festive lights twinkled in the bare branches of ancient oaks and evergreen pines. The cold air smelled of mulled wine, cake, and a whiff of desperation. Or maybe that was just him, trapped in this itchy Santa suit.

Marla and Mrs Bellbottom had gone all out for Hazelbrae's first Christmas Village Fair, transforming the grounds into a festive dream. Stalls, covered in red and white striped tarpaulin, stood on the frosty grass, hawking everything from knitted scarves to Mrs McTavish's infamous shortbread, guaranteed to chip a tooth.

There was a charm to it all, though. Familiar faces bustled about, cheeks ruddy from the cold and the generous servings of Niall's mulled cider. Mrs Bellbottom fussed over a group of children, handing out steaming cups of hot chocolate. For all her eccentricities, his former teacher had a heart of gold. And Marla flitted from stall to stall like a Christmas fairy on speed. He'd never admit it out loud, but their efforts to bring the community together warmed his shrivelled little heart.

It almost – almost – made up for the fact that he was sweating his baws off in this ridiculous red polyester suit.

'What in God's name have I got myself into?' He eyed the growing queue of overly excited children. A gaggle of mums huddled nearby, giggling and throwing not-so-subtle glances his way.

Naw, thanks, ladies. I'm awright.

He'd tried to keep his escapades strictly elsewhere. This was his community. He was their postie. God forbid, what would happen if… Whispers spreading like wildfire through Kilcranach's gossip mill. Hushed voices and knowing looks as he made his rounds. A cold weight settled deep in Jack's guts at the thought. It wasn't just about keeping his reputation intact. No, it ran deeper than that. The idea of mucking it up, of becoming the local pariah, pulled an icy scrape down his back.

He almost heard his aunt's disapproving tsk. 'Jack MacGregor, what would your mother think?'

Christ, as if he needed that ghost rattling around in his head. As if his maw had ever thought about anyone or anything but herself and the bevvy.

Don't go there. Not now.

Twenty-nine years ago. He pushed the thought away. Now, he was Jack the postie – good for a laugh, keeping everyone at arm's length while staying close enough to belong. The last thing he needed was trouble fucking up the life he'd built here. Better to keep his dick adventures to places where he was another face in the crowd. No expectations, no disappointed looks. No risk of running into anyone at the shops, or worse, delivering their mail the next day.

He couldn't afford gossip getting back to Melissa. The 50/50 custody truce was precarious enough as it was. Jack Jr. had been an accident, Beth an attempt to make the family feel whole, and Phil the last-ditch effort to save it. And when it had all fallen apart, Melissa hadn't seen him as fit to be a father. That's why she'd pushed for full custody.

Maybe she hadn't been completely wrong. Jack knew he'd made mistakes. But he loved his kids more than anything in the world, and the thought of losing time with them ripped his heart out, plain and simple. They'd eventually found a balance. For now.

'If it isn't Kilcranach's very own Saint Jack.'

That voice. It knocked something loose in him, like missing a step on the stairs. Trish sauntered up, camera in hand. She looked fucking edible in a chunky knit jumper, curls peeking out from beneath a reindeer headband.

'The opposite of a Saint.'

Trish adjusted her glasses, cheeks flushing. 'Oh, I know.'

He coughed. 'Come to capture my descent into seasonal madness?'

'Just documenting the event.' Her eyes darted everywhere but his face.

'I see. Because nothing says "Christmas spirit" like a sweaty postie in a dodgy beard.'

Trish lifted her camera, and his gaze zeroed in on the slight indent of her bottom lip, where she'd clearly been worrying it with her teeth.

Click.

'I couldn't resist. Um…because this is prime blackmail material.'

Jake's mouth hooked upward. 'This is some seriously *mail*icious intent.'

She snorted, then caught herself. 'A postie making mail jokes.'

'It's all about the delivery.'

Her laugh burst out, warm and genuine like a bass string plucked just right.

'It's not that bad. The beard, I mean. Really brings out your eyes.' Her gaze lingered on his mouth for a heartbeat too long before snapping back up.

'Och, I feel like a joke.'

'Jack, relax. You're a postie. You wear a silly red outfit every day.'

Some of the tension eased from his shoulders. Their banter felt easy, natural. Jack squashed the warmth blooming in his chest.

'Aye, but I don't normally have this much padding.' He patted his foam-stuffed belly for emphasis. 'Or quite so many weans clamouring for my attention. I'm used to three max.'

Trish lowered her camera. The lens cap dangled precariously, and he had to fight the impulse to secure it for her.

'Don't you have some artsy shots to take?' he deflected.

'Go on, capture the magic of mulled wine and kids hopped up on sugar.'

Trish laughed again, the sound doing funny things to his insides. 'Alright, alright.' She winked – *actually* winked – before disappearing into the crowd.

Jack watched her go, admiring the way she moved through the festival. She meandered from stall to stall, camera raised, slipping in and out of moments like a ghost. She was almost invisible to others.

Not to him, though.

Trish captured small moments most people would miss. The way Janet Bellbottom's eyes crinkled when she laughed. The look of joy on a toddler's face as they bit into a candied apple. Hamish McTavish sneaking a nip from his hip flask when he thought no one was looking.

That again.

Once or twice, Jack had considered saying something to Hamish, but it wasn't his place. Alcoholism was an epidemic in Scotland, and Jack had a bit of a genetic disposition for addiction. The last thing he wanted was to end up like his maw, especially with three kids. It was why he usually kept his intake under control and why last night's two beers had been one too many.

Jack kept watching Trish weave through the crowd. The way she held herself apart… Observing but never taking part, never joining in. It rubbed him the wrong way.

A pull on his synthetic beard snapped Jack back to reality as an eager wee face peered up at him. 'Santa!' A small voice piped up.

Right. Back to the job at hand.

'Ho, ho, ho, young Grant!'

The boy hesitated. 'Do I no ken you fae somewhere?'

. . .

The afternoon wore on in a blur of sticky fingers, biscuit crumbles, and increasingly outlandish Christmas wishes.

'A real, live unicorn? Aye, I'll see what I can do, pal.'

Jack was just about ready to call it quits when he spotted a tiny figure hovering at the edge of the grotto. Iona Moretti, a little girl of five, clutched a crumpled piece of paper in her tiny fist. Her eyes were wide with wonder and trepidation. Her parents stood a few yards away, having a chat with Eddie.

Iona took a hesitant step forward, then froze. He knew that look; it was the same one Beth got when she was overwhelmed. Before he could say anything, a flash caught his eye. Trish materialised next to the Moretti girl, kneeling down to her level.

'Hello there,' Trish said softly. 'What's your name?'

'Iona,' she whispered.

'That's a beautiful name. I bet Santa would love to hear it.' Trish's voice was warm and patient. 'Do you want to show him your list?'

Iona nodded, still uncertain.

'How about we go together?' Trish held out her hand. 'I'll be right there with you.'

Jack watched, transfixed, as Trish gently led Iona towards him. The tenderness in her eyes, the easy way she connected with the child... It stirred something in him, a buried ache. A fleeting image of stable family life, of lazy Sunday mornings and bedtime stories and lots of people around one big table.

He swatted the thought aside like an annoying fly.

Naw. Been there, done that. Didn't work. That ship has sailed. Stick to what you know, MacGregor.

But as Iona climbed onto his lap, her small hand still clutching Trish's, something warm and stubborn lodged itself in Jack's chest.

Trish smiled, her camera forgotten at her side. For a moment, their eyes met over Iona's head. Something passed between them. And whatever it was, it sent his pulse skipping.

'Freedom!' Jack declared, peeling off the itchy beard. He was undressing in Hazelbrae's salon, surrounded by the detritus of his Santa costume. 'Sweet fucking freedom.'

A soft snort from the doorway made him whirl around. Trish leaned against the frame, camera dangling from her neck, eyebrow arched in amusement. 'Tad dramatic, don't you think, Braveheart?'

He cleared his throat, suddenly aware he was half-naked. Luckily, only the top half.

'Easy for you to say. You weren't the one wrapped in synthetic fur all day.'

Trish's eyes dropped to his chest, then quickly away. 'Poor Santa baby,' she teased, but her voice held a hint of breathlessness.

'Careful there.' He aimed for casual and missed by a mile. 'Your perverted tendencies are showing.'

Trish rolled her eyes, but her cheeks darkened. 'Please. I'm a professional.'

'Aye, a professional perv.'

Her laugh eased the awkward tension. 'You wish, Postman Pat.' She raised her camera. 'Hold still. I want to capture this…transformation.'

Jack leaned against the wall, half-closing his eyes, and grinned. 'From jolly Saint Nick to village heartthrob in one easy step, eh?'

'More like village comic,' Trish muttered, but her smile was fond.

The camera clicked as she moved around him. Jack felt oddly exposed, and not just because of his state of undress. He didn't like being photographed, though it was less intrusive with her.

'So,' he said, desperate to fill the silence. 'Enjoying your Highland Christmas season?'

Trish lowered the camera. 'It's…different. Good different.'

'We do know how to throw a party.'

'That you do.' She paused. 'Jack, I—'

The salon door burst open, Marla's voice cutting through whatever Trish had been about to say. 'There you are! I need help with the— Oh!'

Jack grabbed his shirt, suddenly feeling like a teenager who got busted making out behind the bike sheds. 'Just, uh, de-Santafying.'

Marla's gaze flicked between them. 'I see. Well, when you're done, we could use a hand in the kitchen.' She retreated and left them in awkward silence.

'Right.' Trish rubbed at an invisible smudge on her camera body. 'I should go and help.'

'Aye, me too. Have to pick up the menace.' Along with the last bit of his dignity.

7

Trish nestled into the overstuffed armchair, her laptop balanced precariously on her knees. Her attic room at Hazelbrae was a cosy cocoon, all soft lamplight and antique charm. Frost silvered the windowpanes. The promised snow hadn't arrived yet, but it was in the air. Ice crystals shimmered like powdered glass scattered across a velvet cloth.

Trish sipped her tea, scrolling through the day's photos, each click a tiny time capsule of Kilcranach's Christmas magic. A group of kids, faces smeared with chocolate, beamed up at the camera. Mrs Bellbottom, resplendent in her leopard coat, doled out hot cocoa with military precision. Hamish McTavish stealing a swig from his flask immortalised in pixels.

Her lips quirked like she was sharing a secret with herself as she scrolled through the images, her fingers hovering over the trackpad. The warmth of community connection radiated from each shot, a contrast to the loneliness she'd felt in Edinburgh and London.

And then…Jack.

Trish's finger hovered over the trackpad. There he was,

Santa suit half-shed, jacket open, chest bare, that cocky grin lighting up his face, eyes half-lidded in an expression that was pure sin.

Her gaze traced the defined planes of Jack's torso. She zoomed in, drinking in every detail. A small scar near his ribs. She wondered what the story was. The faint trail of hair disappearing beneath his waistband. His abs were a master-piece of light and shadow, each ridge and valley begging to be captured in black and white. Or touched. Definitely touched.

No way this came just from lugging parcels. He had to be working out. A tremor teased at Trish's lips before she caught it with a quick bite. The thought of Jack, sweaty and focused, lifting weights in some dimly lit gym sent a torrid rush through her. The play of muscles beneath his skin, the way they'd bunch and release with each movement. His grunts of exertion primal and raw.

Oh, boy.

Trish shifted in her seat. She was getting turned on again just by imagining him. This was insanity. Her mind wandered back to their reckless moment in the pub – the pressure of his body, the rough scrape of his unshaven jaw, his deep voice tickling her ear. And then his words, laced with self-debase-ment: 'I'm a fuck-up, plain and simple'.

It hit too close to home, like a film negative of her own self-doubt. God knew she'd beaten herself up with similar thoughts often enough. Or heard that sort of thing from others.

Too awkward, too intense, too much. And yet, somehow, never enough.

Trish had been so used to the idea that if she wasn't what people wanted, she'd rather be invisible.

Marc's voice floated through her memory: 'You're impos-sible to please, Trish. Chasing something that doesn't exist. Do you have to analyse everything to death?'.

Said the analyst… Men in finance. The fucking worst.

Trish shook her head, banishing the thought. Jack saw her differently. When he looked at her, she felt like a photograph developed in a darkroom, slowly emerging from the shadows. Not a project to be fixed or a disappointment to be managed, but becoming herself.

Her heart raced with a new kind of thrill. The kind that made her want to be seen, to be bold. To stop overthinking. The shots of today were good. No, they were brilliant. Raw and real and alive.

Trish selected the photo of Jack and a few others from the fair and typed out a caption: 'Kilcranach's unconventional Santa brings the heat (and the mail). #HighlandChristmas #SexySanta'. The way the light sculpted Jack's body… It was art, wasn't it? And if posting those pictures happened to show certain people that she wasn't just the safe, predictable Trish anymore… Well, that was just a bonus.

Here's to making people see and feel seen.

Without blinking, she hit 'share'.

A knock interrupted her thoughts. 'Come in!' Trish closed her laptop.

Marla breezed into the room, brandishing a bottle of wine and two glasses. 'Thought you could use a nightcap after all that festive chaos.'

Trish's eyebrows shot up. 'Marl, you're a bloody mind reader.'

Marla poured two glasses of Bordeaux and plopped down on the bed, wine sloshing dangerously close to the rim of her glass. 'So, spill. What's the deal with you and Jack?'

Trish took a long sip. 'There is no deal.'

'Bullshit.' Marla's eyes twinkled. 'I saw you today. And don't think I've forgotten about that cupboard incident. The image of his moving arse is tattooed on my brain forever.'

A tell-tale blaze worked its way up Trish's neck. 'Ancient history.'

'Mm-hmm.' Marla took a sip. 'And the way you were eyeing him like the last slice of pizza? You're not as subtle as you think, Trishy.'

'I was not—'

'Please. I've seen less hungry looks at an all-you-can-eat buffet.'

Trish groaned and buried her face in her hands. 'Is it that obvious?'

'Only to anyone who knows you.' Marla's tone softened. 'Listen, I get it. Jack's...Jack. He's fun and a good bloke, deep down. But...'

An uneasy tension pulsed through Trish's middle as if every nerve beneath her ribs anticipated a hit.

Here it comes.

'He's...complicated. Three kids, an ex-wife who's a right piece of work when it comes to him and the kids, and a history of... Let's just say he's not known for his commitment.'

'Thanks for the warning, but I'm a big girl.' Trish's voice came out harsher than intended.

Marla held up her hands. 'I know, I know. It's just... You're still raw from Marc. And Jack, well, he's got more issues than a newsstand. Before the internet. You should take care of yourself, love.'

Pressure pinched behind Trish's navel. She understood Marla's concern, but a tiny, petty part of her bristled. Was her friend truly worried about her, or more about maintaining the balance of her new life? Either way, she couldn't blame her for it. And she wouldn't. The more Trish got to know this place, the cosier it felt. And what it had done to heal Marla's heart from all the grief... Immeasurable.

'We're just friends, Marl.' The little lie tasted bitter on her tongue. Because that's what they'd agreed to, not what she actually wanted. 'Nothing's going to happen.'

Marla's eyebrow arched. 'Nothing? Not even a repeat performance?'

'Nope.' Trish popped the 'p'. 'Strictly platonic.'

'Uh-huh. And I'm the tooth fairy.'

Trish got up and refilled their glasses. 'Look, I appreciate the concern. But it's fine. We talked about it. We're friends without benefits.'

'If you say so.' Marla didn't seem convinced. 'Just be careful, okay?'

Her concern was well-meaning, but it grated. Trish didn't need Marla's commentary to remind her of the glaring 'extremely bad idea' flashing in her mind every time she thought about Jack. Much like her own, his life was a maze of complications she had no business wandering into. Not after everything it had taken to untangle herself from Marc's shadow. Still, her friend's worries felt like a spotlight aimed at something Trish was trying to keep in the dark.

'I'm not some damsel in distress, Marl. Put down your sword. I can handle myself.'

'I know. But you're my best friend, and I don't want to see you hurt.'

The sincerity in Marla's voice doused Trish's irritation. She softened, guilt gnawing at her insides. 'And I love you for it, Babes. But really, there's nothing to worry about.'

Marla studied her for a long moment, then she nodded. 'Alright. But if he does anything stupid, I'll personally ensure his next delivery is to the bottom of Loch Ness.'

Trish laughed, the tension easing. 'Deal.'

As they chatted about the success of the Christmas Village Fair and Marla's plans for Hazelbrae House, Trish savoured this rare one-on-one. She'd come to Scotland to escape, to find herself as an artist, but mainly to spend long-overdue quality time with her bestie. They hadn't spent enough time together over the past year. No room for distractions, not even from Sexy Santa and his tempting package. She wasn't about to muck it all up by falling for the local postie.

Trish's phone buzzed like an angry hornet. She fumbled for her glasses, squinting at the screen. Her Instagram and TikTok notifications had exploded overnight, a flood of likes, comments, and shares.

'What the fuck?'

She tapped the app, and her stomach dropped as she saw the cause of the commotion. The photo of Jack had gone viral. Over 100,000 likes and climbing.

'Bollocks.'

Trish browsed through the comments, her face burning hotter with each one:

Forget milk and cookies, I'm leaving out whisky and a box of condoms for this Santa 🎅

Someone's been VERY naughty this year 😈

Where do I have to apply to be his Mrs Claus? 💦

Marry me, Santa Daddy! 🧔

Does he deliver packages year-round? Asking for a friend 📦👀

Forget James Fraser. I want sexy Scottish Santa to call me Sassenach. All. Night. Long. 🍆

Trish buried her face in her pillow with a long sigh. Panic welled up in her chest. What had she been thinking? She'd just wanted to share a bit of Highland charm, not unleash a tsunami of thirst across the internet. And as a photographer, she knew better than to post anyone anywhere without asking. Yes, the vendors and main partici-pants of the fair yesterday had signed consent forms, including Jack.

But this had been kind of a private moment.

The photo had already been reposted by multiple accounts, many of which had far larger followings than hers. The sheer momentum of it had spiralled out of control. Worse, some of the reposts had sparked duets and memes. Jack as 'Sexy Santa' becoming a full-blown social media phenomenon. People weren't just sharing the image; they were creating content around it, adding hashtags, captions, and even mock marriage proposals.

Deleting the original post wouldn't make much difference at this point, and a small, guilty part of her worried it might even look worse. The whole thing felt like trying to bail out a sinking ship with a teacup.

Trish groaned and peeked at her phone again. 'Jesus fucking Christ,' she muttered and tossed the phone aside. She flopped back onto her back, staring at the ceiling. The antique chandelier seemed to mock her with its cheery twinkle in the dim morning light.

How was she going to face Jack? He'd probably think she'd done this on purpose, some desperate ploy for atten-tion. Or worse, he'd be furious that she'd exposed him to this circus without his permission.

A gentle rap on the door startled her.

'Trish?' Marla's voice came through the wood. 'You awake, girl? We have gallons of fresh coffee downstairs. Extra-evil, pitch-black, just how you like it.'

'Be right there!' Trish called back, her voice unnaturally high.

She hauled herself out of bed, catching sight of her reflec-tion in the mirror. Her curls were a defiant tangle, eyes puffy from sleep. She looked like she'd been stuck in a hedge.

'Perfect. Just how I want to look when facing the music.'

After attempting in vain to tame her hair into something resembling order, Trish threw on some clothes.

As she fumbled with her camera, an idea surged up. Maybe this was a gift. She could spin it. Use it. Turn it into something that grabbed people by the collar. Bring some well-deserved attention to Kilcranach and Hazelbrae.

'Silver linings,' she told her reflection. 'Find the good shot in the mess.'

But first, Trish had to find Postman Pat to inform him about his little celebrity status and her hand in it.

Each heartbeat felt like a flashbulb going off in Trish's chest as she approached Jack's van on Hazelbrae's driveway, its red paint faded and chipped like her resolve. She found him hunched over a mountain of parcels, his brow furrowed in concentration. The sight of him, so ordinary and unaware in his shorts, made her guilt surge. Her carefully prepared explanation evaporated like mist.

Trish took a deep breath.

Here goes nothing.

'Jack?' Her voice cracked. 'Got a minute?'

He glanced up with a smile. 'For you? Always.'

'I, um, need to show you something.' She pulled her phone out of her back pocket.

Jack's eyebrow quirked. 'If it's an artsy shot of my abs or my arse, I'm flattered, but—'

'No! I mean, yes. But...' Trish gripped her phone. 'Remember the photos I took of you yesterday? The Santa ones?'

'Aye.' Jack's brows drew together, wary.

'See, I may have...posted one. And it might have...gone a little bit viral.' She squinted and held her index finger and thumb just a hair's breadth apart.

Jack's jaw dropped. 'You what?'

Trish winced and thrust the screen at him, bracing herself for his reaction.

'Holy shite.' A muscle in his jaw ticked. 'Is that…me?'

Trish nodded miserably. 'I'm so sorry. I posted it last night with the other pictures, thinking it was just a bit of fun. To showcase all Kilcranach has to offer. I never imagined…'

Jack raked a hand through his hair, making it stand on end. 'One hundred thousand likes? For my silly Santa outfit?'

Then he scrolled through the comments, cheeks flushing. 'Is that a haiku about my abs?'

'It is,' she squeaked meekly. 'And there's more… The *Highland Herald* wants an interview with Scotland's sexiest Santa.'

'Bloody hell, Trish. This is…a lot.'

'I know.'

Tension rolled off him in waves, but it wasn't anger. Not quite. The usual laid-back Jack was slipping beneath the surface, his expression caught somewhere between disbelief and something darker. A flicker of fear sparked behind his eyes, a shadow that seemed to tighten his jaw and stiffen his shoulders.

'Melissa's gonnae have a field day if she sees this. I'm not some…internet sensation.'

A hard twist settled under Trish's breastbone like someone had wedged a stone between her ribs. This wasn't just about a viral photo or silly comments. Jack's life wasn't simple. He had responsibilities, a past, and people who could twist something as harmless as a photo into something far messier.

'God, so sorry. I should've asked first, I can take it down. Not sure what good it'll do, but I can try. I'll explain it was a joke and—'

'Wait.' Jack said, cutting her off. His tone was sharper but not harsh. More like someone trying to get a grip on something slippery. Then the tension seemed to loosen, his mouth curving into a slow, cautious smile as he read the comments. 'Some of these are actually pretty funny.'

Trish pointed to a reply from a local bakery offering him free mince pies for life.

'So, should I take it down?'

'Naw, it's awright.' Jack sighed, his shoulders slumping. 'It's not every day a postie goes viral as a thirst trap. It's just… I like my quiet life, you know? Delivering the mail, playing with the band. This feels a wee bit…'

'…overwhelming?'

He nodded. 'Aye. That's the word.'

She bit her lip, an idea forming. 'What if… What if we used this? Turned it into something positive?'

Jack's brow furrowed. 'How?'

'People are clearly charmed by the whole Highland Santa thing. We could get you a social media account, do a proper photo series, showcase Kilcranach. Boost tourism, maybe raise some money for the community centre?'

'I dunno. I'm no model.'

'You don't have to be.' She went up on tiptoe. 'Just be yourself. That's what people are responding to.'

'And are *you* responding to it, Shutterbug?' Jack's gaze caught hers, locking her in place like she'd been yanked into focus. Trish's pulse galloped. She opened her mouth, but no words came out.

'Cat got your tongue?' His voice was low, teasing.

'I… um…' she stammered, desperately grasping for a witty comeback. Her mind unhelpfully supplied images of his pecs and abs instead.

'That would be tragic.' He leaned in closer, his breath warm on her ear. 'If I recall correctly, your tongue was *very* talented.'

A molten twist flared low in her belly, like metal softening in a forge, and her thighs clenched without permission.

He let out a chuckle. 'Relax, I'm just pressing your buttons. It's…fun.'

The way he pronounced 'fun' made it sound like he had a *very* specific kind of it in mind. Heat and relief flooded through her.

'So, um, you're not angry or in trouble or anything?'

'Angry? I could never be angry at you, Shutterbug.' His grin was wicked. 'Though I might need your help managing this newfound fame. Think you're up for the job?'

The air between them crackled with a tension that had zero to do with viral photos and everything with the way his hand brushed against hers as he handed her the phone back.

'I used to be in marketing and a social media manager before I went all-in with photography, so…sure.'

'Oh, look. Scotland's sexiest Santa and his personal paparazzi, thick as thieves.'

Trish whirled around to see Marla sauntering towards them. The teasing tone in her friend's voice made nerves flutter in Trish's gut. She'd promised Marla and herself that nothing would happen with Jack, and here she was, looking for all the world like she was going back on her word.

'We were discussing strategies.' She took an instinctive step away from Jack. 'There's been a bit of a viral post with Jack.'

Marla cut her off. 'I know. I'm messing with you, Trish.' She winked at Jack.

Trish's cheeks flamed. She could've kicked her friend.

'I'd best be off,' Jack said. 'Places to go, presents to deliver.' He gave a mock salute. 'Thanks for the heads-up about the madness.'

Her heart betrayed her with a traitorous thump as he rode off on his trusty steed, or rather, drove off in his battered red mail van.

Fuck.

Reality barrelled Trish over like a gritter. Thanks to her

impulsive hit on the share button, Jack was internet-famous, and every female within a hundred-mile radius was sliding into his DMs.

What do I care? This is a benefit-free friendship.

Because she hadn't come to Kilcranach to fall vagina first for Sexy Santa. And yet here she was, practically gift-wrapping herself for him, with fate playing the part of a smug little elf.

Yippee-ki-yay.

8

J ack slumped onto the sofa, dodging a scatter of Lego traps underfoot. The living room looked like a tornado had hit a toy store. Not that its usual state was much better. This was his part-time dad/bachelor's den.

Atop the coffee table stood a chipped mug bearing the faded slogan 'World's Best Da'. In the corner, a guitar stand held Jack's prized possession – a lovingly battered Fender Stratocaster. Next to it, a small amp served double duty as an end table, supporting a teetering stack of children's books and a framed photo of Jack with his kids, all pulling silly faces at the camera.

He'd spent the last hour wrangling the kids into bed, a process that involved two bedtime stories and one impassioned debate about why unicorns and octopuses couldn't be kept as pets. The five-year-old wanted a different story than the seven-year-old, and the nine-year-old didn't want to admit he still liked stories at all. All of them sleeping in one room didn't make it easier, either.

Now, in the blessed silence, Jack reached for his phone. The moment he turned the flight mode off, it erupted like popcorn in a microwave. Notifications flooded the screen, a digital tsunami of likes, comments, and DMs.

'Fuck me sideways.' He was clicking through the chaos. The inbox of the new Instagram account Trish had created was a minefield of thirst traps, desperate pleas, and border-line sexual harassment.

Sexy Santa, slide down my chimney!

Got a special package for me?

Christ, the puns were worse than his own. And that was something. A text from Trish popped up on his screen.

> TRISH (21:13) How're you holding up, internet sensation?

Since they both had access to the account, Trish was reading all of it, too. Somehow, that made him feel icky. Jack didn't mind a bit of female attention, in general. It was harmless, a laugh if anything. He could handle the dirty talk, the winks, the not-so-subtle innuendos. But knowing Trish was seeing all this?

Jack's stomach plummeted as if missing a step in the dark. He moved on the sofa, suddenly restless, as if Trish's gaze was on him right now instead of his inbox. The thought of her lumping him in with the picture these strangers had cooked up in their heads – a grinning chancer who'd shag anything with a pulse – made his skin crawl.

Jack's thumb hovered over the reply button. He typed out 'Grand, drowning in tits and terrible pickup lines, as you know,' then deleted it. Too tasteless. Too much. He stared at the blinking cursor, feeling the weight of her somewhere behind the screen.

Jack settled for a noncommittal: 'Surviving. Barely.'

He tossed the phone aside. The constant pinging felt like tiny hammers against his skull. Pseudo-fame was a fickle mistress, and right now, she was being a pain in the arse.

Even his Area Delivery Manager had got in touch, 'Jack, I've seen the buzz about your Santa photo. Just a heads-up: if any reporters approach you, pass them along to comms. And maybe save the fake beard for your off-hours?'

The fact that it had crossed his boss's desk niggled at him.

Jack's gaze landed on a framed picture of him and the kids, taken last summer at the beach in Applecross. His hair was windswept, his smile easy and genuine. That bloke looked nothing like the 'Sexy Santa' plastered across the internet. He'd always been just a face in the crowd. The postie. Niall's mate. The guy who'd fumble through a guitar solo at the pub on Friday nights. The bass player. Now he could add 'meme' to his meagre CV.

The sound of tiny feet padding down the hallway snapped him back to reality. Phil appeared in the doorway, clutching his favourite stuffed penguin.

'Da? I had a bad dream.'

Jack opened his arms, and Phil clambered onto his lap, a warm, drowsy bundle of a boy and his penguin.

'What was it about, wee man?'

Phil's bottom lip trembled. 'There was a big, scary monster. And he was eating all the Christmas presents.'

Jack brought his knuckles to his mouth to suppress a chuckle. 'Sounds terrifying. But you know what? I bet that monster just needed a friend. Maybe if we left him some cookies, he'd share the presents instead of eating them.'

Phil's mouth was set in a little o. 'Really?'

'Aye. Monsters are like people. Sometimes they do silly things because they're lonely or afraid.'

As he spoke, Jack's phone buzzed again. Another notification, another stranger clamouring for a piece of him.

Phil yawned, snuggling closer. 'Can I sleep with you tonight?'

Jack hesitated. The warmth of his son's small body against his chest, the trust in those sleepy eyes… 'Awright. Just for tonight, wee man.'

He carried Phil to his bedroom and tucked him in, then slid under the covers himself. His son's breathing evened out almost immediately, but sleep eluded Jack. His thoughts tumbled over each other.

A few months back, he might've had a laugh about 'Sexy Santa', soaking up the banter and the winks like a right cocky git. Now, the thought just grated, as if the shine had worn off without him even noticing.

And Melissa… She could potentially use this against him, paint him as some kind of half-arsed porn star. But he was showing up now, wasn't he? Helped with homework, knew which ones liked strawberry jam and which one needed the crusts cut off. She could wave around whatever photos she wanted; he was a good da these days. Besides, it wasn't like he was doing anything dodgy. A bit of Christmas cheer for the village. Nothing worth losing sleep over.

The memory of their last custody fight still stung, though. The way she'd laid it all out in court – every missed parents' evening, every time he'd chosen a gig over bath time. Back then, he'd been too busy chasing his own tail to see what really mattered. For months after the divorce, every handover had been a battleground.

'You're not responsible enough,' Melissa had declared.

The worst part? She hadn't been wrong. He'd been coasting, treating fatherhood like a part-time job. Until the day her solicitor had handed him the papers requesting full custody, and reality had slapped him awake. He'd started stepping up. Really stepping up. Parent-teacher meetings. Swimming lessons. Doctor's appointments. He'd learned to plait Beth's hair, mastered Phil's bedtime routine, and helped Jack Jr. with his times tables.

Phil rustled beside him, mumbling something about penguins in his sleep. Jack pulled him closer.

The pit in his stomach deepened as his phone vibrated again.

> TRISH (21:57) Don't let it get to you. It'll blow over in a few days. And you're still going to be just Jack.

A thorny lump formed in his throat. Just Jack. Was that enough? Had it ever been?

He thought of all the times he'd fallen short. Jack knew that he'd been a shite husband and father during the first few years.

But in his defence, he'd never learned how to be part of a normal family.

He was working on it. Too late for his marriage but not too late for his kids. Hopefully.

Jack's fingers itched to reply to Trish, to pour out his fears and insecurities. How weird it felt that the world went nuts for an image that wasn't him, the guy who barely kept his head above water. But what would be the point? She'd be gone soon, back to her fancy life in Edinburgh or London or fuck knew where. And he'd still be trying to piece together some semblance of a life worth living. For his adorable, wee terrors.

Phil stirred in his sleep, his tiny hand reaching out. Jack took it, marvelling at how small and fragile it felt in his own.

This. This was real. This mattered.

Jack closed his eyes, letting the steady rhythm of his son's breathing anchor him. For now, in the quiet darkness of his bedroom, he was just Jack. A dad. A postie. A work in progress.

• • •

Jack fidgeted with the Santa suit, feeling like a right tit as he stood in the Blue Bonnet's back room. The pub's familiar aroma of old pine wood, wet stone walls, and stale beer did little to calm his nerves.

He'd agreed to one more photo. Just one. For Trish.

There was something about the way she'd asked. Not pushy, but hopeful. The way she'd smiled, a flicker of gratitude even before he'd agreed, like she'd already known he wouldn't disappoint her. And hell, maybe he didn't want to. Maybe he liked the way it felt to have someone believe in him, even for something this daft. And really, what harm could it do? One picture to keep the train rolling for five more minutes, to keep Kilcranach on the map. That was all.

But now, faced with Trish's camera, he felt about as comfortable as a nun in a strip club.

'Relax, Postman Pat.' Trish adjusted her camera settings. 'Pretend you're delivering presents, not parcels.'

'Aye, because that's my everyday, isn't it?' He rolled his eyes, but a reluctant smile broke through.

Gwen strolled over, wearing her usual black pointy hat. 'Jack, you look like you're about to face a firing squad, not a camera.'

'Might prefer the firing squad.'

Trish's laugh loosened something in his chest. 'Come on, big guy. Show me your charm. I know it's in there somewhere, I've seen it.'

Jack squared his shoulders. 'Right then. Only this once.'

'You know I need to take many shots to get just one good photo, right?' Trish said, circling him like a hawk sizing up its prey.

'Not with me, you don't,' Jack replied with a grin. 'I'm a one-shot wonder.'

'Hate to break it to you, Postie, but one shot never does it for me. I'm a woman of…high professional standards.'

As Trish manoeuvred him into one pose after another,

Jack's guard slipped. Her warmth and energy had a way of wrapping him in, turning the clumsy moments into something intentional. The way she honed in on details – his hands, the tilt of his head – made him forget he was supposed to feel like a numpty.

'Now, hook your thumb in your waistband,' Trish instructed, her voice slightly breathless. 'And...bite your lip.'

Jack complied, feeling daft. But the way Trish's eyes widened, colour rising across her face, made his skin too tight for his body. He held her gaze, letting a hint of challenge seep into his expression.

Click. Click. Click.

'Brilliant.' Trish lowered her camera.

Was it his imagination, or did her hands tremble slightly? Gwen's wry expression from behind the bar told him it wasn't all in his head.

After the shoot, they huddled around Trish's laptop, scrolling through the avalanche of comments and questions flooding the Santa photo.

'Here's a good one,' Trish said. '"Dear Sexy Santa, will you marry me and my three cats?"'

Jack snorted. 'Sorry, lass. I'm more of a dog person.'

As they bantered back and forth, responding to increasingly absurd proposals, Jack felt every nuance of Trish's presence. The soft bump of her arm against his, the scent of her shampoo, the way her eyes creased at the corners when she laughed. It was...nice. Comfortable.

And out of bounds. Friends without benefits didn't sniff each other's hair.

'You've got an eye,' he said as she closed her laptop. 'The way you capture things... It's something else.'

Trish ducked her head, a glimmer of a smile teasing at the corners of her mouth. 'Thanks, Jack.'

He opened his mouth to say more, but her phone pinged, shattering the moment.

Her lips parted, a tiny gasp slipping out as she read the e-mail. 'Oh my God. It's *Wanderlust Magazine*. They want me to do a spread on Highland Christmas! Apparently, their photographer backed out. They've seen the viral post with your photo and the village pictures.'

Jack's insides took the express elevator down to his shoes, even as he plastered on a smile. 'That sounds brilliant. When do they need it by?'

'One week – which means I'll have to stay a bit longer.' Her voice fizzed with excitement. 'But it also means that, if it goes well, they're offering me a regular gig. A steady job as a staff photographer. International travel, Jack! This could be huge for my career!'

As Trish rattled off details about the assignment, his initial excitement curdled into apprehension. Words like 'quaint' and 'romantic' and 'rustic charm' landed wrong.

'Sounds like they want a fairy tale version of Kilcranach.' He tried to keep his tone light. 'Not exactly the real deal, is it?'

Trish waved off his concern. 'Yeah, but it's only a bit of holiday magic, Jack.'

'We're not some theme park attraction, Trish.' The words slipped out before he could stop them. There was no malice in what she was doing; he knew that. She wasn't trying to make Kilcranach into something it wasn't. She just...looked at it differently. Where he noticed quiet corners, bad roads, and hard graft, she found postcard landscapes and stories waiting to be told. And maybe that was the problem. Because people like her – who saw Kilcranach as something to frame, not to hold – never stayed. Not for long.

A crease formed between her eyes. 'I know that. But this is a massive opportunity. Don't you see how important this could be for me?'

Jack bit back a sigh. That was the kicker, wasn't it? He *did* see. All too clearly. 'Course I do.'

As she turned back to her phone, already making plans,

something old and bruised stirred behind Jack's ribs. He'd seen that look before, that hunger for something bigger. That irresistible itch. It never ended well for stuck-in-place blokes like him.

His gaze fell on Gwen behind the bar. She raised an eyebrow, a silent question in her gaze. Jack shook his head minutely. No use getting attached. Trish would be chasing her dreams across glossy magazine pages. And he'd be delivering the mail, raising his kids, and living his quiet life.

It was better this way.

9

The thing was HUGE. Like, fucking *massive*. Not just length but the girth, too. Trish had no idea how it was supposed to fit.

How many men does it take to wrangle one ginormous Christmas tree through a double door into a ballroom?

At least three, by the looks of it.

Niall grunted. 'This bloody thing's got a mind of its own.' He glared at the pine as if it had personally offended him.

'It's what they call a beast.' Jack tried to manoeuvre his end without stepping on Bert's foot. 'Why did you have to fell the mother of all trees, mate?'

Bert, who had somehow managed to wedge himself sideways between the door frame and a particularly obstinate limb, snorted. 'Aren't you supposed to be a professional tree guy, Niall?'

'Haud yer wheesht and pull.'

Bert laughed.

Trish watched from the sidelines, arms folded and lips quirked in a half-smile. She was reminded of a circus act, with each man playing his part in the slapstick routine of man versus tree.

'Do you need help, guys?'

'We're awright,' Niall fumbled with the rope securing the tree's netting, which promptly slipped from his grasp, sending a cascade of needles onto the polished floor. Jack cursed under his breath as he stumbled to regain his footing while Bert, now freed from his wedged position, shot Trish a wry glance.

'Awright, eh?' Bert dusted off his jacket. 'I think we've established that's a lie.'

Niall, his face reddening, growled, 'Shut it, Bert. We just need…a bit more…finesse.'

Trish's half-smile stretched into a wide grin as she pushed off from the wall, strolling over to the three guys. 'Do you mind if I take a picture? Men against nature, that's an intriguing motif.'

This was great for her *Wanderlust* Highland Christmas job. The camera shutter clicked, followed by Trish's snorting laugh. 'Scots Succumb to Evergreen Overlord.'

'Careful, lass,' Bert joked, 'we don't take too kindly to overlords here in Scotland.'

Accompanied by lots of grunting, the tree finally cleared the doorway, and the trio exhaled collectively.

As the last branch was wrestled into submission, Trish lowered her camera. ''Tis the season for mortal men to be humbled by flora.'

And one step closer to getting her assignment right. At least, that was her hope.

Two hours later, the eleven-foot pine was standing there, looking all tall and smug, decked out from tip to trunk and ready for Marla's big debut tree-lighting. Trish's finger hovered over the shutter button as Niall reached for the switch. The room buzzed, faces glowing in the flicker of candles and fairy lights like they were all waiting for some magic to happen.

Click.

The second the tree blazed to life, gasps rippled through the small crowd as if someone had just announced free booze and food. Trish's camera whirred, catching every wide-eyed, awestruck expression. But even as she framed her shots, doubt gnawed at her gut like a cat with a grudge.

Is this enough? Will it be 'high concept' enough for Wanderlust and their highbrow Photo Director Seraphina?

She'd already sent in a batch of photos, and the lukewarm response still burned.

'Nice, but we need more,' Seraphina had said, with all the enthusiasm of someone ordering dry toast. 'We want that expected surprise. Something familiar but fresh.'

Trish pressed her lips together, flipping through her shots. They were good – capturing the joy, the sparkle in everyone's eyes, Marla's hand slipping into Niall's like they were in a cheesy rom-com. But were they 'extraordinary'? 'Fresh and familiar'? Or just…plain predictable?

A tug on her sleeve yanked her out of her spiralling thoughts. She looked down, and there was Phil, grinning like he'd just won a gold medal. 'Did you see? I helped with the top bit!'

Trish crouched down, getting on his level. 'Did you now? I'd say you nailed it, kiddo.'

Phil puffed up his little chest, glowing with pride. 'Da lifted me up real high. I was taller than a giraffe!'

The second she heard that familiar chuckle, her insides tingled.

'Nearly took out my back in the process.'

Trish straightened up, trying to ignore the way her pulse sped up just looking at him. Jack standing there, all casual and happy, did things to her. Warm, fuzzy things she wasn't ready to deal with.

'What an acrobatic stunt.' She picked imaginary lint off her jeans. 'I'm surprised you didn't topple the whole tree.'

Jack's smile turned sly. 'What can I say? Man of many talents here.'

'Really?' Trish shot him a teasing look. 'What other secret skills are you hiding, Postman Pat?'

Every unspoken word crowded the space between them like static before a storm. Jack opened his mouth to fire back, but before he could, a small hurricane named Beth crashed into his legs.

'Da! Da! Hot chocolate time! You promised!' She shoved a bunch of candy canes into his hand. 'We can use those.'

Jack smiled, stuffing the sweets into his pocket. 'But only if you've been on your best behaviour for Auntie Marla.'

Beth's eyes went wide, all innocence. 'I have. I've been an angel!' She twirled on the spot.

Trish bit down on a laugh, remembering how Beth had turned the banister into a glitter-bombed winter forest earlier.

'An angel, eh? I take your word for it. Guess that means hot chocolate's on the menu then.'

As Jack wrangled his herd towards the refreshment table, something twisted low in Trish's gut. Longing? Envy? Perhaps a weird cocktail of both. She stuffed the notion into her inner darkroom, lifting her camera and zeroing in on the villagers instead.

Mrs Bellbottom strutted in her leopard print blouse, looking like she'd just burst out of a maximalist Christmas catalogue. Meanwhile, Gwen was sneaking what looked suspiciously like whisky into the punch bowl for the grown-ups, her green hair catching the light as she grinned like she'd just got away with murder. And Marla... Jesus, Marla was glowing, nestled against Niall's chest like she'd won the romance lottery.

Which she most definitely had.

Click.

Trish snapped away, fingers flying, capturing it all. A gust rattled the windows, and her focus shifted. Outside, the snow had started, fat flakes swirling down in a postcard-perfect scene. Her pulse kicked up. This – this would be the money shot. The kind of thing *Wanderlust's* picky Photo Director would kill for. Probably. The idyllic backdrop for those dreamy winter shots. Even though lasting snow was rare here in Scotland's west, that was what people expected. The universal fantasy.

Trish made her way to Marla, who was deep in conversation with both Bellbottoms.

'This snow is fab.' She nudged Marla with her elbow. 'Perfect timing for those photos.' Her voice was bright, but a sliver of anxiety tightened her chest.

Marla beamed like a child on Christmas morning. 'Isn't it stunning? Niall says it's the first proper snowfall in years. Except for that January blip...' She flashed Trish a grin, eyebrows doing a little dance that screamed 'you know what I'm talking about.'

Trish had heard all about Marla and Niall's fateful, steamy-stormy, snowy night at least two million times.

'Kilcranach's about to turn into a postcard. Let's hope we're all right.' Marla's gaze slid over to where Niall was standing, chatting with Bert by the fire, a mug in hand, looking like a lumberjack fantasy. Marla's expression softened, all gooey-eyed affection. And while Trish was genuinely thrilled for her bestie, the whole thing was tinged with a bittersweet awareness of her own situation.

Thirty-six, single again, and struggling to make my dream career work.

'Och, dearie, this snow's nothing to worry about,' Janet Bellbottom chimed in. 'So long as we're dressed properly – not gallivanting about in open-chested, flimsy Santa suits.'

She leaned in slightly, dropping her voice as if about to reveal a secret. 'Not that I'm biting, though. This fish swims in a different pond entirely, as you know. But even I must admit, our Jack's looking quite the picture.' She gave Trish a knowing wink. 'Or should I say, the internet's favourite "Sexy Santa"?'

Trish coughed into her mulled wine.

Marla rolled her eyes with a pointed grin. 'Mrs Bellbottom, you've been trawling through those comments, haven't you?'

Mrs Bellbottom grinned, unabashed. 'Can you blame me? It's harmless fun. Besides,' she patted Trish's arm, 'we should be thanking this one for putting Kilcranach on the map. Mind you,' she added, 'I'm not sure the village can handle those ladies all clambering to see a certain postie's…deliveries.'

Trish's face burned. She shouldn't have posted that picture without thinking it through. 'It wasn't meant to blow up like—'

'…confetti at a hen do?' Marla cast her a glance somewhere between amusement and something more guarded. 'Don't worry, it's not like they're hunting Sam Heughan here. Although…'

Her gaze lingered on Trish for a beat longer than usual, a shadow of something unreadable crossing her eyes. A slight unease unfurled in Trish's chest.

Jack waded through the throngs of people, Niall at his side. Every few steps, another cheeky jab was thrown his way, and Jack took it all with that signature grin. But Trish noticed the faint clench in his jaw, the way his fingers tapped a restless rhythm against his leg.

'Oi, Jack!' Bert called out from the back. 'When's the calendar dropping? I need something to jazz up my bookstore window!'

Laughter spread through the crowd, and Jack didn't miss

a beat. 'Sorry, lads. This festive dad bod? Strictly limited edition, reserved for a very special someone – me.'

Dad bod. As if.

Those muscles? Burned into Trish's brain like a guilty pleasure, every ridge and dip. Completely unfair for a guy who claimed he lived on whatever the kids didn't finish.

She noticed the way the people lit up around him, leaning into his easy charisma. Jack wasn't just a postman here. He was a pillar, sewn into the quilt of this place in a way she could barely comprehend.

Prickling unease crawled along her skin as Trish looked at the notifications. A fresh wave of thirsty DMs flooded in for Jack – or rather, 'Sexy Santa' – each one hornier than the last:

Santa, I've been a very naughty girl. Come spank me. 😏

Milk and cookies? Nah, I've got something else for you to munch on, babe. 🍆

It was pathetic; she really shouldn't care. They barely knew each other and were just becoming friends. But every message was like a jab to the ego. Her self-doubt crept in, a sour undercurrent to the festive cheer. Each shameless flirt, every suggestive emoji, was like a glowing neon sign flashing, 'NOT YOU'. Not tall enough, not sleek enough, not hot enough. Whatever that even meant.

That one time in the linen closet had probably just been a slip for him.

Trish knew damn well how a camera could bend reality – hell, she was trying to make a living doing just that. Angles, lighting, pose, make-up, a little bit of Photoshop magic, and voilà, anyone could look like a half-decent goddess. But even with all that knowledge, the primitive part of her brain was still whispering, *not you.* Her body – real, unfiltered, and unapologetically hers – suddenly felt like it didn't quite belong. Not in the glossy, Instagram-perfect world those other women seemed to float through without breaking a sweat.

And certainly not in Jack's bed.

Her passion for analogue and digital photography? Definitely not the sort of thing that got a man's blood pumping.

Nerd.

She'd heard it so many times before: at boarding school, from Marc, even her parents.

Maybe that closet fumble had been a fluke. A bit of charity work from a nice guy helping a friend's friend through a post-breakup crisis.

The idea stung more than she cared to admit.

Marla's voice broke through her reverie. 'You okay, Trishy? You look like you've seen one of my ghosts.'

Trish slapped on a smile. 'Just the festive spirit, I guess.' She waved vaguely toward the snowy wonderland outside. 'And I'm only haunted by those damn *Wanderlust* shots.'

Marla's brow crinkled. 'You've been fretting over that for days. Chill out, it's Christmas time. Try relaxing for once.'

'Easy for you to say,' Trish muttered, stuffing her phone back in her pocket. 'You inherited a castle, a hunk, and a whole damn village. Lucky cow.'

Marla laughed, totally unbothered. 'I know, right? And now our postie's a local celebrity.'

Trish forced out a laugh, but it felt like eating sandpaper. 'Yeah, who knew delivering the mail could be so…marketable.'

'But seriously, I'm getting worried about this whole "Sexy Santa"-thing,' Marla went on, her brow knitting. 'It's great for business, sure. But there are only so many tourists a tiny community can handle. Just yesterday, a bunch of gals trampled through Fiona's flowerbed, looking for "that Highland Hottie". What if some nut job shows up demanding a private meet-and-greet with Father Christmas? Or worse,' she lowered her voice for dramatic effect, 'what if they start stuffing their old knickers in the post box?'

Trish snorted. 'For fuck's sake, Marl. You're not making any sense.'

'Am I not?' Marla shot back with a raised eyebrow.

Before Marla could grill her any further, Niall's voice sliced through the room. 'Oi, Jack! The *Highland Herald* wants to know if you'll do a centrefold. Maybe with nothing but a sack of letters?'

'I'd have to charge extra for that, mate. Premium goods don't come cheap.'

The room burst into titters, but Trish's stomach flopped. She'd started this. One click of her camera, one post, had thrown Jack into this bonkers spotlight. Various websites and newspapers had even dangled money for an exclusive interview, but Jack had declined, fierce and unbending in a way that didn't match his usual easy-going swagger. He didn't want it to snowball any more than it already had, he'd said, and passed all inquiries straight along to the Royal Mail's media relations team to handle the circus.

There was so much more to him than the cheeky, chill postie act. She'd seen it in those quiet moments. The way he was with his kids, how his face lit up when he talked about his band, his connection with his community, the unexpected softness beneath the bravado.

Her gaze was drawn to him across the room, and the moment he noticed, Jack threw her a wink that hit her like a spark to dry tinder. For a heartbeat, the noise fell away, and it was just them sharing a private moment.

But reality snapped her back. By Christmas, in two weeks, it all would be over. His fame, along with their no-benefits-friendship. Trish squared her shoulders, raising her camera like a shield. She had a job to do.

'Holy Mother of Mary's undercrackers!' Janet Bellbottom's

voice cut through the festive chatter like a rusty chainsaw. 'Will ye look at that snow ootside!'

Everyone turned to the windows, where swirling white chaos had replaced the gently falling flakes. The wind whipped the flakes into a frenzy. Visibility was down to approximately bugger all.

'Oops,' Marla muttered, peering through the frosted glass.

'That's looking worse than the Beast from the East,' Janet Bellbottom said. 'Remember that? Easter, and we were snowed in up to our eyeballs.' She shuddered dramatically.

'Pablo Escobar thinks this is too much snow,' Fiona added dryly.

Niall, Hazelbrae's estate manager and ever the pragmatist, pushed his way through the crowd. 'Right, I'll go have a gander.'

He pulled on his wax jacket and returned a few minutes later, shaking snow from his sleeves. 'It's proper shite out there. Roads are blocked, drifts piling up faster than Hamish's tab on karaoke night. We're stuck. No way down the hill. Unless you want to end up with a broken leg.'

A groan rolled through the crowd like someone had just cancelled Christmas.

Jack, who'd been leaning back, taking it all in, clapped his hands together. 'Looks like we're having a Hazelbrae sleepover.'

His children exploded like they'd won the toy jackpot. Beth did a happy twirl, Phil leapt up like a spring, and even Jack Jr. smiled.

Trish's chest did that weird, clenchy thing as she watched the chaos unfold. Red hair flying, cheeks rosy, all grins and giggles, Jack's children were pure joy. Completely oblivious to anything, like mini Tasmanian devils with a talent for making you grin whether you wanted to or not. They were so cute it was almost criminal.

Trish helped Marla toss blankets and pillows at the

stranded guests – those who couldn't be moved into one of the guestrooms. The grand ballroom was quickly turned into a provisional camp, with people sitting on the floor like it was some sort of rustic Christmas-themed overnighter. Air mattresses and blankets scattered everywhere, the tree twinkling in the background, giving the whole scene a weirdly cosy vibe.

'I think that's everyone settled. I'm so glad we only have regular B&B guests and no NHS staff here at the moment. Too much chaos to recover from burnout,' Marla said, hands on her hips like she was commanding an army. 'Trish, you're an absolute legend. Thank you.'

Trish forced a grin, though she felt like her body had been run over by a herd of reindeer. 'Hey, happy to help. How often do you get to play hostess during a mad *snow*pocalypse?'

'Thanks, honestly. But you seem shattered, babes. Go on, head up to your room. I've got this.'

'You sure?'

People were huddled with hot chocolate or tea, and Mrs Bellbottom had a captive audience of kids, probably spinning some wild tale. Jack was sprawled out on a pile of blankets with his children draped over him like tiny, ginger-haired puppies. His eyes found hers, and he smiled – one of those secret smiles that reached right into her chest, making her heart trip over itself.

Marla waved a hand in front of her face, breaking the spell. 'You still with me?'

Trish blinked. 'Yeah, sorry. Just…thinking about tomorrow's shoot. Angles and light and stuff.'

Marla's eyebrow shot up. 'Uh-huh.'

'What?'

'Nothing.' Marla's voice was all light and breezy, but something lurked underneath. 'Just… Don't forget that you're leaving.'

That hit harder than it should have. Trish tried to laugh, but her sternum felt like a tensed fist. 'Oh, trust me, I know. Now, if you'll excuse me, I've also got a hot date with my laptop and a thousand raw files.'

Trish retreated to her attic room. She sank onto the bed, her camera a comforting weight in her hands.

As she worked on the day's shots an hour later, a soft knock at the door made her jump.

10

J ack's knuckles hovered over her door, his heart thrumming an erratic beat. He cleared his throat, willing his voice to sound casual. 'Trish? You decent?'

Part of him wished she wasn't.

He told that part to shut the fuck up.

A muffled thud, followed by a string of colourful curses. 'Hang on!'

The door swung open, and there was Trish, a beautiful mess of curls framing her pink cheeks. Her glasses teetered halfway down her nose, one side caught in the loose strands tumbling over her face. His fingers were begging him for permission to nudge them back into place.

'Jack? What are you—' Her eyes landed on the steaming mug in his hand. 'Is that Gwen's punch?'

'That and a cheddar sandwich.' He grinned, offering it to her. 'Wasn't sure I'd seen you eating. I'll eat it if you don't want it.'

Trish snorted, making grabby hands for the mug and the plate. 'Sounds delightful.' She stepped back, allowing him entry. 'Come to chat strategy for the next round of Sexy Santa posts?'

Jack's gaze swept the small room with sloping ceilings and exposed beams. The old servants' quarters, much cosier now than they'd ever been. Tastefully done. A thick rug muffled the groan of the wide plank floorboards, and a trace of something warm and smoky wafted through the air, coming from the little wood burner huddled in the corner. Trish's laptop balanced precariously on the corner of the box spring bed, surrounded by memory cards and cables. Organised chaos.

Pretty much like my life.

He also noticed the dark circles under her eyes. 'Thought we could go over some photos. And...' He hesitated, rubbing the back of his neck, '...you seemed a bit off earlier. Wanted to check in.'

Trish's shoulders tensed. 'I'm fine. Just work stuff.'

'Aye, because "fine" involves hiding away and working yourself into the ground.' Jack levelled her with a look, a slow tilt of his head. 'Come on. Talk to me. Remember how we had a long chat at the kitchen table on opening day?'

They'd sat there for hours after their impulsive encounter in the linen cupboard.

Trish's laugh was brittle. 'I told you all about my break up. It was more a therapy session.'

'Naw, I liked getting to know you.'

Not true. He'd loved it. Loved how naturally conversation had flowed between them, from music to art to life's messier parts. She'd been raw that night. Fresh from her breakup, disappointed in her career, feeling like she was constantly proving herself. And Jack? He'd listened. Not with the half-ear he usually reserved for conversations, but with something deeper. He'd shared small bits of his own story, too. About co-parenting, about music being his secret language, about feeling stuck but not unhappy. That night, he'd glimpsed something rare in her. Someone who saw the world differently, who understood what it meant to find refuge in creativity.

Trish sighed, sinking onto the plush rug at the foot of the bed. Jack joined her, their shoulders touching. The brief contact was enough to spark a thrill that surged through his entire body.

'It's stupid.' She took a sip of punch and wrinkled her nose. 'Jesus, what's in this? Jet fuel?'

Jack huffed a laugh. 'Gwen's secret recipe. Best not to ask.'

Trish set the mug aside, pulling her laptop onto her crossed legs. 'Since you're here…' She pulled up a folder of images, her fingers flying over the keys. 'These are from the tree lighting tonight.'

Jack leaned closer. The first photo on her screen was a close-up of Mrs Bellbottom's hand. Wrinkly, aye, but holding a mug as if it was the Holy Grail. Steam rising like a wee cloud escaping the cold. Gwen's hair, bright green and tangled up with tinsel like a Christmas tree. Another image showed Niall standing by the fire, looking all broody and moody – but staring at Marla like she was the only woman in the room. Which she was for him. Trish had captured his mate's essence.

And then, amongst all that art, a photo of himself and the wee ones. Phil up on his shoulders, pointing at the tree like he'd discovered a new planet. Jack Jr. sceptically clutching his hot chocolate. And Beth snuggled against Jack's leg, eyes wide with wonder. Not posed or anything, just…them. Somehow, she'd made the moment look special and timeless.

He absolutely loved the way she saw the world. Saw them.

'Trish, these are… They're incredible.'

A puzzled line appeared above her nose. 'You think? Don't know. The lighting's off in this one, and the composition here—'

'Stop.' Jack's hand covered hers, stilling her scrolling and clicking.

Trish turned her head, and her eyes met his, uncertainty

swimming in their depths. Jack fought the urge to pull her close and tell her how amazing and talented she was until her ears would bleed and then some. 'You've got a gift. A real, honest-to-God talent.'

Her laugh had a fragile edge. 'Right. That's why my photo editor's about ready to bin the whole project. And I need that job. I want it so badly.'

'Fuck your editors.' The vehemence in his voice surprised even him. 'They're idiots if they can't see your talent. You're an artist, and that's that.'

Pink spread across her collarbone like she'd downed a shot of whisky. 'I… No one's ever called me that before just like that.'

'What? Brilliant? A bloody artistic genius?'

She ducked her head, a curtain of hair hiding her face. 'Stop it.'

'Make me.' His words settled in the air between them, a fuse waiting for a spark.

Trish cleared her throat and toyed with the hem of her jumper. 'So, um, what about you, Mr Rockstar? When's the next gig?'

Ah, deflection. That was his go-to move. Now, he found himself on the receiving end and wasn't at all sure how he felt about that. Especially because she'd put her finger straight into one of his wounds.

Jack's laugh was hollow. 'Rockstar, right. Because a postie turned viral joke playing covers in a pub is the height of musical achievement.'

'Oh, piss off.' Trish's elbow connected with his ribs. 'You're talented, Jack. I've heard you play.'

'And I'm sure it sounded fab after Gwen's punch.'

Trish narrowed her eyes. 'Stop that. You don't get to sit there and tell me how brilliant I am while tearing yourself down.'

A taut warmth unfurled in his chest at the defiant protectiveness in her voice. 'Trish…'

'No!' She turned to face him fully, her knee pressing against his thigh. 'You're an incredible musician, Jack. And a loving father. And…' She trailed off, her gaze dropping to his lips.

She just stared, and he stared back until his pulse roared in his ears.

Her eyes, framed by those crooked glasses, held entire galaxies he was desperate to get lost in. 'You're lovely, Trish. It's the way you see everything. Like you've got this light inside you, and it spills out through every single shot you take.'

'Stop it. Seriously.'

'Why?'

Trish's fingers wrapped around the edge of her laptop. 'Because… Because I don't know how to handle this. Compliments.' She drew in a ragged breath. 'And I don't want to think you're a liar.'

'I'm not. Don't you dare call me that.' He didn't want to push her, even though he hated seeing her so harsh on herself. Jack leaned back against the bed, his fingers drumming an absent rhythm on his thigh. 'Okay, Shutterbug. Then tell me how you ended up behind the lens.'

Her eyes lit up, setting him on fire in the process. 'Funny story, actually. It started with my dad's old Polaroid…'

As she talked, her hands flew around like she was conducting an orchestra, nearly taking out the punch. Jack barely heard her words, too busy watching those curls bounce with every gesture like they had a life of their own.

'…and I realised I could freeze time. Capture moments no one else noticed. No, *discover* them.' She paused, her gaze distant. 'It was freeing. And it helped me to get through boarding school.'

'Boarding school, seriously? Sounds posh.'

Trish took a gulp of the punch and winced. 'Possibly. But that place was mostly crawling with bullies and bitches.'

Jack gave a slow nod, sensing the tip of an iceberg. 'And why did your parents send you off to that hellhole?'

Better to keep her talking than have her flipping the spotlight back on him and his own messed-up past. Deflection, it worked.

'It's what they thought best. My dad was an ambassador for Brazil. He's now retired. My mum's a human rights lawyer. They had very specific expectations of their only child. Art was acceptable as a hobby, but a career? Never.'

She gave a wry laugh, and it stung him. 'Mum wanted a mini-lawyer. Dad… Well, he wanted me to be another achievement, I think. Politics, business. Not a nerdy girl with a Leica.'

A slow, heavy pull anchored itself in Jack's chest. Didn't she see it? 'And yet here you are, taking the world by storm with that camera of yours.'

She scoffed. 'Hardly. I've only ever been doing it professionally for about two years. Before that, I worked in marketing. My parents have their money, but I don't want any of it. And they wouldn't give me a penny, anyway. Not as long as I'm not doing what they want me to do. I'm still hustling for every gig, paying my own bills, trying to prove I'm not some trust fund kid playing at being an artist.'

'Is that how you see yourself?' The question hovered between them like a thick fog.

'Sometimes. When the rejections and the bills pile up. Which they do.' She lifted one shoulder, but the casualness seemed forced. 'It is what it is. Can't choose your family, right?'

'Aye, but you can choose your path. And you chose to create.'

Trish's head dipped. 'Yeah, fat lot of good it's done me. My last relationship certainly didn't appreciate it.'

Jack's eyebrows shot up. 'The infamous ex? Marc, wasn't it?' He was starting to loathe the sound of that name.

Trish nodded, her mouth twisting. 'He freaked out when I left my job to pursue my passion. Mr "Why can't you stay in your real job?" himself.'

Jack shook his head. 'Sounds like he was afraid of a talented woman with a backbone and a dream.'

'Joke's on me, I guess. Ten years down the drain. And he's getting married in Spring while I'm getting nowhere.'

Jack's fingers dug into his leg. He suppressed the need to reach out, reassure her, tell her that she was fabulous, valued, and absolutely fucking awesome. Instead, he bumped her knee with his. 'That's his loss.'

'Is it, though?' She held his gaze, a glint of something raw breaking through her usual guard.

Vulnerability? It hit him square in the chest. Whoever had dared to dim her light, Jack was inclined to rearrange their face with his fists.

She glanced away, fingers absently wandering along the rug's pattern like it held all the answers. 'You know…that day, Hazelbrae's opening…'

Jack's pulse spiked. 'Aye, what about it?' His voice was casual. He was a master at pretending nothing rattled him, even when everything did.

And fuck, it did.

Since the divorce, he'd been deliberate about keeping things simple, about dodging anything that felt like strings. Sex had been his escape hatch, his way of sidestepping the tangled mess of emotions.

The day of the opening, he'd told himself it was just a one-off, something they both wanted. Bit of fun. He'd kept his head clear, or so he'd thought, sticking to his rule of light and breezy.

But now, with every look her way, that rule felt flimsy, stretched thin against something he hadn't accounted for.

Had he gone along with it because he thought she needed it…or because *he* did?

The more he turned it over, the more the edges of his own reasoning unravelled. It wasn't like he hadn't felt the spark that lingered a beat too long every time she was around. Hell, maybe he'd been waiting for the excuse to get closer all along. The thought dug in like a barb lodged under his ribs.

Trish's voice came out so soft he almost missed it. 'I…I wasn't thinking straight. I…needed something, someone, to make me feel alive.'

'I know,' Jack murmured, locking eyes with her. The honesty staring back at him knocked him sideways. 'I was there.'

'I didn't… I mean, it wasn't just…' She forced in a breath. 'You were kind and funny. You made me smile, and you saw me. Not the awkward photographer or fucked-up daughter or not-lame-enough-to-be-a-wife-girlfriend. Me.'

Pressure built under Jack's ribs, like his heart was stretching to hold her words. 'I—'

'And then I fucked it up.' She let out a laugh, edged and empty. 'Your text… I freaked. I thought perhaps you slept with me out of pity or—'

'You think I pitied you? Christ, Trish.' Jack softly took her chin between his index finger and thumb, words slipping from him like a confession. 'I saw you across the room. Laughing with Marla, but those eyes of yours…' Jack's hand skimmed the back of his neck. 'They held something else. Like you were daring the world to try and dim your light.'

He leaned closer as if the words themselves weren't enough to bridge the distance. 'I couldn't look away. I couldn't help but want to be close to that, to you. Not just because you're beautiful but because there's something real about you. I couldn't have stayed away if I tried. Not from the kind of woman who makes a guy feel like he's just been hit by lightning and still wants to chase the storm.'

A tiny gasp slipped from her mouth like she wasn't sure whether to speak or breathe. 'Jack…'

'No, let me finish. You walked up to me and started chatting about… What was it? Light and shadow in the ballroom?'

One corner of her gorgeous mouth curled up. 'The way it hit the chandeliers.'

'Aye, that's it.' Jack's gaze softened. 'And I thought, "Who the fuck is this girl, talking about light like it's magic?" Because to you, it was. Is.'

The tip of his nose brushed hers. 'And the way you helped Marla with her event? The way you've got your friend's back? That kind of loyalty is a fucking turn-on.' Jack's throat tightened as he tried to find the right words. 'So no. It wasn't pity, Trish.' His gaze drifted to her full, soft lips. 'And then… You were…like you'd been *starving* for it. Like you needed every bit of me.' His voice dropped to a low, gravelly tone. 'You were lovely, so pure in your need for me. It was fucking hot. Your body, the way it responded to mine… Like we were speaking the same language.'

Jack's mind whirled like a drunken gyrocopter as he replayed the words that had tumbled out of his gob. He'd laid it all out, no holds barred, no charming deflections. Then, his brain smacked him with a revelation. He wanted that again. Her raw, desperate need. The way she looked at him like he was the only thing that mattered.

He caressed her chin with his thumb, forcing her to face him. 'I don't think friends without benefits is working for me, Shutterbug.'

'Oh, well… That makes two of us.'

Jack's pulse kicked into overdrive as he leaned in, his eyes darting between hers and the soft curve of her lips, waiting to be kissed. The faint scent of Gwen's punch lingered on her breath, sweet and spicy. His hand slid over her cheek, holding her face. And she leaned into his palm as if that was the only place where she could find peace.

Jack held his breath, every muscle taut. Her tongue flicked across her lips, and a surge of heat shot straight to his groin. The pulse quivering at the base of her throat, the way her lips parted just enough… He lowered his head, his breath teasing hers, the fine hairs on his skin tingling.

'I'm going to kiss you now. Not a soft, polite kiss. The kind that ends up with you riding my cock all night. If that's not what you want, tell me now.'

Trish's eyelids fluttered like butterfly wings, nothing but hunger behind them. The world narrowed down to the two of them. He waited for her consent. She had to say it.

'Please kiss me, Jack.'

With a groan that was half relief, half desire, he closed the gap. His mouth fell against hers in a bruising kiss, a kiss like a collision. A low growl rolled from his chest as her plush lips parted for him, inviting the thrust of his tongue inside her hot mouth. He kissed her with long, hungry, powerful strokes. His hand gripped her jaw, holding her in place. If this was a dream, he never wanted to wake up. She made a small, needy sound in the back of her throat, and it rippled through his entire body. His hand drifted into her hair, rough fingertips dragging along the sensitive skin of her nape.

She broke the kiss. 'Are we making a mistake?'

Jack reached out, his fingers gently tilting her chin up so that she was forced to meet his gaze. 'Does this *feel* like a goddamn mistake to you, Trish?'

'No.'

Jack leaned in again in a slow, deep kiss. Her little tongue slid against his, velvety soft and slick and endlessly sweet.

This kiss… He felt, in the pit of his stomach, a churning, molten fire. It was in the tightening of his chest, the way his heart skipped a beat before punching hard against his ribs. It was in the tingling of his fingertips as they traced the dip of her waist.

Fuck.

'Jack?' Her voice was barely above a whisper against his lips.

'Aye?'

'I like you.' The words slipped free, unguarded.

That confession hit him low, spreading through him with a slow burn, an ache threading through his ribs. 'I like you too, Shutterbug. More than I should.'

'But? I can hear a but.'

'But you're leaving. And I'm here. With the kids, and my job, and—'

'…a whole life,' she finished. 'I know. And I have this amazing opportunity in London. And there's Marla.'

'And Niall. It's complicated.'

The logs popped in the small burner. Outside, the wind flung snow against the windows.

'So, what now?' she finally asked, her voice slicing through the charged silence.

'I don't know. But I do know I'm not ready to say goodbye.'

Trish covered his hand with hers, marvelling at how perfectly they fit together. 'Me neither. I don't like unfinished business.'

'Hate it.'

'God, so much hate.'

'Maybe we'll make this a night to remember. The night we finish our business.'

'Yes. But Jack, the thing is I never fi—' she started, but he cut her off with a hungry look.

His heart pounded like a fucking kick drum. 'Shhh,' he murmured, inching closer. 'Did you enjoy it?'

'What?'

'Did you enjoy being fucked in the linen closet?'

Trish nodded, nothing but a small jerk of her head. 'Y-yes.'

'Even with Marla barging in?'

She exhaled. 'Yeah, she kind of ruined the moment.'

'Aye, too bad. I wanted to hear you scream my name when you came all over my cock.'

She was silent for a moment. 'The thing is…'

Jack waited, the silence filled only by the crackling fire. 'The thing is?'

She looked up at him, eyes all puppy-dog wide. 'It wouldn't have mattered. I've never…come around anyone's cock. I've never…finished that way.'

Jack blinked, processing this bombshell. 'Never?' Something twitched inside him. Not lust, but a strange protectiveness. A need to fix it. To prove to her how wonderful she was. How worthy and desirable. 'Looks like we've got a lot more unfinished business than I thought.' The corner of his mouth quirked up. 'And I'm the postie to deliver.'

Trish smiled and nodded. But he heard the faint catch in her breath. She was nervous. So was he. But fuck, he wanted her. Wanted to taste her, to feel her come undone. To give her the grand fucking finale she deserved.

To make the world right.

Jack feathered his lips over her pulse point. 'No more holding back.'

'Agreed.'

Carefully, he took off her glasses and put them on the rug beside them.

'But…,' she said, 'then I can't see you properly.'

'See me with your lips, your hands. You use your eyes too much, Shutterbug. They're getting in the way of your pleasure.' His lips brushed against her skin. 'Tonight,' he whispered, his voice thick with promise, 'I'm going to make you *feel* stars. One way or another.'

11

'It's not all about the dick and the climax.' Jack placed a soft kiss on her collarbone and another to the hollow of her throat. He traced the frantic rhythm of her pulse with his tongue.

He needed to rein himself in, not rush this. Not with her. He was playing a different game here, a more deliberate one.

'Tonight is about what feels good.' His fingers intertwined with hers. 'I'm going to make you forget all about the destination and enjoy the journey.' He stood up and reached out a hand. 'Come here.'

Jack pulled her up and found the hem of her jumper. Slowly, he inched it upwards. Trish lifted her arms to help him as if she couldn't wait to be skin-on-skin with him. Her bra – plain black cotton. No frills, no flourishes, no nonsense. Practical and real. She wasn't trying to be sexy, to put on a show. She was herself. That was all he needed. And fuck, the way her little nubs strained against the thin fabric... A zap of lighting straight to his cock.

Plain cotton doing it for you, MacGregor? Who knew?

Jack leaned in to press a kiss to the swell of her breast. 'Dear God, I've wanted to do this again for three months.'

He smiled as she let out a soft sigh. His hands cupped her breasts, thumbs teasing her nipples through the thin fabric. She came alive under his touch. 'You're doing a damn good job of getting me hot and bothered, Shutterbug.'

She moaned at his words.

The sentiment was clearly mutual.

Good.

Her hands hesitated for a moment before sliding under his t-shirt. 'If the hundreds of ladies in your DMs knew that I'm the one getting to fuck Sexy Santa…' She trailed off, voice laced with self-deprecating humour.

'You're not. You're getting to fuck *me*, Trish.'

Jack peeled off his shirt and jeans with the practised ease of a man who'd lost count of the number of times he'd undressed for this very purpose. Her pupils dilated as her gaze fell onto the festival tent in his boxers, main stage. It made him smile.

His palms tracked her body's contours. Waist dipping, hips flaring. He hooked his thumbs into her sweatpants and tugged carefully, like unwrapping a gift. His knuckles slid along her legs, the firmness of her muscles, the softness of her curves.

His lips skimmed her ear, his voice a husky murmur. 'Tell me what gets you off. What makes you feel good? I want to hear it from you.'

Something glimmered in her gaze, and her palm landed on his skin like a brand. He felt mapped, claimed, combustible.

'This,' she whispered. 'The way your heart beats against my palm.'

His brain went haywire. He hadn't seen that coming. 'Aye, I like that too.'

Jack dropped onto the rug, pulling her down with him. 'Lie back.' Propped on an elbow, watching her. 'Trust me?'

'Yes, I do.'

Her genuine smile knocked the air out of his lungs. Fuck. That trust was dynamite, set to detonate something fundamental inside him. He wanted to guard it. Cherish it.

Jack dug the candy cane from the pocket of his discarded jeans, the ones crumpled on the floor, like their inhibitions. He peeled back the wrapper and traced the striped hook over her collarbone. Time to play and ease her tension, take her mind off things, make her relax. He twirled it between his fingers and rested it against her lips.

'Suck on it like you sucked my dick that day,' he said. 'Do it slow. Make my cock jealous.'

'Are you…serious?' Surprise flicked across her face before it melted into something else. Something…pliant. 'That's *not* the same.'

'Oh, baby, I know.' He grinned. 'Go on.'

Her tongue darted out, tracing a languid swirl around the candy. Her full lips closed around the stick. And she sucked. A long, deep draw. And another.

In. Out.

Fuck.

Jack tracked the movement of her lips like a laser. That pink tongue darting, teasing. She was playing along, and Christ, she was good at it.

In. Out. In. Out. Each draw a provocation.

Her eyes flicked and collided with his. And there – raw, naked – he saw it, that yearning to please. To be witnessed. To matter. She wanted to make him happy.

'That's it.' His voice was a low growl. 'You're doing so well.'

She made little smacking noises, and damn if he didn't feel that mouth of hers right on him, hot and slick. He was hard as a rock, his dick pushing against his boxers like it was trying to bust out of jail. But this wasn't about him. He wanted her loose, playful, at ease.

'Show me how bad you want it.' He plucked the candy from her mouth.

She reflexively tipped forward, trying to capture it again, but Jack pulled it just out of her reach. Her tongue swept her lips, chasing the lost sweetness.

'Say pretty please, and I'll give it to you.' He trailed the candy cane down her body, dipping into the valley between her breasts, skating over her stomach, leaving a trail of goose-bumps. 'Because good girls get what they beg for.'

'Jack,' she gasped, melting against the rug, every muscle unwinding in a slow surrender – as if she'd been waiting a lifetime to say this one word. '*Please.*'

His gaze roved over her, taking in the flush of her skin, the rapid rise and fall of her chest. She was pure, unfiltered need. And fuck, he matched her pulse for pulse.

'Shhh,' he soothed, following the subtle line from her waist down to her thigh towards the seam of her thong. 'Just feel, baby.'

Jack hooked his fingers beneath the elastic, sliding it aside. 'It's only you and me.' He slipped the candy cane between her thighs, pressing it against her clit, circling it. 'Feel that meeting your sweet spot?'

She nodded, her teeth sinking into her lower lip, but he craved more. He wanted her words. 'Tell me, Trish. Tell me how it feels.'

'Tingling,' she whispered. 'Cold.'

Jack shot her a wicked smile. 'Then we have to warm it up a little.' He traced the line of her wetness. With a deliberate pace that made his own pulse thunder, Jack eased the candy cane inside her, just an inch.

His voice dropped. 'Such a horny girl, all soaked and ready.' Jack twisted the candy cane, pushing it deeper, drawing a moan from her. He brought it to his lips. 'Mmm… you're delicious. Here, try some.'

Her eyes fluttered open, and she leaned forward, her

tongue tentatively touching the candy cane. Her lips sealed around it, drawing it in. Tasting herself.

'That's it, baby. That's how sweet you are.' He put the candy cane aside. His smile stretched wide. 'Let's find out how much sweeter you can get.'

Jack's heart thumped in his ears as he settled between her thighs. His lungs seized mid-breath at the sight of her laid out like a goddamn feast. 'You're so fucking gorgeous.'

All soft pink flesh and glistening wetness, the delicate curls of her dark hair shimmering. The bead of her clit, the way her sex parted... He pushed his thumbs into the yielding flesh of her thighs, easing them wider, making space for himself.

This was it. The moment he'd been dreaming about since September. The scent of her arousal, thick and heady, made his mouth water.

'Beg nicely.' His breath fanned over her slick sex. 'Tell me what you want.'

Her hips bucked. 'Jack, I...' A broken sound.

'What do you need?'

'I...need your...your mouth...' She gasped. 'Right here.' Her hands dug into his hair, and she hiccupped, *'Please.'*

A charge rippled through him at the desperation in her voice.

He dipped his head, his tongue lashing out to taste her. She was fucking exquisite, her flavour bursting on his tongue. He groaned, the sound vibrating against her flesh, and her back arched off the rug.

It wasn't the way her taste grabbed him. It was something deeper that drew him in, that made his heart race and his cock pulse and his mind go blank. It was the way she responded to him. The way she felt in his hands, in his mouth. When he touched her, she dissolved. Genuine. Vulnerable. Pure. Like he was the only man who made her feel this way.

Jack savoured every shiver that rolled through her body. He circled her clit with his tongue, flicked at it lightly, then pressed flat against it.

'Fuck, Jack!' Trish's voice was strangled. 'Jesus Christ...oh *fuck...*'

'I'm glad you're enjoying it.' With a smile, Jack slid one digit inside her, and her walls rippled around his finger, so hot and soft. 'You enjoy that, too? I bet you fucking love it. And I bet you need more.'

She could only moan in response, pushing her hips against his face. He pumped his finger harder, stretching her.

'Yes! I...' Trish whimpered, her head thrashing from side to side. 'Please...I need...'

He licked a slow stripe up her sex. 'Tell me.'

'I need...to come,' she sobbed. 'Please, Jack... God. Ohhh God.'

With a deep groan, Jack plunged his middle- and ring finger knuckle-deep into her. He curled them and felt her clench around his digits.

Yes, baby. Give it up.

He pumped harder and deeper. Like he had something to prove. Trish reared up, her trembling thighs clamping around his head. His tongue flicked mercilessly over her clit in sync with his hand.

'Fuck, Jack!' Trish cried out, her voice strangled. 'You're going to... I'm so cl-close... Don't stop, please don't stop!'

His own hips twitched as she flew apart with a choked scream, her back arching off the rug. And from between Trish's trembling thighs, Jack felt the ground shift. Her orgasm crashed over her like an avalanche, her body convulsing as a rush of slick, sweet arousal flooded his tongue.

Fuck. Fuck, fuck, fuck.

The sheer intensity of her release... Keeping his fingers buried deep, he was drunk on her pleasure, gasping between laps as her thighs shook. He gentled his touch as she came down from her high.

Trish slumped back on the rug, legs splayed, chest heaving. Sweat glistened on her skin, her pulse thundering beneath his tongue. He placed tiny, tender kisses on her inner thighs.

'That was…' Her voice was raspy, breathless. 'Wow. Holy… Wow.'

She tugged at his hair, and Jack climbed up her body, drawn by her grip.

He looked at her with a contented grin. 'You're a force of nature when you come.' Then he kissed her damp temple. 'Made me want to gather up all those pretty cries and never let them go.'

She breathed out a laugh and trailed a finger down his chest. 'So, Santa, what's next on your naughty list?'

Jack shuddered at her touch. He rolled his hips, letting her feel how achingly hard she'd made him. 'I'm thinking…' He dragged his tongue along the shell of her ear. 'I want to sink my fat cock into you and fuck you so hard you won't be able to walk straight.'

Trish sucked in a breath. Then she giggled. She fucking *giggled.* 'Okay.'

He nipped at her earlobe. 'Hey, I'm not joking.'

'Oh, I hope not.'

'You don't?'

'I…' Trish's gaze flicked to his boxers. 'I liked how you felt inside me.' Her cheeks caught fire. 'I don't need to come for this to feel good.'

Christ, this fucking woman.

Jack's mouth crooked sideways. 'Looks like Santa's got a very horny elf on his hands.' His hand settled on her ass, fingers sinking into her flesh with a quiet, possessive squeeze. 'You know what I love about this arse?'

Trish raised an eyebrow. 'The fact that it's attached to me?'

Jack laughed, his fingers skating along her globes. 'That's a given. But no, it's this…' He squeezed again. 'It's so round and plump. And it's all fucking mine.'

'Yours?' Her voice was breathy. 'What makes you think I'm going to hand it over?'

'Because I know you want to feel me gripping it while I fuck you from behind. You want to feel me so deep that you can't think because I'm hitting on your prefrontal cortex.'

Her lids drifted shut for a second, and she smiled. 'Can't argue with that.'

Jack got up and shed his boxers, letting them pool at his feet. Her gaze burned over him, drinking him in with a raw, unguarded awe that made his skin spark.

'Like what you see?' He stroked himself slowly, lazily, enjoying the way her pupils dilated and her tongue traced a quick, wet path across her lips.

'Mmm,' she hummed, eyes locked on his dick like a target. 'I don't even need my glasses to see…*you.*'

Jack laughed and reached for his wallet, pulling out a condom. His fingers fumbled like a nervous rookie, the foil crackling. But her half-smile and that quiet, waiting look settled him. He ripped the wrapper. One roll, smooth as a sleight of hand, and done.

'What do you want, Shutterbug?'

Trish turned around and got on her knees, back arched. 'I want the big candy cane.'

God help me.

Jack kneeled behind her, thumbs digging into the soft flesh of her hips. His cock throbbed at the sight. He'd always appreciated a woman with meat on her bones, and Trish was a fucking banquet. He couldn't wait to be inside her, to feel that lush flesh surrounding him, gripping him.

'You ready to take me all the way?'

Trish pressed against him. 'Yes, Jack…I need you…deep.'

He lined himself up, his shaft nudging at her entrance. She

grunted a frustrated little moan, and he almost laughed at how cute she was, her head dropping forward as she tried to push back against him. But he held her still.

She pushed against his hold. 'Please, Jack…'

His balls tightened painfully at her plea. He rubbed the tip of his cock along the smooth lips of her sex. 'Oh, you're going to be feeling me for days.'

And with one slow roll of his hips, he slid into her.

'Oh my fucking God!' Trish's back bowed, fingers digging into the rug. 'Yes! Ah, YES!'

'Fuck, Trish. You feel so good. Dammit!'

The understatement of the century. A big sneeze felt good. Being buried balls-deep inside Trish seriously messed him up.

Jack pulled out slowly, almost all the way, before gliding back into her. His pleasure centre exploded, his brain melted, and his heart along with it.

'That's it, Jack. Yes, yes, yes…like that…'

The sight of her – bent forward, the globes of her cheeks cushioned against his groin – was enough to make him lose control. He mentally told himself to hold on, not to come too fast. But a nuclear blast of sensation scattered his synapses and scorched every nerve ending.

Her body tensed as she pushed back. 'I love this,' she moaned. 'I'm so full…so full… And it feels so good.'

Jack's hips moved faster, his thrusts becoming more urgent, and there was nothing – absolutely fuck all – he could do about it. She keened, and pleasure detonated inside him, white-hot and feral, rewiring his entire circuitry.

'I want you…to come, Jack. I want to…feel you come… inside me. Feel you…'

'Jack groaned, the sound torn from deep within his chest. She clenched around him, her body gripping him, drawing him deeper. The tight heat of her was making him lose his goddamn mind. As if she'd been cast to accommodate his dick. Taking him as if he'd belonged there.

He *wanted* to belong there.

His pulse hammered in his ears, matching the rhythm of their bodies colliding. With each drive into her snug pussy, he bottomed out. Pure bliss.

'Oh God, Trish… Fuck. I can't…' The dimples on her lower back, the curve of her spine, the sight of him disappearing inside her… He felt every ripple, every quiver of her body like she was tuning him to her frequency.

'You're fucking *destroying* me…' Jack barely recognised his own voice.

What the hell was happening? It was too much, too intense, too fucking phenomenal. He dug his hands into her hips. The coil in his guts wound tighter until he thought he might burst.

'Shit.' His hips thrust faster and harder, the wet slaps of their bodies echoing off the stone walls. 'I can't fucking stop.'

'Yes! Yes! Jack… Don't stop… You feel so…right…'

So right.

'FUCK!' Jack came with a roar, his body shaking with the force of it. He threw his head back as he jerked, going as deep as he could. It was almost painful like a part of him was being ripped away and instantly healed.

His body slumped forward as he rode out the last of his release, and his teeth found that sensitive spot where her neck met her shoulder.

Holy mother of… That just rewrote my entire operating manual.

The last time he'd come this fast, he'd been eighteen.

Jack's forehead rested against the nape of Trish's neck, his breath coming in choppy pulls. His mind reeled, body trembling. It was like the sudden crack of ice splitting open beneath his feet, plunging him into depths he'd never expected.

With a soft kiss, he pulled out, disposing of the condom before pulling her into his arms as tightly as he could.

'Trish, that was…' But words failed him. There was

nothing he could say that would do justice to what he was feeling. He nudged her hair with his nose, inhaling something deeper than her shampoo. Essence, memory, possibility. 'You okay?'

Trish hummed against his chest. 'Mmm-hmm. Just...processing.'

Processing. That was one way to put it. He was processing, too. Processing the fact that he'd come harder than he ever had, and not just from the physical release. It was...confusing.

He let his hand wander over her waist. 'Anything you need to process out loud?'

'Maybe later.' She shifted slightly.

The way her leg casually draped over his, like she'd laid claim to him without even knowing it, sent a possessive surge through him, marking his every molecule with her name. Suddenly, he wanted to be the one she'd warm her cold feet with. And he'd never wanted to be that for anyone.

'For now, I'm...enjoying this,' she said.

'Good. Me too.' The quiet was nice, comfortable even, but the silence was also heavy with all the things they weren't saying. Like how she was leaving soon. Like how this whole thing was supposed to be casual and felt anything but.

He kissed the top of her head. 'You smell nice.'

'So do you.'

'That's my aftershave. Got it from the weans last year for Christmas.' He gave her a crooked grin. 'Along with a pair of silly socks.'

She laughed. 'You don't deserve silly socks. Though you *might* deserve a spanking for that candy cane thing.'

'Oh, you fucking loved it.'

'Maybe.' She bit her lip. 'Maybe I liked it a little too much.'

Trish nestled deeper into the pillows, her eyes half-closed. Gone was the tension in her shoulders, the guarded look in her eyes. She looked...peaceful. Happy and calm. His gaze landed on her camera, sitting on the nightstand. An idea sparked.

'Hold still for a second.' Jack reached for her Leica.

'What are you up to now?'

'Nothing.' He fiddled with the settings, hoping he wasn't about to make a complete arse of himself. 'I want to capture this moment.'

'Mm, but I don't like pictures.' Her nose scrunched up adorably.

A quiet ache broke open in his chest. The kind that comes from seeing something precious not recognising its own worth. 'Humour me, eh?'

He raised the camera, framing her in the viewfinder. Her hair was a mess, spread out on the pillow. Her lips were still swollen from his kisses. He zoomed in, capturing the way her eyelashes fanned against her cheek.

He wanted to remember this.

He wanted *her* to remember this.

'You're stunning, properly fucked six ways to heaven.' He snapped a shot.

'Flatterer.' Trish's cheeks pinked. 'Put the camera away.'

'Just stating facts.' He took another photo. 'Besides, it's about time you were on the other side of the lens.' He tried to capture the way the firelight danced in her hair, turning the dark strands to molten gold.

This was her. This was them. Right now.

It was all they had.

'One more. For posterity.' He framed her face in the lens. The soft glow of the bedside lamp swept over the curve of her cheekbone, the swell of her bottom lip.

'Delete that,' she mumbled, drowsy with sleep.

'Nope.' He lowered the camera, rested it on the side table, and laid back next to her. A smug grin spread across his face. 'Prime blackmail material.'

Trish's muffled laugh rumbled against him. 'You're such a git.'

He nuzzled his nose into her hair. 'But you like me for it.'

'Debatable.' She stretched languidly, her leg tangling with his.

He pulled her tighter into his arm, and it was a gut punch how perfectly she fit there. He wanted to stay wrapped up in this moment forever, pretending the world outside didn't exist. Snowed in forever.

She tucked her head under his chin. 'What time is it? I can't see it from here without my glasses.'

'Late.' He glanced at the glowing numbers of the clock on the mantelpiece. 'Nearly one.'

'Already?' She yawned. 'I'm knackered. All that moaning and suppressed screaming takes it out of you.'

He laughed softly. 'You were the one doing the suppressed screaming, Shutterbug.'

'You were the one making me scream suppressedly.' She snuggled closer, her breath warm against his skin. 'So technically, it's your fault.'

A minute later, she was fast asleep in his arms. Safe and sound.

His real fault, though?

Still trying to believe that this was nothing but a bit of fun.

12

T rish blinked, the world swimming into focus through a blurry haze of contentment. Seven-thirty and still dark. She stretched, a delicious ache radiating through her muscles.

He was gone.

A pang of…something tightened her chest. Disappointment? No. A gentle pull. Longing, more like. Her gaze drifted to the bedside table. A candy cane lay next to a folded piece of paper. With a smile, she reached for the note.

Nae worries, it's a different cane. Had to be with the weans when they woke up. Back later. Don't delete the photos. J. x

Trish rolled onto her side and hugged the pillow close, inhaling the few molecules of his scent that clung to the fabric.

Holy shit. Last night actually happened. Not bad for a second round.

The bathroom mirror reflected a smiling stranger. Cheeks stained pink, lips like bruised fruit. Trish noticed the faint marks Jack had left on her neck and ran a finger over the skin.

She stepped into the shower and let the hot water cascade

over her. Her body thrummed like a plucked string. She still felt him inside. Like he'd left an imprint, like he'd reshaped her. And the pulse of his orgasm... She hadn't lied when she'd told him she wouldn't need to come to enjoy it. Making a guy like Jack completely lose it? It made a girl feel like she could take on the world.

That brought up another question, though.

Why me?

It niggled as she rinsed her hair, a wasp buzzing around the edges of her contentment. Jack had women falling over themselves for a shot with 'Sexy Santa'. So why had he come to her room? Convenience? A warm body?

Trish stepped out of the shower and wrapped herself in a towel. They'd both agreed this was a here-and-now thing, something with an expiration date slapped on like a sell-by stamp on a carton of milk. If all went according to plan, she'd be back in Edinburgh, preparing for her move back to London for a full-time position at *Wanderlust*. And Jack would be here, in Kilcranach, with his kids, his band, his life. So why this... this pull towards him? Was it the kick of a man she wasn't supposed to be with?

Trish's camera was heavier than usual as she descended the stairs. The aroma of fresh coffee and bacon wafted up, making her stomach growl.

She paused at the breakfast room doorway, taking in the scene. Marla stood at the buffet with three of her staff. Between the handful of B&B guests, the two Mrs Bellbottoms sat huddled together and shared the morning paper. William Collins nursed a steaming cup of tea. Fiona and Bert bickered over the last scone. Gwen and her parents practised Spanish while Barclay and Muffin wove between legs, hoping for scraps.

And then there was Jack.

He sat at the far end of the big table, surrounded by his children. Beth perched on his lap, syrup smeared across her chin. Jack Jr. dismantled his pancakes while Phil snickered at something only he found funny.

'Kids, this is Trish,' Jack said, casual as anything, 'you've seen her before, right? She's a very good friend. Pretend to be well-behaved and say good morning.'

'Good morning!' Beth said and smiled. Jack Jr. stared at his pancakes, mumbling something unintelligible, and Phil grinned with chocolate teeth.

'Good morning.' Trish rested a hand on her empty stomach like that could stop the circus act happening underneath.

Jack caught her eye and shot her a wink. She gave a brisk nod, but her lips still buzzed with the memory of his kisses.

'Trish!' Marla's voice broke the moment. 'There you are, sleepyhead. Come grab a plate before the vultures devour everything.'

'Will do.' Trish forced her feet to move and piled her plate high, grateful for the distraction.

When she returned to the table, Jack Jr. pointed to the fruit basket with his fork. 'I want one of those to make banana split pancakes.'

'Banana split pancakes?' Trish set her plate down and took a seat.

Junior nodded, his expression serious as though he'd just invented the idea.

'Good choice.' Quietly, she reached for a banana in the fruit basket. She always carried a small sewing needle in her jacket pocket, a habit she'd picked up after too many broken straps and emergency repairs on the go. Keeping her movements quick and subtle under the table, she used the needle to make tiny, invisible cuts under the banana's peel.

Then Trish turned the fruit in her hand. 'Wanna see something cool?'

Phil's head popped up like a meerkat. Beth twisted on Jack's lap to watch. Even Junior lowered his fork.

'It's a whole banana, yes?' Trish asked. 'You can all see it?'

Three nods.

Slowly, she peeled back the skin to reveal it was already sliced into perfect discs.

'Whoa!' Phil gasped.

'How did you do that?' Jack Jr. asked and pinched his eyes.

'Magic,' Trish winked as she handed it to him.

Beth clapped her hands, and Phil immediately lunged for another banana in the basket. Junior inspected his prize, shaking his head in awe. Even Jack gave her a look like he was seeing her through his kids' wide-eyed wonder.

A tiny, smug thrill of pride zipped through Trish. It was a trick Mrs Kaminski, her favourite cook back at the Velasco-Whitmore household, had taught her when she was about ten. Not her mum or her dad.

A chuckle rippled from the end of the table. Trish glanced up to find Janet Bellbottom giving her a knowing look. She and her wife had also stayed on the top floor last night. 'Sleep well, dearie? Thought you might have had a nightmare.'

Trish nearly choked on her coffee. 'No. All good, thanks. Tired from all the excitement.'

'Aye, it was quite the night,' Sylvia Bellbottom chimed in. 'With the snowstorm and all that…'

'Speaking of snow,' Niall said. 'I'm afraid we're still stuck on this hill, at least for a few more hours.'

'Okay,' Gwen piped up, 'how are we tackling this?'

'I suppose we should start digging out.' Marla slid into the seat next to Niall. 'Though I wouldn't mind being snowed in a bit longer.' She blew a kiss at Niall, who blushed like a lovesick teenager.

Bit nauseating. But stupid cute.

As the chat veered into light-hearted teasing, Trish snuck a few glances at Jack finishing breakfast with his children. Such a patient, loving dad. The polar opposite of her own father, who had rarely ever been there, even before boarding school.

It was a problem. An even bigger problem was the way his arm flexed when he poured orange juice. And the stretch of his t-shirt over those broad shoulders when he reached for the napkins? Totally unfair. Trish raised her camera, snapping a quick photo. She couldn't help herself.

'Stalking me again?' Jack asked with a teasing lilt in his voice.

Trish let the lens drop, warmth inching up her neck. 'Documenting the domestic bliss.'

'Bliss? Please. More like controlled chaos.' Jack grimaced as he glanced out the window at the snow-covered landscape. 'Guess Kilcranach will have to survive without their special tracked deliveries today. The van's not conquering those roads. And the hill's impassable, no chance of walking. I'd be more likely to end up in a ditch than anyone's letterbox. So domestic is all I'll be.'

She smiled. 'I'm sure your fans would love to see Santa in full dad mode. Syrup stains and all.'

Jack quirked an eyebrow. 'Careful now. You're treading dangerously close to paparazzi territory.'

Trish snapped another shot. 'I'm a professional. This is art.'

'That's true. You're an artist.'

A jolt, sharp and startling as cold air hitting her lungs, shot straight to Trish's core. He'd said it, just like that. No qualifiers, no dismissive air quotes. *Artist.* As if it were the most normal thing in the world. For years, she'd fought for that word, clawed for it, defended it against the sneers of Marc and the dismissals of her own family.

And here was Jack, handing it to her like a cup of tea.

'Cheers,' she mumbled, her voice a little thick, a little wobbly.

Yep, she needed a moment.

Trish took her coffee and walked over to the window seat. A pristine white blanket, a fresh start. Except all she wanted to start was another round in her room with Jack. Preferably on all fours.

'Stunning, isn't it?' Niall's voice beside her snapped Trish out of her thoughts. 'The snow transforms everything. It's usually too wet and warm here in the West for it to stick. But when it does…magic.' He gestured towards the view.

'It is.' Her gaze lingered on the untouched expanse of white, a sudden ache in her chest.

'You awright?' Niall's brow furrowed. 'Marla's been a wee bit worried about you.'

Guilt pricked at her. Marla deserved better than a friend distracted by a fling with her boyfriend's pal and an insane work assignment. They hadn't seen nearly enough of each other in the past twelve days. 'I'll slow down.'

'Good. She'd like that. And me, too.' Niall squeezed her shoulder before moving off to help Marla with breakfast.

Trish turned back to the window. She was a fleeting visitor, leaving footprints in the snow. Footprints that would soon be erased.

'Right,' she announced. 'I'm going to head out and get some shots of this winter wonderland.'

Trish battled the tripod down the stairs, its legs clattering against the oak banister. Bundled in her puffy coat, she was basically a human sleeping bag on a mission.

'Whoa there.' Jack's voice came from the bottom of the staircase. 'Need a hand?'

'Possibly.' She gripped the tripod tighter and hoped her voice didn't betray the chaos happening under all those layers.

Jack bounded up the steps, two at a time. 'Let me help before you break your neck. Or worse, your camera.'

His knuckles brushed hers as he grabbed the tripod, and a hot flash jagged across her nerve map like lightning. Trish sucked in a breath that tasted like pine bark and raw masculinity. Dizzying. Dangerous.

Don't think about last night. Don't think about his hands on your hips, his mouth on your —

'Where to?'

'The gardens, to capture some Highland magic.' She hated how breathless she sounded.

He hefted the tripod as if it weighed nothing. 'How about I play pack mule for you? Give you a hand out there?'

Trish's stomach cartwheeled. An hour alone with Jack, surrounded by snow? Sounded like heaven. And potential disaster with a capital D.

'What about your little ones?' She tipped her chin toward the breakfast room.

Jack turned, addressing the two Mrs Bellbottoms who hovered nearby. 'Ladies, would you mind keeping an eye on the wee terrors for an hour? I promised Trish I'd help with her shoot.'

Janet clapped her hands together. 'We'd be delighted! Won't we, Sylvia?'

Sylvia nodded. 'Absolutely.'

'Brilliant.' Jack grinned, turning back to Trish. 'Sorted. Shall we?' He put on his coat.

'Sure you don't mind?'

'Who else is going to make sure you don't end up face-first in a snowdrift?'

A glow stirred under her ribs. 'Okay, Postman Pat.'

As they headed towards the door, Trish traded a glance with Marla. Her friend's eyebrows arched slightly, there was a glimmer of concern – or was it disapproval?

Message received: stop or proceed at your own risk.

But with Jack already holding the door, bailing now would've been an Olympic-level feat of awkwardness.

Outside, the December air was crisp and cold. Trish inhaled deeply, the scent of snow and pine and damp earth filling her lungs. It was…grounding. Quarter to nine and the sun was just rising. Her boots crunched through the fresh snow as she followed Jack into the garden. The white blanket stretched before them, broken only by the stark silhouettes of frost-covered trees. She lifted her camera, capturing how the morning sun painted the snow in soft pinks and golds. The whole scene looked like it was waiting for something.

'So…' Jack's voice cut through the snowy silence that felt as if someone had hit the mute button on the world, '…what's the plan?'

Trish lowered her Leica. 'We start with the gazebo. The way the snow's settled on the roof…'

Jack nodded, adjusting his grip on the tripod. 'Let's go.'

'Okay, here's a question,' she began in an attempt to fill the silence, 'how long have you lived in Kilcranach?'

'Born and raised in Glasgow, actually. A proper Weegie. Ended up here when I was ten.'

A beat of silence stretched between them, something unspoken riding beneath his words.

'Oh?' Trish's intrigue radar pinged. 'What's the story?'

'Short version or director's cut?' Jack's steps faltered for a moment. 'Bit of a complicated one.'

'Whatever you're comfortable with.'

When he spoke again, his voice was quieter. 'Maw was a wreck. She had an addiction and couldn't handle a kid. My da had buggered off before I could walk.' He sighed, running a hand through his hair. 'One day, I confronted her. Told her she was killing herself, kicking and screaming and all that.' He paused, something hard and brittle in his silence. 'Next thing I knew, I was on a train north, dumped with a relative I barely recognised. My aunt Sarah took me in, here in Kilcranach.'

Another beat. 'And then… My mother died. Overdose, fifteen years ago. I'd never seen her again since that day when she'd put me on the train.' The words came out flat, stripped of emotion.

Trish's heart clenched. 'God, Jack. I'm so sorry. I didn't mean to—'

He shrugged, but she noticed the tension in his shoulders.

'Ancient history now. Can't change the past. And you can't choose your parents, like you said.'

They reached the gazebo, and Trish busied herself setting up the tripod. Her thoughts swirled like snowflakes. It explained so much about him. But not nearly everything she wanted to know. Because she did. She wanted to know everything about him.

'Now you tell me,' Jack's tone was lighter now, 'what's the Marc update?'

Trish laughed, the sound echoing in the crisp air. 'That ship has well and truly sailed.'

'It has?'

'Very much so.' Trish straightened, meeting Jack's eyes. 'Turns out, ten years with someone who doesn't get you and wants you to be someone else… It's exhausting. It took me a while to see it, but we wanted different things. Still… After such a long time, even a mutual break-up hurts like a bitch. It took away a chunk of my confidence and optimism, I guess.'

Jack nodded. 'I hear that. My ex and I… We were like oil and water by the end.'

Trish's curiosity was already halfway out the door before she could stop it. 'What happened there?'

Jack rubbed a hand down his face. 'Melissa and I were together in school. You know, deep teenage love.' He laughed. 'She was my first, so there's that. But then she moved away to England for uni and a career. This place wasn't enough for her. I was left behind, heartbroken. When she came back ten years later, we just picked up where we'd left. Kind of just happened, like putting on old trainers. Then we got pregnant. Junior was an accident, but we wanted it to work and got married, even though we both sensed we shouldn't. We were fighting all the time, mostly about money. And then we had Beth to become more of a family and Phil to save it.' He sighed. 'Didn't make anything better, of course. The exhaustion, the fighting. Bottom line: I was never good enough for her. Just a postie.' Jack's smile was rueful. 'But that's all over now. We're making it work, for the weans. But it's tough; she wanted to get full custody just to spite me. Now we're co-parenting. It's a fragile peace.'

'I don't know her, but she sounds like a bit of a cow.' Trish nodded and turned back to her camera, lining up a shot of the snow-laden trees. 'Marc never wanted kids. Said they'd cramp his lifestyle.'

Jack snorted. 'I don't know him, but he sounds like a bit of a prick.'

Her laugh bubbled up from deep in her chest. 'He was. Is. God, what was I thinking?'

'We all make mistakes, that's how we learn. People can be lessons, too.'

'Clearly.' Trish laughed, the tension easing. She pointed to a spot overlooking the frozen pond, the bare branches of the willow trees dusted with snow. 'This'll do.'

Jack set down the equipment. 'Nice view. Though I prefer my landscapes with a bit more…curve.' His stare carved into her, a knowing glint in his eyes.

'Focus, Postman.' She busied herself with adjusting the tripod.

'Aye, focus.' His voice was low. 'That's what I'm trying to do. You're making it hard.'

'It or *it*?' Trish's heart thudded so fiercely she half-expected it to echo.

'Don't ask if you can't handle the answer.'

She cleared her throat and toggled through the camera settings. 'I, um, I need to get this done.'

He leaned against a nearby tree with crossed arms and watched her. The intensity of his gaze made her skin prickle.

'Take your time. I'm happy to…admire the view. Bend forward a bit more?'

'Jesus, let a woman do her work.' Trish smiled and calibrated the settings. A tiny snowflake landed on the lens, blurring the image. She swiped it clean. This had to be perfect. *Wanderlust* was her dream gig, her ticket to finally proving herself. Her middle finger to every doubter.

No pressure at all.

Her fingers flew over the camera's controls, muscle memory taking over as she framed the shot. Precision. Obsession. Her weapon and shield.

Trish's phone chimed in her pocket. She ignored it, concentrating on the morning light twinkling on the ice crystals. It pinged again. And again.

'Aren't you going to check that?'

Trish sighed, fishing out her phone. Three texts from the Photo Director at *Wanderlust*. She scanned them quickly, her stomach sinking with each word. 'Fuck.'

Jack raised an eyebrow. 'Everything okay?'

'Not really.' Trish pulled at one of her curls. 'The editor wants more "Scottishness".'

Another chime.

'It needs more…magic.' Trish's jaw tightened, and she wanted to hurl her phone into the pond. 'More magic? What the hell does that even mean?'

Seraphina, with her penchant for cryptic feedback, was driving her insane. 'What kind of magic are we talking about? Pixie dust? Unicorn tears? If I don't nail this assignment, I can kiss the idea of that steady job goodbye. A job as a staff photographer in their London office, with international travel. That is like a unicorn.'

Jack stepped closer. 'Hey. Take a breath. You've got this.'

Trish barked out a sound more rust than mirth, jamming her phone into her pocket. 'Do I? Because right now, it feels like I'm spinning my wheels in a mud pit, getting absolutely nowhere.'

'Stop talking nonsense.' The sincerity in his voice made her core drop into free fall.

'They're not good enough.' The admission came like a fist, bruising and unadorned. 'I'm not—'

Jack's hand on her arm stilled her pacing. 'Says who?'

'Me. My parents. Marc. This annoying editor.' Trish's voice cracked. 'Everyone.'

'Everyone's fucking wrong.' Jack's voice carved granite, brooking no argument. 'Including you.'

He reached out, wiping a stray snowflake from her cheek. His simple touch set off a slow burn under her skin like he'd flicked on a switch she didn't know she had.

'You're brilliant. I mean it.'

Trish met his gaze, struck by the conviction in his eyes. For a second, she almost let herself believe him. Then reality snapped back in place. 'Easy for you to say. You're not the one with everything riding on this.'

Jack's mouth tilted into a lopsided grin as he crouched, scooping a handful of snow. 'I'm just a humble postie.'

Despite herself, a smile crept onto her lips. 'Humble? You?'

'It's not my fault I'm irresistible.'

She rolled her eyes, but the knot in her chest loosened. 'You're insufferable.'

'Ah, but I made you smile.'

Before she could respond, something cold and wet slid down the back of her neck. Trish yelped and glared at him, sweeping the snow from her neck. 'You didn't.'

'Oh, but I did. The question is: What are you going to do

about it?' He grabbed a fresh mound of snow, working it tight between his palms.

Trish slit her eyes. 'Don't even think about it, MacGregor.'

He tossed the snowball in the air and caught it. 'What if I do, Whitmore?'

Trish grabbed a handful of her own snow, packing it into a ball. 'Then you'll regret it.'

This was nuts. The deadline was breathing down her neck like a debt collector with brass knuckles, her career teetering on a knife edge so thin it could slice bone. And yet here she was, about to launch snowballs at a walking testosterone billboard who looked like he'd been ripped straight from a postal service pin-up spread. The belt of tension Seraphina's texts had wrapped around her chest? Gone, replaced by a surge of giddy recklessness.

A wicked grin spread across her face. And with a flick of her wrist, she launched the snowball. Then she ducked behind a frost-crusted pine, lungs burning, heart thundering a punk rock rhythm.

They chased each other through the garden, slipped and skidded like drunk figure skaters on the icy ground. Trish's sides ached from laughing; her cheeks stung from the cold. Jack's boot snagged on a hidden root, and the next thing he knew, they were tumbling in a flurry of snow and limbs, rolling through the snow like a pair of clumsy otters.

When they finally stopped, Trish found herself on top, straddling his hips. Snowflakes dotted his lashes, melting as he blinked up at her.

The world reduced to breath, touch, and the electric space between them.

That's when she felt it.

The hard length of him pressing against her core. At his size, it wasn't an easy secret to keep. A slow, simmering heat spread through her, contrasting the icy snow seeping into her jeans.

'Oh.'

She shifted, half of her basking in the thrill of having this effect on a man like him. After all those years of feeling like wallpaper, suddenly she was...desired. The other half? Still couldn't wrap her head around it. She bit her lip and pushed against him, tilting her hips back and forth, and the groan that rumbled out of his throat shot straight through her.

'Is it because I'm such a hot mess? Nothing sexier than a neurotic photographer who can't get her assignment right.'

All traces of playfulness vanished from his face, and his voice was raw. 'No. It's the way you laugh. It's so fucking beautiful, it makes me hard.'

The air stuck somewhere between Trish's lungs and lips, like a swallowed hiccup. There was no hint of teasing in his eyes, just naked want and something...deeper, almost pained.

Her icy fingers teased the line of Jack's jaw, the stubble on the edge of bone and skin. She lowered her head, and their breath combined in warm puffs. She shouldn't be doing this. He shouldn't either. Snow fell around them, silent and soft, a cover of white muffling the world and all doubts.

'Jack,' she whispered and couldn't hear her voice over the pounding of her heart.

His hand came up, fingers tangling in her damp curls. 'Trish.'

And when she kissed him, she didn't think about deadlines or editors or friends or the miles that separated them.

All she could think was how happy he made her.

13

J ack's world shrank to the press of Trish's lips against his. Soft. Warm. Insistent. Snow was seeping through his jeans, but all he could focus on was her. The taste of her. Coffee and something sweet – leftover syrup from breakfast?

A sigh leaked from her mouth to his, and she wrapped her hands around his face, pulling him into a kiss that devoured all oxygen and reason. Pulse roaring, his heart tried to pulverise every internal boundary. Christ, when was the last time a simple kiss had felt like that? This was… Fuck. It was like coming home after a long day, like sinking into a warm bath.

Her hair tickled his cheeks, still wet from their snowball fight. His fingers tightened around her head, desperate to keep her close. The weight of her body on top of him, the way she fit against him… It felt right.

And fuck, he was hard. Painfully so. All from her laughter. That sound had shot straight through him. He wanted to hear it again. To be the cause of it. To make her laugh like that every bloody day.

Whoa there, postman. Slow your roll.

Trish pulled away. Her eyes were wide behind her

smudged glasses. A speck of moisture glistened on the frame, and her lashes touched the glass as she blinked, trying to focus on him. 'We probably shouldn't.'

'Aye', he agreed, even as he tilted his chin up to capture her lips again. 'We probably really shouldn't.'

But he didn't stop. And neither did she.

Jack's tongue traced the seam of her lips, drawing them apart. It was like drinking sunlight. She made a small noise, halfway between a whimper and a moan. Her hips rocked against his, and Jack bit back a groan. Christ, he was hard enough to drill through concrete.

'You feel that?' He bucked his hips up to meet hers. 'That's what you do to me. You make me so fucking hard, I can barely think straight.'

Crimson crawled up her throat, and her breath came in quick pants. Her pupils were blown out, reflecting the stark white of the snow and the deep green of the pines. She pushed her mound against his length again.

'Trish,' he gasped out between clenched teeth. 'I'm going to come like a teenager if you keep doing that.'

The way she reacted... Her breath hitched, and she ground down harder.

'Oh, you *like* that, don't you?' He thrust up again, his cock throbbing with every beat of his heart. He felt her heat, even through their layers of clothing. 'You like hearing how thick you have me. How good you make me feel.'

Her hands gripped his shoulders tighter. 'Yes.'

She was rocking against him in a rhythm that threatened to break him. Jack groaned, and his head fell back against the snow. Cold needled through his hair, a stark contrast to the hot pressure building inside him. Her lips found his – wet, urgent – a kiss that was pure, unfiltered need.

He wanted more.

So much more.

But not now. Not here.

With a herculean effort, he stilled her movements. 'Wait, Shutterbug. We really need to stop.' His gaze darted towards Hazelbrae. There wasn't a clear line of sight; there were snowy pines and all that, but still. 'Too many potentially prying eyes.'

Trish rested her forehead against his, and he felt her smile. 'Okay.'

It didn't just warm him; it set off a chain reaction that had his own lips curving before he could catch up with the why. His muscles loosened, every inch of him humming with a contentment he hadn't realised was possible. It wasn't just joy. It was deep, bone-set happiness that snuck up on him.

'Thanks for taking my mind off things.' Her breath tickled his cheek.

'Turns out that's my favourite thing to do, Shutterbug.'

As they lay there, Jack soaked it all in like he was storing up warmth for the winter. And then it hit him, hard and fast, like someone had yanked the air from his lungs – how long it had been since he'd felt this close to someone. Not just sex but this…connection. This easy laughter. Real intimacy.

Jack pushed the thought away, focusing instead on Trish's body against his. In another life, this could've been something real. If she didn't live over a hundred miles away. If she weren't his pal's girlfriend's best friend. If he were the type to get tied down. Which he wasn't. Not anymore.

Even as the thought took shape, a sneaky voice at the back of his mind chimed in, reminding him of something he wasn't ready to face. Trish was the first person in a long time who made him wonder if he could be that guy. The one who'd stick around, who'd make her coffee every morning. The one who'd support her dreams, cheering her on.

Daft notion. It wasn't like she was going to stay here. It wasn't like he was going to leave. It wasn't like he was looking for forever.

But what if forever was looking for him?

Jack gave a quick cough, trying to shake off the knot tightening in his chest. Getting all choked up right now was the last thing he wanted. He shifted, willing the sudden pressure off his ribs like it would disappear if he moved the right way.

'I don't usually have time for this.' He tried to sound casual. 'Between the weans and work... Been a while since I've just, well, arsed about like this.'

'Me neither.' Trish lifted her head, her eyes meeting his. 'I've been so focused on my career, on proving myself... I forgot how good it feels to just let go and have fun.'

'That's what I'm here for. I'm the fun guy.'

'That's not all you are.'

Jack's chest constricted as she rolled off him. It was like someone had ripped away his favourite blanket. He stood, knocking flakes from his jeans.

'We should head back.' He offered her a hand. 'Before we freeze our arses off.'

Trish nodded, her cheeks glowing from more than just the cold. As they trudged through the snow, Jack's synapses fired wild and random. The banter, the snowball fight, that kiss... It all felt natural. Easy. That was what worried him. He knew better than to let himself think it ever could be easy. He'd been down this road before.

Let someone in, and they leave. Things fall apart. Keeping it simple, casual – that was how he survived.

As they neared Hazelbrae, Jack's steps slowed. He wasn't ready to share her with the others yet.

Numpty.

He closed the heavy oak door behind them and stomped the snow off his boots as they stepped into the castle's entrance. Chatter from the ballroom spilled out into the hallway.

'Where are my little monsters?' Jack scanned the room.

Marla looked up from where she was chatting with Bert

and Niall. 'Oh, hey there. Your kids are outside in the snow. Trish, how'd the photos turn out?'

She shrugged, avoiding Marla's gaze. 'The light was a bit tricky. We'll see.'

Jack raised an eyebrow. He'd seen the way she handled that camera, like it was an extension of her. She was a visual genius, and he wasn't just saying that because he fancied her.

Because he did. He did fancy her.

The front door burst open, and in tumbled his three snow-covered kids, followed by Gwen and the two Mrs Bellbottoms, all rosy-cheeked and grinning.

'Da! We built a snowman!' Beth exclaimed, taking his hand.

'I can see that, darlin'.' Jack laughed, ruffling her hair. 'Thanks for watching them. It really takes a village, eh?'

Mrs Bellbottom waved a dismissive hand. 'Och, wrangling the wee ones was our pleasure. But we're knackered now. The land of nod awaits, dearie.' She linked arms with Sylvia, and Jack watched as the two women mounted the stairs, steps slow and steady.

Trish cleared her throat, drawing their attention. 'Hey, um…I was thinking about baking some Christmas cookies. Would you guys like to help?'

Jack caught the hopeful lilt in her words, the way she bent slightly to meet their eye level, a careful balance of confidence and nerves. His jaw tightened. Was she nervous? For his kids' approval? It made something in him twist, a mix of protectiveness and…something else.

Beth's eyes lit up, but Jack Jr. squinted like she'd just offered him Brussels sprouts. Phil just blinked at her, thumb in his mouth.

'Depends. What kind of cookies?' Junior asked.

'Simple ones,' Trish replied. 'Just lots and lots of butter and sugar?'

She didn't push, didn't overwhelm, just offered herself up like this was the most natural thing in the world.

'Can we make reindeers? With red noses?' Beth bounced on her toes.

'Snowmen!' Phil chimed in.

Junior, ever the pragmatist, crossed his arms. 'Only if Da helps.'

Trish tossed a glance Jack's way. 'What do you say? Up for some baking?'

Something tugged inside, like a string being yanked just hard enough to throw him off balance. The fucking way this woman looked at him. And including his children… Who was he to say no? They were still snowed in here for a while, anyway.

'Suppose I could lend a hand. Can't have you lot burning down Hazelbrae's kitchen now, can we?'

Marla clapped her hands together. 'Great. You lot handle the baking and keep the kids occupied. The rest of us will tackle that snow drift blocking the driveway and the path.'

As the others bundled up to head outside, Trish gathered her camera equipment. 'I'll just drop the tripod off in my room. Meet you in the kitchen in five?'

Jack nodded. The thought of being alone with her and the kids felt like slipping on a comfortable jumper he'd forgotten he owned.

Trish disappeared up the stairs, her camera bag slung over her shoulder. He put his hands in his pockets, fingertips snagging on a crinkly candy cane wrapper.

Oh, aye. That happened.

And he'd fucking loved it as much as she had.

Which could only mean one thing: he was going to fuck this up somehow.

Jack's ribs felt like they were cinching in, locking down his lungs. He'd been there before. Melissa, all her promises and plans. His own dreams of having a family. It had all gone to shite. Jack wasn't a naïve eejit. He'd learned long ago that love was something he was monumentally rubbish at, that it was best not to count on anyone. Not since his maw had packed him off to his aunt's with nothing but a rucksack and a 'Be good for them, Jackie.' The memory pricked at him, sharp as the day it happened.

Jack wrestled with Phil's snow-caked boots. The boy squirmed. 'Hold still, wee man.'

Then he hung up the kids' coats next to his own.

'Cookies! We're making cookies!' Beth chanted, jumping up and down.

'But only if you promise not to eat all the dough this time, you little snack monster.' Jack glanced at his other two, who were grinning from ear to ear. 'Let's get washed up and ready for operation Christmas cookie.'

Fifteen minutes later, Jack found himself smack in the middle of Hazelbrae's big basement kitchen, surrounded by chaos. Flour dusted every surface, and his kids were arguing over who got to stir the batter. Trish stood in the midst of it all, laughing and trying to maintain some semblance of order.

'Alright, alright.' She held up her hands. 'How about Junior stirs, Beth adds the chocolate chips, and Phil can help me roll out the dough?'

Jack leaned against the counter, crossing his arms. 'And what do I do?'

Trish looked up. 'You? You get to clean up the mess.'

He let out an amused huff. 'Fair enough.'

As they worked, Jack noticed the little things. The way Trish's hands, dusted with flour, looked so pretty. Short nails, no fuss, but neat. Like her, in a way. She'd bite her bottom lip or stick the tip of her tongue out when focusing, this tiny tell that said she was properly on it.

Beth cracked some daft joke, and Trish let out a full-volume laugh, rich and warm. He wanted to capture that sound, bottle it up, and keep it for himself.

Jack's attention snapped to Beth when a sharp yelp broke through the floury chaos. She clutched her hand, her lower lip wobbling, tears pooling but not quite spilling.

'Caught my finger in the drawer.' Beth held out her little hand.

The tip of her index finger was red, the tiniest swelling already starting. But before Jack could react, Trish was there, crouching to Beth's level. 'Oh, sweetie. Let me see.'

Beth hesitated, glancing at Jack, then back at Trish, before offering up her hand.

Trish took it gently, cradling Beth's fingers in hers. 'Hm. This needs a little magic, I think.' She leaned in, her tone conspiratorial. 'Do you know what Mrs Kaminski told me when I was your age?'

Beth shook her head, curiosity edging out the tears.

'She said if you sing a little song, the pain gets bored and goes away.'

Beth blinked. 'Bored?'

'Bored.' Trish grinned and began humming a low, soothing melody as she rubbed gentle circles over Beth's knuckles with her thumb.

It took Jack a second to recognise the tune. Sounded like *The Girl From Ipanema*.

'See?' Trish said. 'The magic's working.'

Beth sniffled, eyes huge as the redness seemed less alarming. 'It doesn't hurt so much now.'

Trish smiled. 'All better. Now, let's give that drawer a warning. Hurt you again, it'll have me to deal with. And then we put some ice on your finger.'

Beth pointed her red finger at the wood. 'You hear that?'

Jack blinked, a knot pulling tight somewhere he hadn't

even known was loose. Trish didn't belong here, not really. But somehow, in this moment, she fit better than anyone had a right to.

'Da, look!' Phil held up a misshapen lump of dough. 'It's a snowman!'

Jack's brow shot up. 'It's definitely something.'

Trish snorted as she held an ice cube to Beth's finger. 'Hey, don't knock the abstract art.'

For a moment, Jack just stood there, watching. The way Trish played with his kids, laughed with them, comforted them, and even took the time to explain how reindeer's antlers grow and shed each year… It was too picture-perfect. Like life was dangling a carrot in front of him, only to yank it away when he got too close. That nagging feeling gnawed at him.

Yet, as he watched her forehead crinkle while she tried to keep up with Phil's rapid-fire 'But why?'-questions, Jack felt it – something slid into place. It had no business being there. And worse? It was skirting dangerously close to the line he'd drawn, the one he'd sworn never to cross again.

Hope.

That was what landed you in trouble.

He cleared his throat, turning away to tend to the kettle. 'Hot choc and extra marshmallows for everyone, right?' His voice came out too loud. He winced, forcing a laugh. 'Christ, I sound like Mary Poppins.'

Jack chanced another glance at Trish, catching her faint smile. Humour, keeping it light… This was his shield against the world. A lifetime of practice, of dodging the emotional landmines that were his own childhood, his own mistakes.

Jack Jr.'s voice pulled him from his thoughts. 'Da, can we make green cookies? Like the Grinch?'

Jack ran his hand through his son's unruly hair. Junior squirmed while his dad's fingers found the one spot that always got a reaction, right at the crown, where the hair stuck up like a coo's lick. 'I don't think we have green food colouring here, mate.'

'I'll check!'

As Jack poured the hot chocolate into the mugs, he felt Trish's gaze on him. He refused to meet it, refused to let her see the chaotic thoughts swirling in his head. He couldn't trust himself not to…

What exactly was he afraid of? That she might look at him like Melissa did, with disappointment? Or worse, with pity? He was a small-town postie with three riotous kids, no money, no prospects, no plan. He couldn't afford to get tangled in this fake domesticity.

And he wouldn't dream of holding her back.

Trish would be gone soon, back to her life in the city, her stellar career. And he'd be here, same as always. Just him and the kids.

Trish reached out, her fingers touching his where they both gripped the spoon. She looked up. There it was, that barely-there smile of hers, the kind that slipped out unannounced and gripped him by the balls. She could've dragged him all across town with that smile, and she had no fucking idea.

This was exactly what he'd been afraid of. But he couldn't look away. Her hair was piled atop her head in a bun. The light caressed the curve of her cheek, the line of her neck. He shouldn't be noticing things like that. Not with his kids around. And it was that – her with his children – more than anything, that had the dread coiling in his stomach.

Because he was falling.

Falling for her, falling for the life he'd never dared to let himself want. And the terrifying part? He knew she'd catch him. Catch him and hold him up.

Jack shuddered. He had no idea what to do with this feeling. The way she fit into their little world like that special chord, the one that made the tune work. Yank it out, and there'd be nothing but noise where the music used to be. All of it was right in a way that scared the piss out of him.

Because nothing good ever lasted. Not for him, anyway.

14

The mixing bowl trembled in Trish's hands, a subtle vibration she couldn't control. Every thought was scattered like pieces of light caught in a prism, still fractured from that kiss in the snow.

That brain-fizzling, heart-wrecking, absolutely panty-melting kiss.

'Oh, for Christ's sake,' she muttered as she fumbled with the whisk. Her glasses were fogged up, and not from the temperature change. She'd come in here to bake cookies, not to relive every scorching second of that snog.

Calm down, Whitmore.

Trish's eyes settled on her Leica that rested on a nearby shelf like a watchful guardian. This sleek, black piece of magic gleaming under the kitchen lights was her third eye. Even as she reached for the sugar, her mind was composing shots.

Jack Jr. perched on a stool by the counter, measuring out flour with a concentration that seemed beyond his nine years. Beth, down on her knees, was rummaging through the cupboard, hunting for the biggest mixing bowl. Meanwhile, Phil sat cross-legged on the floor and stole licks of butter whenever he thought no one was watching. Jack stood by the sink and rolled up his sleeves to wash his hands.

Her stomach did a weird little thing, like a camera shutter clicking too fast. She'd always had a thing for forearms, and Jack's? Spectacular.

'You're pretty handy in the kitchen,' Trish commented as Jack deftly cracked an egg with one hand.

'I've had practice. Comes with the territory when you've got three wee ones to feed. But this is my only cool move; I'm showing off.'

He flashed her that boyish grin again. The kind that had no business pulling the ground out from under her, leaving her knees with the stability of wet paper.

Trish glanced over at the kids, who were now arguing over who got which cookie cutter. 'They're lucky to have you.'

Jack looked at his children with so much love Trish's insides turned soft as spun sugar.

'I'm the lucky one.' He added a pinch of flour to his fingertips and flicked it gently towards them.

The kids yelped and laughed as the flour sprinkled down like gentle snow, instantly capturing their attention.

Trish grabbed another spoon from the drawer. She handed it to Phil with a wink. 'Here, I think this one's bigger. More choc chips for you.'

Phil beamed. This was nice. But nice was something you got used to. Nice was something you started to expect. She knew better.

The first batch of dough had firmed up in the fridge, ready for tiny hands and star-shaped cutters.

'Who's ready to cut some cookies?' Trish asked into the kitchen.

'Me!' all three kids shouted in unison.

Trish stole a sideways peek at Jack, who was helping Junior roll out the dough, his large hands gentle and patient.

'Like this, pal.' Jack pressed the rolling pin firmly, and his mini-me nodded, mimicking his dad's movements.

This was what she'd missed growing up. The simple, unpolished everyday moments that were magic because you shared them with people you cared about. It was like staring at a photograph of a moment she'd never captured. Her own childhood had been all starched tablecloths and polished silverware, while the kitchen remained a foreign territory staffed by professionals. She'd never known the joy of spilling flour, licking spoons, or feeling someone's warm hands over hers, guiding her through a recipe. She was experiencing FOMO for a past she'd never had. Nostalgia for something that should have happened but never did.

Jack looked up, his gaze sliding into hers with an electric kind of ease. A slow smile pulled at the corner of his mouth, and Trish's pulse faltered. There was something incredibly attractive about a man who was so good with kids.

'Trish, look!' Beth pointed to a speck of dough shaped vaguely like a reindeer. 'I made Rudolph!'

Trish's smile deepened. 'That's brilliant, Beth! Make sure to give him a big, red nose.' She handed the girl a small tube of red icing.

Beth squeezed the icing onto the dough with more enthusiasm than precision. Trish reached out, steadying the girl's hand. 'Like this, sweetheart.'

Beth looked up at her. 'You're good at this.'

'Thank you.'

Trish tore her gaze away, focusing hard on wiping down the counter in front of her.

Jack moved in closer. 'You having fun?'

Trish nodded. She was afraid if she opened her mouth, she'd say something stupid. Like how much she loved this. How much she loved being here with him and his children. How much she wanted to stay but couldn't.

Jack turned back to the table and picked up a cookie

cutter. 'Right, let's keep fingers out of drawers and icing out of hair, aye?'

Trish almost tasted the memories in the making. The scene before her was too precious not to capture. She reached for her camera and wrapped her fingers around the familiar grip like a lifeline. The low winter sun squeezed through the garden-level windows of the souterrain kitchen, throwing angled beams across the stone floor like spotlights. Patches of light danced over worn wood and glinted off copper pots, casting a play of shadow and shine that was almost too damn perfect to be real. Through the viewfinder, the world narrowed to a series of perfect moments.

Jack's strong hands guiding Beth's smaller ones as they cut out star-shaped cookies.

Click.

The flour dusting Junior's nose as he peered intently at the pictures in the recipe book.

Click.

Phil's tongue poking out in concentration as he decorated a lopsided snowman.

Click.

Trish adjusted her aperture, honing in on the way the light laced through the golden strands in Jack's hair. He looked up, snagging her gaze like he'd been waiting for it.

Click.

'Thought you were helping, not documenting.'

Trish lowered her camera. 'This light is too good to waste.'

But it wasn't just the light, was it? It was the sense of belonging that radiated from every flour-dusted surface. It was everything she'd always wanted. But wanting meant risking. The possibility of losing.

Trish raised her camera again, focusing on a close-up of Jack's hands as he helped Phil roll out more dough. The faded ink on his knuckles, the slight roughness of his skin – she catalogued every detail.

Click.

Because memories were safer than hopes. Photographs couldn't break your heart.

As the children were busy doing the shapes with the cookie cutters, Trish felt Jack's warmth seep into her back. He dusted a gentle kiss on the nape of her neck, a whisper of contact, and she instinctively backed away.

'The kids…'

'Busy.'

She glanced at the three, still blissfully focused on their creations. Trish turned to face Jack, her voice barely above a whisper, 'Just reminding you, we've got company.'

'You're a natural with them, you know.'

Trish blinked up at him. 'What do you mean?'

Jack nodded towards his three children. 'You're great with them. Fun. Patient. Kind. They really like you. Even Junior.'

Her skin heated again. She hadn't thought much about being a mum. Not because she didn't want to be, exactly, but because it had always felt…out of reach. Like something other women did. Marc hadn't wanted kids, and if she was honest, she hadn't fought him on it. How could she when the idea of a wholesome family felt so foreign? She'd been certain she'd cock it up somehow.

'Thanks. But it's easy to like them right back. They're so sweet.'

Jack's laugh was low, more felt than heard. 'Right now they are. But you wait until bedtime.'

His lips whispered softly against her temple; then he sauntered back towards the large, old oak table in the centre of the kitchen. With a gentle nudge, Jack helped his daughter shape the reindeer's legs, guiding her hands. 'Like this, darlin'. Nice and careful.'

Trish busied herself with the baking tray, hands on autopilot. But that pull inside her wouldn't let go. A gnawing itch coiling in her gut.

Her career looked like a mess, a jumble of half-baked ideas and failed attempts. Thirty-six, and she was still clawing for recognition, still struggling to make a steady income from the thing she loved. Marc had always expected her to mould herself to his life. He'd never understood her passion for photography, had never seen the way she could capture the essence of a moment, the way she could tell a story through a single frame. He'd wanted her to be his small, well-bred, agreeable trophy. A perfectly packaged partner he could display without ever having to deal with her ambition or fire.

His fucking head had exploded when she'd quit her marketing job.

But Jack… He'd only known her for three months. And yet he encouraged her, even when she was feeling like a failure.

A knot jammed up in her throat, coming out of nowhere like a rogue wave, clogging her airway.

Jack's voice cut through her thoughts. 'You okay?'

Trish blinked, realising she'd been staring at the same spot on the counter for who knows how long. 'Yeah, sorry. Just thinking.'

One of Jack's brows shot up. 'About Santa and his naughty elf?'

'Oh, shut it,' Trish laughed, flicking a bit of flour at him.

Jack grinned and reached out to sweep the flour from her cheek. His touch lingered. 'Make me.'

She wanted to. God, how she wanted to. But the kids were right there, and this wasn't real. This was a Christmas castle daydream. The kind of holiday magic you'd find in a Netflix film. Beautiful, heart-warming, but fading as soon as the credits rolled.

'You're staring into the void again, Shutterbug,' Jack murmured, low enough that only she could hear.

Her smile widened. There was something about the way he used the nickname, the playful tone that made her feel…

seen. Like she was part of something. This man, with his dad jokes and his kind eyes and his ability to make her smile even when she felt like crying.

Be rational. Be reasonable.

This was just baking. It wasn't a date or anything. They simply happened to be snowed in together and had to keep the kids occupied. But she wanted to lean into him, to feel his arms wrap around her, to hear him laugh at something she said. She wanted to be part of this.

Stop it, silly. You're here to take photos.

It wasn't real. It couldn't be. Jack wasn't the type to settle down. Kids or no kids, he never stayed in one bed for too long. And even if he were, she wasn't the type to be settled. Not here. She had a career to launch and couldn't just stay here, lost in the land of more lochs than locals. Trish shook her head, pushing the thoughts away. This was just a Christmas fling, at best.

When the first batch was done, Junior, Beth, and Phil pounced on the cookies like a pack of wild little wolves, their laughter echoing through the kitchen.

'We're gonna show them to Marla and Gwen!' Beth declared. And off they ran.

Trish wiped her hands on a dishcloth, surveying the mess in the kitchen. 'That was an experience.'

Jack let out a snort of laughter, rinsing a bowl under the tap. 'Chaos is their natural habitat.'

Trish leaned against the counter. 'I can't even imagine handling three on my own. Even if they're…nice little people.'

'Nice, hey?' His voice dropped, laced with amusement and something else. 'You know what's nice?'

Jack stepped closer behind her and slipped his arm around her waist underneath her jumper. His breath skimmed her skin, just enough to stir up trouble, and his hand found the bare warmth just above the waistband of her sweatpants.

'What on God's green earth are you doing?'

'Shhh. Don't want to draw attention, do we?'

She kept her eyes on the counter, on the remnants of dough and scattered chocolate chips, as he moved lower, dipping beneath the waistband.

'Behave,' she whispered, but the words came out with the conviction of a cooked noodle.

'Where's the fun in that?'

His fingers dipped lower and teased the edge of her briefs, prickling her skin into tight, responsive bumps. The cotton folded and stretched between his knuckles. Her breath seized, a tiny tremor threading through her ribs.

'Feel that?' His voice scraped low against her ear. 'How your body's already saying yes? Now *that's* nice.'

He slipped underneath, finding her slick and swollen. Two fingers pressed deep, ruthlessly precise, sinking into her. Her muscles gripped him reflexively, a compulsive pull. Her breath scattered in uneven pulses.

'Fuck. God.' Trish's hands gripped the smooth edge of the counter. She felt every callous on his fingertips, every ridge. Her eyelids drooped, and her teeth clamped down, stifling the sound rising in her throat. As Jack withdrew, the absence burned like a sudden draft against wet skin. Her heartbeat pulsed so hard it felt like it might give her away.

She risked a glance over her shoulder. Jack's eyes held hers, dark and unblinking. He raised his hand and slid his tongue across his fingers. The slick sound was barely audible over the hum of the oven, but it shot through her like a spark, lighting her up.

'Mmm…still sweet. And still sweet.'

'Jack, what is this…with us?'

'I don't know. But I'm enjoying it. Very much.'

The way he stretched 'very' – that raw Scottish burr – sent flames licking down her spine. Her ribcage felt compressed, each breath harder and harder to control. She turned to face him, her hips pinned against the counter's edge. His presence warped her gravity, each cell rotating – until she aligned completely, inevitably toward him. She should put some distance between them. But her body refused.

'Jack, we can't—' she started, but her words were cut short as his thumb skimmed along her lower lip.

'Can't what? Can't enjoy this? Can't let ourselves feel something for a moment?'

She closed her eyes as he rubbed his nose against hers, infinitely gently. His breath mingled with hers, warm and sweet from the cookies.

'This isn't real,' she whispered, even as her hands found their way to his chest, feeling the racing thump of his heart beneath her palms. 'It… It can't be.'

The room fell quiet for a beat like the universe hit pause.

'Aye. I guess you're right.'

Trish's heart dropped a million feet as Jack stepped away with a pained frown on his face. The loss of his warmth felt as if someone had snuffed out the only candle.

'It's as real as Santa Claus.' His voice was too calm, and the huge kitchen suddenly felt too small, too intimate. 'I should go and check on the kids.' He turned around.

As he left the room, Trish released a trembling breath. She stared at the doorway, half-expecting him to return. But he didn't.

This wasn't supposed to be anything more than a bit of fun during the holiday season. So why did her chest fold in on itself like an empty cardboard box at the thought of leaving them behind?

15

Everything felt too small like the walls were closing in. Jack's boots scuffed against the worn stone steps as he ascended from the kitchen through the narrow stairwell.

Trish's words lodged in his head: 'It's not real.'

She was right, of course. This wasn't real. It couldn't be.

But fuck if it didn't feel like it.

Jack's palm settled on the banister's worn grain. The distant sound of his kids' laughter drifted down from above. A posh lass like Trish, with dreams bigger than this postcode's entire horizon? She'd never be satisfied with a small-town postie. And he'd be damned if he'd clip her wings, keep her from soaring by tying her to this forgotten corner of the world. She'd suffocate here faster than a butterfly pinned under glass. She'd grow resentful of him.

Jack resumed his climb, each step feeling heavier than the last. He reached the top of the stairs. Shoulders back, chin lifted, mouth stretched into a grin so manufactured it could've been stamped from tin. Then he pushed open the door to the ballroom.

His kids were huddled with Gwen near the Christmas

tree, their faces sticky with cookie crumbs. And there it was. The thing that made Kilcranach home.

His people.

Not blood-bound, but bonded by something more stubborn: chosen connection.

They'd been his lifeline when his mother's rejection dropped like a shit-ton of ice water, when grief rattled through him after his aunt's death, and when his divorce shredded everything. They'd scooped him up – him and his kids. Jack owed them. Big time. And getting tangled with Marla's best friend? That'd be like taking a sledgehammer to the only goddamn foundation he'd managed to cobble together. He already felt like he was punching above his weight just having her here. Trying to make her part of *his* world? That'd only end with him losing her. And probably everything else that kept him steady, including the people who'd stuck by him when he needed them most.

Marla lurched an eyebrow. 'How did the baking go?'

Jack shrugged. 'Grand. Though I think we used every bowl in the place.'

Janet Bellbottom, back from her nap, perched on the arm of a nearby chair. She peered at him over her glasses. 'How's our lovely photographer doing? Still snapping away?'

Trish's face, lips parted like she'd been caught mid-sigh, slipped into Jack's thoughts. He pushed it aside. 'Cataloguing the chaos, I think.'

Their stares scraped the back of his neck. Unspoken questions hung in the air, thick as bog mist. These people had witnessed every spectacular MacGregor nosedive. The thought of another crash twisted in his gut like a damn corkscrew. Pity. Those knowing side-glances. Disappointed murmurs.

Not. Fucking. Again.

He loved this community, but it didn't take much for folks to start talking, and the wrong story at the wrong time could tip the scales. Jack snatched a cookie, ramming it into his mouth. Sugar disintegrated into sawdust, coating his throat like regret.

Gwen's gaze cut through the small talk and pleasantries like she could see through his bullshit. Which she probably could. He shifted his weight, and the floorboards creaked beneath his boots. He had to get out of here; the air felt too thick with expectation.

'There's enough batter in the kitchen to wrap the whole castle,' he said in the direction of his children. 'So, who wants to bake more cookies?'

Three sets of eyes lit up like the Christmas tree last night.

'Okay, wee monsters. Back to the kitchen for round two.'

The kids cheered, already scrambling towards the door. His phone buzzed in his pocket, a jolting tremor against his thigh. He fished it out. Melissa.

Fuck.

Jack held up a finger. 'Hold your horses. Just gotta…' He trailed off, answering the call. 'Aye, Mel?'

He turned away, trying to shield the conversation from the room's collective gaze.

'I need to talk to you about Christmas.' Melissa's voice was clipped.

Jack closed his eyes briefly, bracing himself. This was never good. He kept his voice as neutral as possible. 'What's up?'

'Craig and I are going on holiday in five days. Two weeks in Magaluf. We've just been invited by clients of his, but the kids can't come. So I'll need you to take them. Over Christmas and Hogmanay. We'll be back on January second.'

Jack's organs went sideways, every cell running for an emergency exit. Two weeks? Smack in the middle of Christmas and Hogmanay? How the fuck was he supposed to wrangle that logistical nightmare?

'Mel, you know that Christmas is my busiest time. The post office—'

'Och, don't give me that, Jack. I saw the photos. You playing "Sexy Santa".' Her voice dripped acid. 'If you've got time for that shite, you've got time for your own children.'

Mortification flash-froze his blood, every capillary going arctic. The photos. Of course, she'd use them like a weapon.

Jack glanced back at the room. They were pretending not to be watching or listening. But they were. He wanted to disappear, to dissolve into the floorboards and become one with the dust bunnies.

Jack gripped the phone tighter. 'It was just a little harmless fun, Mel.' He spoke quietly, aware of the ears around him.

'Fun?' Melissa scoffed. 'While I'm here busting my ass trying to make ends meet, you're gallivanting around half-naked? Really responsible, Jack. As always.'

He could almost see her, arms crossed, eyes flashing. He squeezed his eyes shut to make the image disappear. 'That's not fair. You know I take care of the kids just as much—'

'Do you?' she cut him off. 'Because from where I'm standing, it looks like you're more interested in playing rock star and viral sex symbol than being a father.'

Her words stung like frostbite. He glanced at his kids. He was trying, dammit. 'You know it's not easy—'

'Easy?' Her voice rose half an octave. 'You want to talk about easy? I could tell you how often I—'

'At least you're not alone, Mel.' He couldn't keep the bitterness out of his voice. 'You've got...*Craig*.'

There was a pause, a beat of silence that spoke volumes. 'Aye, I do. And he wants to take me away for a bit. Is that so wrong?'

Jack sighed, rubbing the heel of his palm across his jaw. 'No, it's not wrong. But neither is asking for a little understanding. I can't just drop everything—'

'Can't or won't?'

Anger punched through him, skin radiating fuck-you fire. 'Listen, I'm not saying no, awright? I'm just saying it's fucking complicated.'

'Complicated.' She laughed, a harsh sound. 'Life is complicated, Jack. Grow up.'

Jack bit back a retort. 'Mel, it's not...' He started, then stopped. What was the point? She'd already made up her mind. 'Fine. It's not like I have a choice.'

'No, you don't. It's your turn. You've left me hanging dry for years. It's your flesh and blood. So, have a nice Christmas. And I'm sure all three are happy to stay with you. Fewer rules and all that. Bye now.'

The line went dead. Jack stuffed the phone back in his pocket, his hand clenching into a fist. He turned back to the room and forced another smile.

'Everything okay, Jack?' Marla's words came as though she'd already clocked whatever he was trying to hide and was daring him to deny it.

Jack nodded, his throat tight. 'Just Mel being Mel.'

He looked at his kids, their faces bright with anticipation. Guilt churned low in his gut, like a bad pint settling in his stomach. It wasn't that he didn't want them for Christmas. More like he wanted to fully be there for them. And he couldn't.

Fuck. Jack dragged a hand over his face. As usual, he'd have to wing it somehow.

Another thought crossed his mind. Trish deserved better than the messy reality of his life. Three kids, an ex-wife who treated him like a stray dog – for good reasons, to be fair – and a job that barely paid the bills. He pictured Trish trying to navigate the chaos of his mornings. The frenzied search for matching socks, the spilt cereal, the constant bickering.

She'd hate it. She'd run.

The room was too warm, the scent of pine and cookies

cloying. The heaviness of Melissa's words still pushing down on him like a sodden wool blanket.

'Right, cookie monsters. Let's get back to baking and get you a few sandwiches for lunch.' He shepherded the kids towards the kitchen, thinking about logistics and childcare for the next two weeks.

Descending the stairs, Jack's thoughts careened like a drunk driver. The viral photo, Melissa's demands, Trish's smile… Everything collided in a wreck of guilt, want, and worry.

What the fuck was he playing at?

The kitchen's warmth hit him like a wall as he opened the door.

'Triiish!' Jack Jr., Beth, and Phil yelled in unison.

His kids were bouncing around like sugared-up gremlins, hyped for another round of flour fights. Jack's chest cinched, not with love – he had that in spades – but with a stab of parental panic. He adored those little maniacs, but the constant pressure? It was like trying to herd cats while juggling flaming knives.

Jack stalled mid-threshold. Trish stood backlit by the oven-glow, glasses askew, a chocolate constellation smudged across her cheek.

She looked up, her grin bright enough to rival the kitchen lights. 'Hey. Just in time to get roped into round two.'

Flour dusted her cheeks, and her tongue poked out in concentration as she prepared something on a baking sheet. Jack's heart seized like a fist as he watched Trish carefully arrange the cookie letters. J, B, P.

Not just any letters.

His kids' initials.

Something geological realigned inside him, tectonic plates grinding. The truth punched him square in the sternum: he was fucked. Monumentally, catastrophically fucked.

He was…*falling in love*?

He gripped the counter, steadying himself. The weight of it settled in his chest, warm and terrifying. Trish was…everything. Brilliant. Kind. Sexy without trying. Funny as fuck. The way she saw the world, capturing beauty in the smallest moments…

He wanted to cup her face in his hands, to brush away that smear of chocolate on her cheek with his thumb. To taste it on her skin. To memorise every freckle, every laugh line. To tell her he was falling. Falling so hard he might not survive the landing.

The words jammed in his throat. His fingers drummed against the counter, a restless rhythm that matched the beat of his heart.

Trish's smile widened, a small dimple appearing in her left cheek. 'Come on, Postie Pat. Your turn to get messy.'

He buried his hands in his pockets, attempting to look casual. Like he wasn't about to spontaneously combust. 'What's the plan?'

'These are for the kids.' She gestured to the tray, where J, B, and P were taking shape in perfectly formed cookie dough.

His fucking heart.

'They'll love that.' His voice came out rough, so he gave a little cough to smooth it over.

'Da! Look!' Beth held up a cookie. 'That's me! B for Beth!'

'Mine's a J,' Junior declared, grabbing his cookie. 'And it's got green sprinkles. Nice.'

Phil glared at his cookie, head tilted. 'What's that?'

'That's your letter, wee man. P for Phil.' Jack's hand settled lightly on Phil's head.

Junior took a big bite. 'Did Trish make these just for us?'

'Aye, she did.' Jack's words scratched the back of his throat.

'Why?' Junior asked.

Trish shrugged. 'Because I thought it was cool.'

'It is', Junior said and grinned.

Beth's feet shifted in a little dance. 'Can we make some for her too?'

'What letter does Trish start with?' Phil asked.

'T.' Junior said. 'Like turtle.'

'Or tiger!' Beth added.

'Well, then,' Trish wiped her floury hands on her apron, 'who wants to decorate the next batch?'

Beth squealed, grabbing a bowl of sprinkles. 'Me! Me! Me!'

Jack Jr. pointed at a tube of icing. 'Can I do the green one?'

'Sure!'

Suddenly, Trish's phone rang. She fumbled it free from her pocket, and the brightness in her face dimmed as she glanced at the screen. 'Sorry, I need to take this.' With a tight smile, she stepped back, muttering a clipped, 'Hi, Seraphina.'

Jack's ears perked up, catching the tension in her voice like static in the air. 'Yes… What? Tomorrow? Yes, they're… Look, I'm a bit—' Trish's voice was tight. 'No, that won't be a problem. Of course not.'

Jack tightened his gaze as she paced, one hand gripping the phone, the other twisting her curls. Something was off.

'Sure, I can call you back. Five minutes? Okay. Goodbye.' She ended the call, her shoulders sagging.

'Everything fine?' Jack asked.

She untied her apron, draping it over a chair. 'Work stuff. Deadline's been moved up. I need to go edit those photos asap. You okay to finish baking without me?'

'Of course.' He picked up a stray sprinkle from the counter.

Beth pouted. 'But we're not done decorating!'

'I know, sweetheart.' Trish knelt down, giving each child a hug. 'You'll have to show me your masterpieces later, okay? Can't wait to see them.'

Trish straightened up, and Jack froze as she leaned toward him. In that microscopic moment before contact, the universe contracted. Her lips grazed his cheek, barely a whisper of touch. But fuck, it detonated through him like a low-voltage current.

A millisecond kiss. Chaste as a nun's prayer.

And he was wrecked.

He'd snogged women senseless. But this? Freaking out over a kiss on the cheek? This was unheard of.

His children cackled, oblivious to the earthquake happening inside their father.

'Ewww!' Jack Jr. said. 'Da and Trish, sitting in a tree…'

'K-I-S-S-I-N-G!' Beth chimed in.

A molten tide climbed his neck. 'Oi, you wee monsters. Back to your cookies.'

'Later?' Trish whispered, her breath warm against his ear.

He nodded, his voice lodged somewhere between his chest and his throat.

Trish turned and headed for the stairs. Jack watched her go, tightness knotting in his stomach.

Her work call. The deadline moved up. His kids' cookie letters cooling on the tray. All the pieces clicked into a picture Jack didn't want to see. His chest ached like someone had reached in. She'd made cookies for his kids. But now she was running off to edit photos for some fancy London magazine.

16

Sometimes, making magic meant destroying reality, and Trish was becoming an expert at both.

She paced the room, phone glued to her ear, her attention fracturing between the glowing laptop screen and the mess of camera gear scattered on the bed.

'Trish, darling,' Seraphina's voice scraped honey over razor blades, 'as I said, it's out of my hands that the deadline's been moved up. We need your best shots by tomorrow morning. Exceptional, not just good. No room for mediocrity.'

Trish's grip tightened on the phone. 'Seraphina, I've got a ton of editing to do. I'm not sure I can—'

'I have complete faith in you,' Seraphina interrupted. 'You're a professional, aren't you? Besides, we really want to capture that Highland Christmas vibe. Think romantic, whimsical. You know, all those cosy, charming details. That's why we chose *you*.'

Doubt lodged itself beneath Trish's sternum. She stared at her laptop screen, the cursor blinking like a malevolent metronome. 'I don't want to exaggerate. Kilcranach isn't just some postcard fantasy. It's real, and I'd prefer to stay true to that.'

'Trish, do you know why our readers buy our magazine? Escapism. They want a fairy tale that looks just realistic enough. They want to see the magic of the Highlands. Walter Scott, *Outlander*, tartan galore. Give them that.'

'I get it, but I don't want to lose sight of what's real. Kilcranach isn't Disneyland.'

'Disneyland?' Seraphina's long sigh was intentionally audible. 'Just…enhance the charm a bit. You can do that, can't you? We're really counting on you. This *could* be huge for your career.'

Or not if you don't deliver. Subtext received.

Trish's thoughts spun, scenes of Jack and the kids blurring in her mind. Their life here was tangible, real. Replacing that with a polished, artificial image unsettled her. 'I know it's important, Seraphina. I just—'

'You need to deliver, Trish. We love your work, but we need you to step up. Make this happen. Think about how much this means to your future. You want this, don't you?'

Trish's hand trembled slightly as she pushed her glasses up her nose. 'Of course, yes.'

'Fabaroo! Then get it done. We're expecting great things from you, Trish. Don't let us down.'

The line went silent. Trish dropped the phone onto the bedside table, its plastic clatter slicing through the quiet. The attic room contracted, walls pressing inward. Her eyes flicked to the blinking cursor on her laptop screen. She sat down on the bed with a frustrated groan, her fingers tapping on the edge of the computer. Seraphina's words clung to her like a too-tight sweater, smothering her creativity.

This didn't feel like making art. This felt like a chore with an aftertaste of cheating.

Her fingers hovered over the keyboard, indecision gnawing at her. The pressure of turning Kilcranach into a glossy fantasy coiled tight in her gut, sour and wrong.

She leaned forward, clicking open the folder of pictures

from the past few days. Images of Kilcranach filled the screen, each one a snapshot of the life she'd been immersed in. Her fingers tapped the keyboard, the click-click-click echoing in the silence.

She zoomed in on the photo, studying the arc of Jack's lips, the easy warmth etched into his features. The way he grinned had a certain pull. That smile could undo her for good, and damn if she wasn't already halfway there.

Trish's eyes skimmed over the camera gear sprawled all over the bed, each piece a reminder of the dream she'd been chasing for years. Now, staring at it, all she felt was pressure. Failure nipped at her heels, paralysing her. If she couldn't pull this off, what did that make her? The girl who thought she could but never did? Disappointment. Failure. The labels hovered, waiting to stick.

She couldn't let *Wanderlust* down. But she also couldn't let herself down. This was her chance to show that she was more than just a marketing manager playing at photography.

Seraphina's words clanged around in her skull. 'Magic. Charm. Whimsical.' Trish's gut twisted like she'd downed bad milk. She knew what Seraphina wanted.

Tartankitsch.

Snow-dusted heather and Highland coos with frost on their shaggy coats. Stags on the moors and shortbread tins by the hearth. Whisky in crystal tumblers and plaid everywhere: blankets, scarves, even the dogs. Not the emptying villages with 'For Sale' signs where families used to be. Not the second homes sitting dark through winter while locals fought to find a place to live. The daily struggles, the isolation.

Trish's gaze drifted to the window. The snow outside was hiding the imperfections beneath. She knew the truth: underneath were dead leaves, gnarled roots, and mud. Nothing was ever as perfect as it seemed. But snow made it look that way.

Her hand shook as she reached for her camera. The weight

of it was different now, heavier with expectations and doubt. She turned it over in her hands.

I have to be like snow.

Trish gripped her camera like an anchor as she descended the grand staircase. One last shoot. She paused at the doorway, her eyes scanning the room.

People swarmed around the late lunch buffet, balancing plates, the air alive with laughter and conversations. The image of Marla and Niall hit her retinas with the subtlety of a camera flash. A thin ache scratched along her insides. Not jealousy, but close enough to stir that old sensation of being on the outside, looking in. Marla blended into this place, woven into its fabric. Niall, the village, the whole vibe – it all fit her. She was part of Kilcranach's tapestry. Meanwhile, Trish was the voyeur behind the lens.

Suddenly, that role pinched and rubbed in all the wrong places, like trying to squeeze into too-small winter boots.

Marla glanced up and waved at her. 'Trish, grab some grub. You must be starving.' The grin that followed lit up her face, making it clear she wasn't taking no for an answer.

Trish couldn't help but smile back. It was good to see her friend so content and at ease. Trish was happy for Marla. Even though she wasn't really a part of it.

'In a bit. I want to capture some of this first.'

Marla arched a brow. 'Always working, aren't you? That's a fast track to burnout, babe. You've gotta step off the tread-mill sometime. And I must know, I'm running a retreat for NHS personnel with burnout.'

Trish raised her camera, letting the viewfinder's black borders block out everything as a rush of emotions threatened to break through. She fired off a few shots of the scene, honing in on the tiny, unnoticed moments. Each click of the shutter was a comfort, a rhythm that steadied her nerves.

Gwen sidled up beside her, her lips quirking in that way that said she knew exactly what was up. 'You're not fooling anyone, you know. You can't hide behind that camera forever.'

Trish lowered the Leica. 'I'm not hiding. I'm working.'

Gwen snorted. 'Working, my arse. You're avoiding. And Jack has gone home, in case you're wondering.'

Trish's pulse stopped for a second. 'Oh?'

Gwen gave one of those half-hearted, can't-be-bothered shrugs. 'Took the kids and buggered off half an hour ago. With the driveway being finally clear and all that.'

Trish's clutched her camera. 'Makes sense.'

Gwen studied her, a sympathetic tilt to her head. She gestured towards the buffet table. 'Come on, let's get you a sandwich. You seem like you could use a serious snack.'

Trish trailed after Gwen, her thoughts zigzagging like a pinball. Jack had left without saying goodbye? She tried to ignore the sinking feeling in her stomach, the gnawing sense of disappointment.

As they approached the table, Janet Bellbottom bustled over, her leopard print blouse clashing with the festive decor.

'Dearie, I was hoping to catch you. I wanted to thank you for those lovely photos you took of Muffin. He's quite the model, isn't he?'

Trish managed a smile at the thought of the grumpy Border Terrier. 'He's a natural. I'm glad you liked them.'

Trish's gaze swept the room before settling on the vacant spot where Jack and the kids had been earlier. Her throat tightened like it was fighting against her.

Marla appeared at her side, a glass of wine in hand. 'Here, you look like you need this.'

Trish took the glass. 'Thanks, Babes.' She downed it in three sips, which earned her a minorly concerned glance from her best friend.

'Refill?'

'Nope, I'm working.'

Trish clicked through a few shots, capturing the joy and connection on people's faces. Seraphina's critique gnawed at the back of her mind. This wasn't enough. She needed the fairy tale, not the mundane reality.

Her eyes hooked on Janet Bellbottom and her signature leopard print. This could be...

Trish approached her with brightness in her voice. 'Mrs Bellbottom, can I trouble you for a photo? Perhaps by the Christmas tree?'

Janet Bellbottom's grin spread wide, the kind of smile that had probably talked half the village into trouble. 'Of course, dearie. But only if you promise to make me look like a Hollywood starlet.'

'I'll do my best. You've definitely got the glamour.'

She positioned Mrs Bellbottom against the tree, Christmas lights etching silver threads across her weathered skin.

Trish snapped a few shots, then paused, her fingers tapping against the camera. 'Could you perhaps...tilt your head slightly? And maybe a softer smile? And now lift a bauble with two fingers...' One subtle direction after another, a choreography of manipulation.

Mrs Bellbottom raised an eyebrow but pivoted into performance mode. Less Highland ex-teacher, more reluctant beauty pageant contestant.

Trish's insides knotted tighter than a camera strap in a rush, but her finger hit the shutter, her mind already envisioning the edits. 'Are you okay with me submitting them to *Wanderlust*?'

'Sure.' Mrs Bellbottom chortled. 'I don't mind a bit of spotlight. If our dear postie doesn't mind sharing his fifteen minutes of fame.'

'You've already signed a model release. So that's good. Now a little to the left...'

After she was done shooting Mrs Bellbottom, Trish

moved on to Gwen, who was pouring alcohol-free punch into red mugs. 'Could I get a pic of you doing that? Maybe with a bit more of a festive smile and in front of the fireplace?'

Gwen looked up. 'A festive fucking smile? Trish, are you awright?'

Trish let out a laugh, but it sat awkwardly in the air, as stiff as her shoulders. 'Just trying to capture the spirit of the season.'

Gwen shook her head. Then she stretched her lips into an exaggerated smile, showing off her chipped front tooth like an exclamation mark.

I can fix that asymmetry in post.

Trish took the photo. 'Thanks, Gwen.'

'Anytime, hen. Marla's pals are our pals.'

Trish turned and looked straight at Niall, the epitome of the Highlander with his auburn hair and broody aura.

Jamie Fraser has fuck all on him.

Niall was leaning against the wall, his arms crossed over his chest, a slight scowl on his face.

She approached him with slow steps. 'Niall, do you think I could get a shot of you in your great kilt? You know, the one you wore on opening day. It would highlight the Highland charm.'

Niall's scowl deepened. 'No.'

Trish blinked, taken aback. 'What do you mean, "no"?'

'I won't put it on just for a picture; it takes forever. And it makes me look like a cliché.'

Trish's fingers locked around the camera. 'But it would add to the authenticity—'

'Authenticity?' Niall pushed off the wall and scoffed. 'This is authentic, Trish. Me, in my jeans and an old hoodie, having a laugh and a chat with my friends and my woman and my dog.'

Trish's face burned so hot she could've baked cookies on

her cheeks. She lowered her camera, feeling the sting of Niall's words more than she wanted to admit.

'You're right. I'm sorry. I got carried away.'

Niall's jaw unclenched, and the tension drained away, the edge in his voice fading. 'Nae bother. I get it. A man in a kilt is a special kind of Sexy Santa. It's just not me.'

Oh, right. That.

Trish's mind drifted back to Jack. Perhaps he'd seen through her façade to the wreck underneath – the relentless need to prove herself, the fear of failure shadowing every shot she took. The neediness. No wonder he'd slipped away without another word. They might see each other again before she left for Edinburgh, possibly. Somehow, his quiet exit today stung more than it should have.

Trish closed the door behind her with a thud and slumped against the heavy wood. Her pulse pounded in her neck, chasing the wild tangle of her thoughts. Her tiny attic room was spinning.

'Shit.'

Marla had been enthusiastic about letting Trish use Hazelbrae for the shoot – 'It's perfect for the magazine, Babes!' And she hadn't been wrong. The late-eighteenth-century castle was a Highland Christmas fantasy come to life, especially dusted with snow. But forcing people into awkward poses, with fake grins and stiff holiday cheer, twisted Trish's insides like a bad roll of film. This wasn't the Kilcranach she'd come to like. This was a curated lie wrapped in tartan and tied with a bow of bullshit.

And Jack.

No goodbye, no see you later. No note, no text, no word. Probably nothing. Probably just rushed off with the kids, right? Totally reasonable. Except her stomach didn't believe it.

It twisted anyway, churning through too many emotions at once – anger, hurt, fear.

He could've left a note. A text wouldn't have killed him.

Her logical brain tried to calm her down.

Maybe he didn't have time, maybe he'll call later, maybe—

But the maybes weren't helping. They weren't silencing the part of her that had been bracing for this since the beginning.

This is Jack MacGregor, it whispered. *Walking, talking flight risk. You knew this was coming.*

She pressed her palms to her temples, shutting the thought down.

Stop. Don't do this.

But her mind wasn't done punishing her. Because hadn't she known this would happen? Hadn't she told herself he was just a bit of seasonal stuffing, a Christmas temp job for her libido, a holiday boost to her ego? She'd known. She'd prepared.

So why did it feel like the ground had been yanked out from under her anyway?

Trish pushed off the door, legs shaking as she made her way to the bed. Her laptop sat open. She collapsed onto the mattress. Her phone buzzed, jolting her out of her thoughts. She dug it out of her pocket, heart skidding into her throat. Not Jack. Her mother.

MOTHER (14:37) Darling, your father and I expect you for Christmas dinner. The new ambassador's son will be there. Perhaps it is time to discuss your future? You're 36. Time to get you on a proper path. Mummy x

Nausea rolled through her like bad eggnog. Her phone sailed across the bed, landing with a muted thump as her hands knotted into tight fists. Her mother's expectations and her own terror of spectacular implosion crushed her chest. A concrete weight, real as broken bones.

Then she saw it. The message she'd missed. Jack, fifteen minutes ago.

> JACK (13:09) Sorry. Had to get the menace home. And you were right; this isn't real. But it was fun as long as it lasted. Now you focus on your job. Show them what you're made of. See you around. J.

The screen dissolved into a smear of pixels, and Jack's casual words drilled through her ribcage.

Past tense.

She'd already been archived, filed under 'temporary'. The room contracted, oxygen thinning with each shallow breath.

She must have ruined it somehow. Too desperate? Too…herself?

Her fingers lingered over the screen, ready to type a response. What could she say? 'Thanks for the fun fuck'? 'Sorry I'm not worth sticking around for'? 'Guess I failed at being casual, my bad'?

Delete. Delete. Delete.

Trish flipped the phone face-down, but the words had already tattooed themselves into her brain. 'Was fun.' Like a weekend trip to the beach. Like one of those old-school disposable wedding cameras.

The phone's glow cut through the dim room like a neon 'closed' sign at midnight. Jack's message sat there, and the truth scratched along her ribs: she'd never known how to be part of a real family. Her childhood had been all empty rooms, nannies, and that fucking boarding school. Not much in the way of cookie-baking, bedtime stories or sticky kisses.

She typed slowly: *Your kids are amazing, Jack. They deserve someone—*

Her fingers paused. Someone what? Someone better?

Someone who knew how families worked? Someone who could stay? She'd never learned the rhythm of family life. She deleted the message and started again:

> TRISH (14:46) It was the most fun I've had in years. Thank you – and your nice little people.

Her laptop purred lowly, demanding attention. Work. Right. That's what she was good at. That's what she could control. Her index finger tapped against the keyboard. The folder of photos stared back at her. She clicked it open.

The first picture was of Jack and the kids decorating cookies. They looked so happy, so carefree, so…fucking perfect. Like a Christmas card come to life.

She flipped through the images, her gaze lingering on the ones of Jack. That crooked grin, the way his laugh seemed to ripple through him, the way his eyes softened when he looked at his kids… It was too much. Too raw. Too real. Like her camera had caught something she wasn't supposed to see.

Trish snapped the laptop shut. She couldn't handle this. Couldn't look at those damn photos, couldn't face the reminder of letting herself long for something impossible.

But she had to. Deadline looming, career teetering – she couldn't fall apart now, not when she had something huge on the line. With a steadying breath, she cracked open the laptop again and dived into the folder.

And then she saw it.

The perfect shot.

The three kids, their faces obscured by the angle, red hair gleaming in the soft light in different shades. Junior's strawberry blonde, Beth's carrot ginger, and Phil's auburn. The cookies, the decorations, the whole goddamn Christmas magic.

It was flawless. Everything Seraphina wanted.

Trish stared at the screen, her mind racing.

But… Is this allowed?

They'd signed the event release forms, standard stuff. She chewed her lip.

That's probably enough for this.

Their faces weren't even visible, just their hair, their small hands clutching those cookies. It wasn't invasive. It wasn't personal. It was… art. This was a fine line. Her professional side took over, reasoning, rationalising.

It's not like I'm naming them or showing anything identifiable. It's tasteful, it's safe, it's ethical.

She let the thought settle for a moment before it was bull-dozed by desperation.

And it's my only chance.

The winter wonderland shots were good. The eighteenth-century Scottish country house was postcard perfect, and Mrs Bellbottom 'decorating' the tree gave it charm. But this… this was special. This was the soul of the set.

Her fingers flew over the keyboard, thoughts tumbling and colliding in her head like a fast-paced slideshow. She could do this. Crop the photos, edit them, and make them into something…magical. Something that would make Seraphina happy and land her the job.

Something that might finally make her mum stop harping about wasted potential.

Something that would make her forget about Jack MacGregor and his stupid, perfect smile, his sexy forearms, his unparalleled dick, and his soft, huge fucking heart.

Her hands moved in a frenzy, cropping and enhancing, tweaking the lighting and contrast, pulling every last drop of goddamn magic out of the images. And as she worked, she muttered to herself, her voice low and urgent in the empty room. 'Come on, Trish. You can do this. You're a professional. You're not some pathetic girl pining over a guy. You're an artist. You can make this happen.'

Be like snow. Cover the mess with beautiful cold.

17

Jack yanked the handbrake up harder than necessary, the van's metal creaking in protest. Another morning, another round of deliveries. The silence rang in his ears. No kids arguing over radio stations, no tiny voices demanding snacks. Just him and a mountain of parcels.

His phone pinged. Another DM notification. The whole viral Santa thing had mostly died down, thank fuck. Five minutes of fame stretched into about five days too many. At least he'd dodged those newspaper vultures.

The screen lit up with a message.

> MELISSA (09:19) Kids settled in fine. Craig's taking them to the cinema for the new monster movie later.

Great. He'd planned on taking them to see *Creepy Creatures Club*. There went that idea. Jack's teeth ground together. He let the phone glide into his back pocket and grabbed the next batch of packages. Two weeks of Christmas and Hogmanay with the wee ones stretched ahead of him. Dread settled in his gut at the thought of juggling it all.

Church Hill. Jack checked the address twice. His mind kept wandering to Trish. To cookies and laughter and…

No. Focus on the job.

The front opened, and Sarah Campbell stood there in what could generously be called a dressing gown. If dressing gowns were made of see-through fabric and stopped mid-thigh.

'If it isn't Scotland's sexiest Santa.' She leaned against the doorframe, hip cocked. 'I've been *very* naughty this year.'

For crying out loud.

'Mornin', Sarah. Got a parcel for you.' He held out the package, keeping his eyes firmly on her face.

'Why don't you bring it in?' She bit her lip. 'I've got coffee brewing.'

'Can't. Routes to run.' Jack stepped back. 'Need you to sign here.'

Sarah pouted. 'I saw those photos. That body shouldn't be hidden under a postal uniform.'

'I take it Mike's away then?'

Something skittered behind her eyes. A quick, nervous tell. Her husband's business absences were so frequent they'd become municipal conversation, a well-worn story everyone knew but nobody officially acknowledged.

Small towns, smaller secrets.

'Aye.' She scribbled her signature on the scanner.

Jack's mind flashed to Trish in the kitchen at Hazelbrae, flour dusting her hair, glasses fogged from the oven's warmth. She'd been a gazillion times more tempting than any other woman in a fucking negligee.

It's not real…

'Say hi to Mike when he's back, he owes me another round of darts.' Jack tucked the scanner away. 'Have a good day, love.'

'You too, Santa.' Sarah winked. 'My chimney's always open.'

Gie's a break.

Jack walked back to his van. The cold bit through his jacket, but he barely noticed. His chest felt hollow like someone had scooped out everything warm and replaced it with winter.

Back in the car, he sat for a moment, forehead against the wheel. Two days since he'd last seen Trish. Two days of pretending he wasn't checking his phone for messages. Two days of missing her laugh, the way she saw beauty in everything.

The engine coughed to life. Jack pulled away from the kerb, leaving Sarah's invitation in his rear-view mirror. He had three more hours of deliveries ahead. Three more hours to not think about cookie-scented kisses and candy canes.

Jack moved the heavy package in his arms, double-checking the address. 23, Burnside Row. He'd delivered here a thousand times before. Struan Kerr, retired lorry driver, a decent bloke who always had a kind word and usually slipped him two tenners at Christmas.

The door flew open before he could knock. And there stood Struan – all six-foot-four of him – squeezed into a Santa outfit that left about as much to the imagination as Jack's own viral photos had.

'Special delivery?' Struan waggled his eyebrows, striking a pose that made the velvet stretch in alarming ways.

Jack's mind blanked. His mouth opened, closed, opened again. 'I, um...'

'Like what you see?' Struan ran a hand down his exposed chest and over his belly. 'Thought I'd join the party. Can't let you hog all the spotlight.'

A slow blaze spread across the back of Jack's neck. 'Look, mate...'

'You're not the only one who can rock a Santa suit.' Struan propped a hand on the doorframe.

'Christ.' Jack pinched the bridge of his nose. 'I appreciate your enthusiasm in taking the piss. But I've got rounds to finish.'

'Spoilsport.' Struan grinned and took the package. 'The missus thought this was hilarious, by the way.'

'Brilliant.' Jack handed over the signature pad. 'Just what I needed to hear.'

'Och, come on. It's funny! The whole village is talking about it. You're famous.'

'Lucky me.' Jack logged the delivery. 'Tell Margaret I said hi.'

'Will do. And Jack?' Struan's eyes danced with amusement. 'If you ever want to do a double act…'

'Ta-ta, Struan.'

Back in his van, Jack dropped his head against the headrest. His phone buzzed, probably another Instagram notification. He'd thought about turning them off a dozen times, but the settings were a bloody maze.

Maybe it was Melissa with more demands about Christmas.

Instead of checking, he started the engine.

This whole 'Sexy Santa' thing had gone sideways, twisting into something Jack never signed up for. Always another wink, another joke that chipped away at whatever dignity he'd been trying to maintain. It was fucking tiring.

The cosmic joke wasn't lost on him. That's what he'd been projecting into the world. Playing up the charm, letting people see only what they wanted to see.

Don't let anyone look too deep.

But he was more than just a six-pack and a cheeky grin. He was a father who read bedtime stories, built blanket forts, and kissed scraped knees. A friend who'd hold your hair back after too many pints and never mention it again. A son who'd lost his mother way too early to addiction.

The muscles in Jack's shoulders bunched like twisted rope, a tension headache brewed at the base of his skull. He jabbed at the radio, needing noise – any noise – to drown out the loop playing in his head. Static crackled through the speakers, matching the restless energy crawling under his skin.

Each house on his route now felt like a potential ambush, another chance for someone to reduce him to that bloody Santa photo. Jesus, even Struan – solid, dependable Struan – had turned it into a joke.

Maybe they were right. Maybe that's all he was.

The brass knocker on the Bellbottoms' door gleamed despite the grey December morning. Jack balanced the parcel against his hip, reaching for it.

'Jack MacGregor!' The door swung open before he could knock. Mrs Bellbottom stood there in a leopard print jumper. 'Perfect timing. I had a feeling you'd show up, and I just put the kettle on.'

'Naw, I've got rounds to—'

'Nonsense. You look like you need a cuppa.' She stepped aside. 'Come on in, dearie. Five minutes won't kill you.'

The scent of Earl Grey and shortbread hit him as he followed her into the kitchen. Nothing had changed since his school days. Same yellow curtains, same ceramic dogs lined up on the windowsill. Muffin looking at him with his signature semi-threatening scowl.

'Sit.' She pointed to a chair. 'You look done in.'

'Just tired.' Jack sank into the seat. 'Been a weird few weeks.'

'Aye, I bet.' She plonked a steaming mug in front of him. 'Our local postie turned pin-up boy.'

'Not you, too.'

'Och, don't worry about me.' She settled across from him, pushing the biscuit tin toward him. 'Though I must say, those photos caused a wee fuss at bridge club.'

Jack sighed. 'Can we not?'

'You know, Jack,' Mrs Bellbottom stirred her tea with deliberate slowness, 'the ladies had quite strong opinions.'

Jack stared into his cup and watched the steam rise. 'Look, about that—'

'Makes you wonder, doesn't it? How quickly folks reduce others to…' She gestured vaguely. 'I saw it often enough in my teaching days. The way some of the boys would talk about girls as if they were items in a catalogue. Young lads strutting about, rating the girls on their looks. As if that's all they were.'

Jack grabbed a shortbread, turning it over in his hands. 'I never…' He paused, the justification hollow in his throat.

Really?

The pattern wasn't exactly the same, but close enough. Meet, shag, move on. He'd always gone for the lookers. What was on the inside hadn't mattered much, not if the outside turned heads. His head. And how often had he walked away, leaving nothing but a casual text behind? How many names had he already forgotten? No real conversations, no genuine connection. Just warm bodies and fleeting pleasure.

The realisation crept in. He'd been doing the same thing all along. Not as crude or public as these Santa photos, but he'd still reduced those women to entertainment. To shells. Keeping it casual meant keeping them at arm's length. Limited their worth to what happened between the sheets.

Sure, it had all been consensual and respectful. Just two adults scratching an itch. But how many times had he snuck out? How many 'had fun last night' texts had he sent and never answered to any replies? He'd convinced himself it was better that way – cleaner, simpler. No messy feelings or complications.

But simple for who?

He'd never stuck around long enough to find out.

Mrs Bellbottom's eyes held no judgment, just that annoyingly patient teacher's gaze that had seen through countless excuses. 'You've never what?'

'Nothing.' The biscuit in Jack's hand crumbled slightly.

She dunked a bit of shortbread in her tea. 'Funny how perspectives change when the shoe's on the other foot.'

Jack flicked crumbs from his fingers. 'Maybe.'

'Speaking of perspective...' She leaned forward. 'How's our visiting photographer?'

His stomach dropped. 'She's...working, I guess.'

'Mmm.' Mrs Bellbottom studied him over her mug. 'Ambitious girl, that one. Reminds me of myself.'

Jack tipped his mug slightly as if weighing her words. 'You were a photographer?'

'Dinnae be daft, no. But I had dreams. Big ones.' She smiled. 'Sometimes they seem impossible to reconcile with real life.'

An uncomfortable weight settled just under his sternum. 'Aye.'

'But here's the thing about ambition.' She tapped a finger against her mug. 'Sometimes we get so focused on one path, we miss the side roads.'

The tightness in his chest squeezed a little harder with each word. 'What if the paths are going in opposite directions?'

'Are they?' She fixed him with that penetrating stare that had terrified generations of children. 'Or do they just look that way from where you're standing?'

Jack stared into his tea. 'I should go. Got deliveries... Christmas and all that.'

'Of course.' She stood, gathering their mugs. 'Just remember, Jack – the best views often come when we step back and look at the whole picture.'

He paused at the door. 'Mrs Bellbottom?'

'Yes?'

'Thanks for the tea.'

She smiled, patting his arm with her small hand. 'Anytime, dearie.'

The door clicked shut behind him. Jack stood on the step, letting the cold air clear his head. His phone chimed – another notification. But for the first time in days, he felt something loosen inside him like a lock easing open. Just enough to make him wonder what might be on the other side.

Hazelbrae loomed ahead, its stone walls catching the last light of day. Jack drummed his fingers on the wheel, that damn package burning a hole in the passenger seat. He'd saved this delivery for last, telling himself it was just practical route planning. Nothing to do with avoiding anyone.

The van's tyres bit into the gravel, sending small stones skittering as he pulled up. No other cars in sight. No camera equipment scattered about. No wild curls catching the winter sun.

His shoulders felt both lighter and heavier at once.

He grabbed the package, boots scuffing against stone as he made his way to the entrance. Marla stood by the doorway, wrestling with a string of fairy lights tangled in a boxwood plant.

'Fucking shitty shit thing.' She yanked at a stubborn knot.

'Need a hand?'

She spun around. 'Yeah. I swear, these lights are possessed.'

He set the package down, reaching for the twisted strand. 'Where's your resident photographer?'

'Finally finished her assignment.' Marla's voice held a note of pride. 'Wait till you see the spread in *Wanderlust* next week. The entire town is waiting for it. To see how much

Tartankitsch it really is. There are bets on a Highland romanticism bullshit bingo in the Blue Bonnet, so I've heard.'

Jack focused on untangling a particularly nasty knot. 'That right?'

'God, yes. Though I didn't know your kids were going to be in it too!'

His fingers froze on the lights. 'What?'

'There's this gorgeous shot of the three of them decorating cookies. Trish showed it to me before she sent the e-mail. Really cute.'

The string of lights dropped from his hands, the cold shock of her words spreading from his chest down to his fingertips. 'She's using photos of my kids?'

'Yeah. They're part of the—' Marla stopped, catching his expression. 'Oh shit. You didn't know.'

'No, I didn't fucking know.' His voice came out rough. 'When exactly was someone planning on telling me?'

'I thought… She must have asked…'

'Aye, well, she didn't.'

Yes, he'd signed a slip, but… Jack scrubbed a hand down his face, and his mind raced to Melissa. 'Christ. Their mother's going to lose it.'

'Jack—'

'Don't.' He held up a hand. 'Just…don't.'

The fairy lights lay forgotten at their feet, twinkling mockingly in the gathering dusk.

Why didn't I set clearer boundaries? Eejit.

He grabbed the parcel and held it toward Marla. 'Need you to sign for this.'

'Jack, come on. I'm sure there's—'

'Sign. Please.'

She took the scanner and swiped her finger. 'She wouldn't have meant—'

He tucked the handheld device back into his bag. 'Doesn't matter what she meant.'

The words came out bitter, coating his tongue like old coffee. He turned away, not wanting to see Marla's face. Not wanting to think about hot nights and cosy afternoons and trust broken as easily as shortbread.

'She still here?'

Marla gave a small nod. 'In her room, packing.'

'Good.'

The oak doors creaked as Jack pushed through them, each step echoing off the old stone walls. His hands balled into fists, his pulse throbbing in his skull.

Third floor. Room 12. The one with the thick rug.

The stairs flew under his feet. A guest moved out of the way, muttering something he didn't catch. Jack's breaths came shallow, his mind spinning with images – his kids' faces plastered across magazine pages, agreements torn apart because he'd been stupid enough to…

He wanted a fucking explanation.

The corridor stretched ahead. Light spilled from under her door.

This time, Jack didn't knock.

18

The door crashed open with enough force to rattle the windowpanes, wood banging against ancient stone. Trish spun around, her heart leaping into her throat.

Jack stood in the doorway like the god of vengeance, jaw clenched tight enough to crack teeth. His postal uniform was rumpled and dusted with snow that was already melting into dark patches.

'What the actual fuck, Trish?'

Her fingers stilled on the half-packed suitcase, a silk blouse dangling between them. 'Hello to you, too. What's—... Are you okay?'

'My kids? Seriously?' His voice was low, dangerous – nothing like the warm, teasing tone she'd grown to love. 'You're using my kids for your fancy magazine spread?'

Ice slid down her spine. She'd known this conversation was coming, had rehearsed explanations in her head. It all made perfect sense, at least in theory. Legally, it was above board. Morally, too. Or so she'd thought. But nothing had prepared her for the raw betrayal in his eyes.

'I'm not using anyone.' The words felt inadequate even as they left her mouth.

'No?' He stepped into the room, the door swinging shut behind him with a thud. His boots left wet marks on the rug. 'Then explain why Marla's telling me my children are going to be in that magazine.'

'It's one photo of many, Jack. A beautiful moment I captured.' Trish straightened, squaring her shoulders against the weight of his accusation. Her chest felt like it might crack from the force of keeping her composure. 'You can't even see their faces or recognise them. At all.'

Why couldn't he understand? She'd spent hours perfecting that image, making sure it was both anonymous *and* magical. A small voice whispered that she should have discussed it with him properly first and not relied on that general release form. But no – she'd done everything by the book, hadn't she? Like everything else in her life, she'd tried so hard to get it right. To do right by everyone. To square the circle.

'That's not the point, Trish.'

'Then what *is* the point?' She crossed her arms, her nails digging half-moons into her skin. 'Because from where I'm standing, you're acting like I committed a crime.'

'The point?' Jack's sarcastic laugh barely had the strength to lift the words. 'The point is, you didn't even ask. You just took what you needed and—'

'I didn't ask?' Trish's voice rose with disbelief. Hurt crystallised into defensive anger. 'You signed a release form. Remember? Before and after the "Sexy Santa"-thing, for yourself and your kids.'

'That was different.' He stepped close enough to let her smell the winter air clinging to his jacket, to see the muscle ticking in his jaw. 'That was me! My choice!' His hands slashed through the air between them. 'Not my children being turned into props for your Highland fantasy bullshit.'

The words struck, yanking the breath right out of her. Yes, this was a commission. And no, she wasn't entirely on board with the brief. And yes, maybe using that picture was a bit of a grey area. But fantasy bullshit? Was that what he thought of her work? After everything they'd shared, talking about dreams and fears and hopes?

'What else am I supposed to think?' He paced up and down. 'We're all just characters in your story, aren't we? Props for your photos. The charming locals, the sexy postie, the cute kids. A backdrop. Perfect for your portfolio. Not real, you've said so yourself.'

'Fuck you.' Her voice cracked. 'You haven't even seen the pictures. I would never—'

'I don't need to.' He stopped, facing her. 'I know how this works. You'll polish everything up, make it all pretty and perfect. Then you'll fuck off back to London—'

'Stop. You can't accuse me of—'

'Of what? Using us?' The warmth had drained from his gaze like water down a storm drain. 'That's exactly what you're doing.'

'No! Jack, no.' She grabbed her laptop, fingers trembling as she pulled up the photos. 'Look. Actually look.'

The screen lit up with images. Frosty gazebo. Twinkling lights. And there – three small figures, backs to the camera, red hair catching the light. Hands in the cookie dough, flour dusting the air like snow.

'See?' Her voice softened. 'If you didn't know, you wouldn't recognise them. They could be anyone's children. I would never exploit them, Jack. Never! Your kids were safe with me,' she continued, softer now. 'I would never... I saw something beautiful that day. A father with his kids, making memories. Real moments. Not posed, not fake. Just...love.'

'But—'

'And perhaps I wanted to capture that. To show the world that sometimes the most extraordinary things are the simplest ones. But you'd know that if you'd bothered to talk to me instead of running away and going AWOL.'

'I've not…' He stared at the screen, something flickering across his face. 'It doesn't matter. You should have asked.'

'I did! You signed—'

'…a general release!' He stepped back, knuckles dragging a frustrated path across his forehead.

'You know what, Jack? You're right. I should have asked properly.' Her voice wavered. 'I…I thought I had. I'm sorry. Would've been different if you could see their faces, of course. But you can't, they could be anyone's—'

'Jesus, Trish! Melissa's already on me about being a proper dad. If this magazine thing backfires, I'm fucked. These aren't anyone's children. These are my kids.'

'And I respect that.' She closed the laptop. 'But you're not really angry about the photo, are you?'

'What's that supposed to mean?'

'You're angry because I'm going back.' She flung the words between them like a challenge. 'Because it's easier to push me away than face—'

'Face what?' His voice was razor-sharp. 'That this was supposed to be a bit of fun and then became…? That you were never going to stay?'

The pain blossomed in her chest like frost patterns on the window pane. 'You never asked me to.'

'Because I'm not an arse. I would never stand in your way. And would it even have mattered?'

'You didn't even try!' Her voice broke. 'You decided I wasn't worth it without even talking to me.'

'Worth it—' He cut himself off and barked out a sound that was half growl, half snort. 'You're the one who said this wasn't real.'

'Because you've made it crystal-clear from the start that you didn't want it to be!' Her eyes stung, and a burn prickled under her lashes. 'When I got close, you pulled away. Like I wasn't good enough.'

'Good enough?' Jack's face twisted. 'You're the one with

the fancy degree and the big dreams. You're too good for me. I'm just a postie with a viral photo.'

'No.' Trish's hands trembled as she shoved the blouse into her suitcase. 'You don't get to do this.'

'Do what?'

'This!' She gestured between them. 'Barge in here and put on a pissed-off show when you're the one who's been avoiding me.'

Jack's adjusted his weight. 'That's not—'

'Don't.' Trish held up a hand. 'Just don't. You want to talk about using people? Fine. Let's talk about your notorious shagging, shall we?'

The words lingered between them as if they'd been etched into the air. Jack's face went blank, that carefully constructed mask she'd seen him wear with others sliding into place.

'Low blow. And that's not the same.'

'Isn't it?' Her laugh splintered. 'You're pretty good at taking what you need yourself.'

Jack flinched like she'd slapped him.

Good. Let him hurt, too.

He raked a hand through his hair, leaving it standing in spikes. 'Christ, Trish. You can't—'

'Can't what?' She lifted her chin. 'Can't care? Can't want more than being your convenient holiday shag?'

The truth escaped like a sob she'd held too long, exposing more than she'd meant to. But she'd been strangling it down for weeks. She blazed with a fury that had nowhere to go but back into herself, punishment for the elaborate fiction she'd constructed: that this could ever be just sex.

'Trish, that's not what this was. I don't know what—' His voice cracked. 'Fuck, you know that's not—'

'Do I?' Trish adjusted her glasses, a nervous habit. 'I don't know anything anymore. I thought...' She hated how uncertain she sounded.

Silence became a third presence. Outside, hail tapped

against the window like nature itself was trying to break through their standoff.

'I can't—' Jack's shoulders slumped. 'Look at me, Trish. I'm a postie who plays in a shite band. I deliver other people's dreams in brown paper packages. I live in my aunt's crappy old house.' He gestured at himself. 'You've got exhibitions and magazine spreads and a whole world waiting. I can barely keep my own life together, let alone...' His voice cracked like thin ice. 'And the kids need stability. Their mum's already on my case about being a proper dad. One wrong move and she'll...' He shook his head. 'I can't go anywhere, and I can't... You're too talented.'

Trish's hands shook as she folded the same shirt for the third time. She'd spent her whole life trying because she was never enough. And here was Jack, assuming she was too good for him? The irony would be funny if it didn't touch that sore, broken place inside her that had never healed.

'So you push me away instead? That's your solution?'

His attempt at a casual shrug failed. 'Better than watching people realise they've outgrown this place. Outgrown—' He stopped himself, jaw tight. 'It's complicated.'

Trish's eyes met his, her vision swimming. 'You don't say.'

For a heartbeat, something vulnerable flashed across Jack's face. Then it hardened, vanishing like frost under fire.

'Face it, Trish. We both knew the script from the start.' He slowly retreated toward the door. 'You'll return to your world of art and galleries. Me? I'm anchored here. Parcels to deliver, kids to raise. You were never going to stay, and you know it.'

But that was the thing.

She didn't know.

Trish hadn't realised until right now how thin the line was between the shiny bauble of a steady job and an alternative she'd never seriously considered. What if he'd simply asked her to stay? Not dramatically, not with grand promises, but simply: stay. What if, beneath her narrative of ambition, there'd been a willingness to consider?

But he hadn't asked. And now, with each breath, that microscopic space of potential was closing, sealing itself shut like a wound.

He hadn't asked because he didn't want to.

The truth burned against her tongue, metallic and urgent, as she met his gaze. 'No, Jack. Maybe it's you who decided I wouldn't stay.'

He'd already turned around. The door opened. Closed. His footsteps faded down the corridor.

Trish stood in the silence, each heartbeat jarring like it was trying to crack through bone. She'd tried to be perfect, to prove herself, to make everything right. But in the end, none of it mattered.

It never did.

Her phone vibrated. Seraphina, probably with more feedback. More demands for fucking magic.

Fuck off.

Trish grabbed her suitcase, stuffing in the last of her clothes. The fabric of her dreams was unravelling, threads of ambition tangling with threads of love until she couldn't tell where one ended and the other began.

She'd come to Kilcranach looking for a story. Instead, she'd found something much, much bigger. And lost it in the same breath.

When she was done packing, she took her suitcase and put on her coat. The door closed behind her with a soft click. No dramatic slam, no thundering echo. Just the quiet sound of an ending.

19

Jack stared at the wiggling icon on his phone screen.

Delete.

The app disappeared, taking with it three years of casual hook-ups and meaningless chats. His thumb lingered on the empty space where the icon had been, like pressing on a bruise to check if it hurt.

It didn't.

At least not that one.

The kitchen timer shrieked, jolting him back to reality. Pasta bubbling over, steam fogging up the window. He grabbed a tea towel, yanking the pot off the stove.

'Da! Phil's eating the raw spaghetti again!' Beth shouted from the kitchen table.

Jack turned to find his youngest crunching on uncooked pasta like it was a snack. 'Out of your mouth. Now.'

Phil grinned, a pasta stick dangling from his lips like a straw.

'I mean it.' Jack held out his hand. 'Raw pasta makes your tummy hurt, remember?'

Beth piped up from the table, where she was allegedly

doing homework. 'Like that time he ate all the cookie dough and—'

'We don't need to revisit that story.' Jack intercepted another pasta stick heading for Phil's mouth. 'Right, who wants proper food?'

Jack Jr. looked up from his phone. 'Is it the red sauce with the bits?'

'Aye, but no bits.'

'Good. I hate the bits.'

'I know.' Jack focused on draining the pasta in the sink, steam scalding his face. 'Now, plates please.'

'Da?' Beth asked as he spooned sauce over her portion. 'Are we still watching the film on Friday?'

'Course we are.' Jack watched his kids dig in. His own plate sat untouched.

His phone pinged. Not her. Never her. Just another notification. Wonderful.

When he finally speared a forkful into his mouth, the pasta tasted like cardboard. Everything did these days. But he forced it down, one mechanical bite after another. Because that's what adults did. They kept going. They didn't fall apart over…

Over what? A woman who'd breezed through town, captured some photos, and moved on with her life?

Christ, he was pathetic.

'Da?' Phil's voice pulled him back. 'Can I have more juice?'

'What's the magic word?'

'Abracadabra?'

Jack sighed and reached for Phil's cup, the plastic Batman logo worn nearly smooth from countless washings. His movements were mechanical, disconnected. Like watching someone else pour juice through a fog.

'Da?' Beth twirled pasta around her fork. 'Will Trish come to film night?'

The juice sloshed over the rim. Jack seized the tea towel, mopping up the spill. 'No, darlin'. She's gone back to Edinburgh.'

'Oh, okay.' Beth's fork clattered against her plate.

Phil pushed his pasta around, sauce all over his chin. 'I liked her cookies.'

'The ones with our letters?' Beth's face did that thing that always made him cave in at the toy shop. 'Those were pretty!'

Jack glared at his plate, sauce congealing into abstract patterns. Two weeks. She'd been in their lives for two weeks, and already his kids talked about her like she belonged. Like she was…

He couldn't finish that thought.

The kitchen fell silent save for the tap-tap-tap of Beth's fork against her plate and the sound of Phil slurping his spaghetti.

This was his life, right here. Three wee souls who needed him, who counted on him. Even if it weren't for Melissa, he couldn't uproot them, upset them, couldn't chase some dream of…what? Playing house with a woman who'd already chosen her path? A great one at that. One that she deserved.

His phone on the table, screen dark. No messages. No missed calls. Just silence.

'Time to clear the table.' Jack set Phil back on his feet. 'Then finishing homework.'

Three groans echoed through the kitchen.

As he loaded the dishwasher, muscle memory taking over, Jack's mind wandered. To hair as untamed as her laughter. To honey-brown eyes behind smudged glasses. And kisses in Hazelbrae's kitchen.

Perfect. It had been perfect.

And that was exactly why it had to end.

Because perfect things never stayed perfect. Nothing did. He'd learned that lesson, hadn't he? Ten years old, standing in his aunt's kitchen, clutching a backpack. Then, watching

Melissa pack her bags to go to uni. And again, when she'd left him and took the children.

'Da?' Beth's voice threaded through his thoughts. 'Can you help me with my maths?'

Jack turned and saw his daughter holding up her homework like a peace offering.

This was what mattered. This was real.

He only wished this reality could include…her.

'I'll try, love.' He dried his hands on a tea towel. 'Let's see what we've got.'

Wednesday night landed Jack in his usual spot for band practice, surrounded by the familiar clutter and musty air of the Blue Bonnet's backroom. Equipment cases and spare chairs crowded the corners like sleeping giants. The last note hung, weighty and thick, before dissolving into the quiet. Jack lowered his double bass, fingers still tingling from the final pull of the strings.

'Well, that was shite.' Niall set his guitar down with a grimace.

'Speak for yourself.' Bert adjusted his drums. 'I was brilliant.'

'Aye, if by brilliant you mean off-tempo.' Niall grabbed his water bottle. 'We need to run it again.'

Jack's shoulders tensed. 'Gary and Linda are with the kids. I should head—'

'Nowhere.' Niall's voice was firm. 'Not until we get this right. Only two days until we play on Christmas day, lads.'

'Och, it's good enough for the Blue Bonnet.' Jack busied himself with his instrument case, avoiding Niall's eyes.

'Right, lads. I'm off.' Bert stood and stretched. 'Fiona's waiting, and ye ken how it is.' He paused at the door. 'Try not to kill each other before Christmas.'

The door closed behind Bert. Jack felt Niall's stare boring into his back.

'Out with it,' Niall said.

'Out with what?'

'Whatever's got you playing like your strings are made of washing line.'

Jack's wry laugh landed with all the conviction of junk mail. 'Just tired.'

Niall crossed his arms. 'This is about her, isn't it?'

'Her who?'

'Don't play daft. I've known you two-thirds of your life, remember? Trish.'

Jack's fingers slipped on the case's clasp. 'There's nothing to tell.'

'Is that so?' Niall's eyebrow shot up. 'Because you've been walking around like someone pissed in your porridge ever since she left.'

Jack's grip tightened on his bass case. 'Leave it, mate.'

'No, *mate*.' Niall's boots scuffed against the floor as he stepped closer. 'You've been off. Playing like shite. Cancelling practice.'

'I've got the kids.'

'Never stopped you before.'

Jack yanked the case shut, metal clasps snapping like they meant it. 'Some of us have responsibilities.'

'That's rich.' Niall's laugh was anything but amused. 'Since when do you care about responsibilities? You've spent three years shagging your way from here to Inverness and back.'

'That's a different story.'

'How?'

'It just is.' Jack's knuckles went white on the handle, the leather straining under his grip.

'Because none of them mattered?' Niall prodded. 'Because none of them actually made you feel—'

'Feel what?' Jack swivelled around. 'Go on. Tell me what I'm feeling since you're such a fucking expert.'

Niall settled onto an amp. 'Afraid.'

The word dropped like a weight on his chest. Fuck. All the barricades he'd been holding onto simply gave way. 'Arse. But aye, possibly.'

'So, what happened?'

'Nothing happened.' The words left an acrid residue. 'She's gone. That's it, end of story.'

'And whose fault is that?'

Jack's head snapped up. 'What's that supposed to mean?'

'It means you're being a right numpty. Did you even ask her to stay?'

'She has a life in Edinburgh. Or London. A shining career ahead of her. I'm not mental.'

'That's not what I asked.'

Jack's face seized up like a rusted letterbox. 'It doesn't matter.'

'Doesn't it?' Niall's tone gentled. 'Because from where I'm sitting, you're both miserable for no reason. Been there, done that. Waste of time.'

'I'm not—'

'Save it. As I said, I've known you since we were boys. You're shitting yourself.'

The truth of it burned. 'I have the kids to think about.'

'The same kids who haven't shut up about baking cookies with her and the banana thing? Aye, they told the Bellbottoms. And Marla. Fifty times.' Niall let out a dismissive grunt. 'So try again.'

Jack's hands bunched. 'What do you want me to say?'

'How about the truth?'

'The truth?' Jack's laugh burst out like a punch – a quick, broken sound. 'Fine. The truth is, I fucked up. I got scared, and I pushed her away. Happy?'

'Getting there.' Niall's eyes held his. 'What scared you?'

'Everything.' The word escaped before Jack could stop it. 'The way she fit. How easy it was. How much I wanted…' He broke off, throat tight.

'Wanted what?'

'More.' Jack's voice folded inward. 'I wanted more. And that terrified the shite out of me. Because let's be real – someone like me? Never gonna measure up to someone like her. Different leagues, different planets. I'm not daft.'

'Up for debate. You know what your real problem is, Jack?'

'Please, enlighten me. Since you really can't seem to stop yourself.'

'You're so busy protecting yourself from getting hurt, you don't see you're already hurting.' Niall's voice carried the weight of every late-night conversation they'd ever had. 'And not just yourself.'

Jack's fingers found a loose thread on his jeans, picking at it. 'They're fine. The weans are—'

'I'm not talking about your children.' The amp creaked under Niall's weight. 'Though Christ knows they adore her.'

'They barely know her.'

'Two weeks, that was enough.' Niall's eyes fixed on him. 'Same as it was enough for you.'

Jack yanked the thread loose. 'What the fuck do you want from me?'

'I want you to stop being a coward.'

The word struck like a knife. Jack's head whipped around. 'Excuse me?'

'You heard me.' Niall's voice didn't waver. 'Remember when your mum sent you here? To live with your aunt?'

Jack's insides compressed. 'Don't.'

'You'd only been in Kilcranach a day,' Niall bulldozed forward. 'She dragged you to Old Harris' birthday party. You looked like a drowned rat, just standing there in the corner. Hood cranked up, fists bunched like live grenades. Like you'd bolt or detonate if someone so much as looked at you wrong.'

Jack's jaw locked, memories bristling back. 'I was ten.'

'Aye, and scowling like a wee fucker.' Niall stepped closer. 'But you stayed. Until we started up some god-awful tune, and you asked if I could teach you the chords. Then you told me—'

'That was ages ago.' Jack's voice hung by a thread.

'And you're still that same scared lad, running from anything that might get close enough to hurt you.'

Jack stood up and marched to the door. 'You don't know what you're talking about.'

'No? Let me tell you this: casual isn't enough anymore. Never was, actually.' Niall's words kept hitting like arrows. 'And that's terrifying.'

Jack's hand found the doorknob.

'Go on then. Run. Ignore. Play it down. Pretend nothing matters. Your masterclass.'

Jack's fingers tightened around the cold metal.

'Or you could try something else,' Niall's words came slower now, careful as tuning pegs, 'like actually telling *someone* how you feel.'

Jack's forehead pressed against the door, wood grain rough against his skin. 'What if… What if it fucks everything up? You and me. Marla. The whole village knows each other's business.'

'Aye, maybe. But that's not why you're standing there with your head against the door.' Niall's heel tapped against the amp.

'Fine.' Jack turned. 'What happens when she realises she isn't happy with…this?' He gestured at himself. 'A small-town part-time single dad who still plays in his former school band.'

'As opposed to what? That London tosser who couldn't handle her? Marla told me about him. What a sad prick.'

'At least he could afford to take her places. Show her things.' Jack's fingers traced the doorknob's edges. 'I can barely afford new shoes for the kids.'

'Jesus, Jack. You think that's what she's after? Overpriced wine and oysters in the Maldives? Have you met her?'

'That's what she's used to. And I think she deserves more than film nights with three kids and frozen pizza.'

'Have you ever asked *her* what she wants?'

Jack's hand dropped. 'If it goes wrong—'

'The real question is: What if it goes *right*?'

The words held suspended in the musty air between them. Outside, snow slipped past the window, each flake dipping through the streetlight's glow like a twinkle of possibility. Appearing and melting away.

'I can't.' Jack's voice came out strangled. 'Not with her being Marla's best friend. Too much at stake.'

Niall stood. 'Och, you're just looking for excuses.'

'I'm being considerate.'

'Naw, you're being a coward.' Niall stepped closer. 'And you bloody well know it.'

Jack's mouth set like dried cement. The pipes groaned overhead, a counterpoint to his frenzied heartbeat.

'If it goes wrong, it goes wrong.' Niall said and put a hand on his shoulder. 'But at least you'll know you tried.'

Jack turned and stared at his friend. 'Since when did you turn all life coach?'

'Must be those self-help books you keep delivering.' Niall's mouth twitched. 'That, or I'm just sick of watching you be a knobhead.'

'Whatever.' A dry laugh slipped out, ragged and genuine. 'Cheers, mate.'

'Anytime. Now, are you going to fix this, or do I need to lock you both in the post office till Hogmanay?'

'I think I'm awright. I'll figure it out.'

'Good.' Niall pulled him into a rough hug. 'Because if I

have to watch you mope through one more practice, I'm replacing you with a better-looking bassist.'

'Good luck. I'd like to see you find one 'round here.'

They pulled back, grinning like the same smartass schoolboys who'd first clicked.

Stars pierced the winter sky like tiny ice chips as Jack trudged home, his bass case bumping against his leg. The snow had settled into a hard crust, each step breaking through with a satisfying crunch. His mind churned with Niall's words, replaying their conversation like a stuck record.

A bark cut through his thoughts. Mrs Bellbottom appeared around the corner, Muffin straining at his lead.

'Evening, Jack!' She waved, her leopard print coat lighting up the streetlight. 'Just finishing our constitutional.'

'Bit late for walkies, isn't it?'

'Och, you know Muffin. He's in charge.' She patted the Border Terrier's head. 'Say, did you see the Christmas edition of *Wanderlust*? Just came out today.'

Jack's stomach dropped. 'No, I haven't.'

'Don't fall over yourself to rush to the shop.' She adjusted her scarf. 'Not a peep about Kilcranach in there.'

'What?' Jack stopped dead. 'But Trish…the photos…'

'Not a single one made it in.' Mrs Bellbottom wore that same knowing look she'd used when catching students passing notes. 'Funny that.'

'But…' Jack's mind raced. 'All the work. The Christmas market shots. The castle. My k—' He stopped himself. 'Everything.'

'Indeed.' She smiled, unperturbed. 'Though I must say, I was rather looking forward to seeing myself decorating that tree. I felt like a star that day.'

'You're not upset?'

'Why would I be?' She guided Muffin away from a particularly interesting lamppost. 'Some things matter more than fifteen minutes of fame.'

'Agreed. But… like what, exactly?' He let out a grunt. 'Purpose? A higher calling?'

'Like being true to yourself.' Her voice carried on the night air. 'Ever notice how people get swept up chasing what they think they *should* want?' Mrs Bellbottom's words drifted between them. 'Always reaching for the next rung, eyes fixed upward. Meanwhile, life's happening right here at ground level.'

Jack traced a seam on his sleeve. 'Sometimes you have to climb though, don't you? To get somewhere?'

'Somewhere.' She gave a soft laugh. 'And where exactly would that be?'

'I don't…' He trailed off, unable to finish. 'The stars?'

'The thing about ladders,' she adjusted her coat, 'is they only go up and down. But life? Life spreads out in all directions. The real gold isn't found by climbing higher and higher. It's found by standing still long enough to see what's there.'

His heart folded like an envelope. 'What if standing still doesn't work for some people?' He couldn't let go of the thought that some folks were meant to chase after dreams while others were destined to remain rooted in place.

She patted his hand. 'The truth doesn't need all those fancy words we dress it up in. It just needs to be spoken. Sometimes it's about finding the courage to express what's in your heart, regardless of where you think it should take you.'

He leaned against the lamppost. 'But what if that truth changes everything?'

'You know what's in your heart.'

The night air felt heavy with possibility. 'And if I'm wrong?'

'Being wrong isn't the worst thing, dearie.' She smiled. 'Never giving yourself the chance to be right, that's the real tragedy.'

The stars above seemed to pulse brighter. Jack's heart thundered against his ribs as understanding clicked into place. Deep and unforgiving, sweeping away every excuse he'd clung to. All this time, he'd assumed she'd used those photos to climb the fancy London career ladder. But they weren't in the magazine. Not one. What the hell happened? Did that editor knock them back? Was Trish gutted about it? Or had she…chosen not to publish them? The thought carved a path through his assumptions.

Whatever had happened, he'd been a complete dickhead, zero context, all knee-jerk reaction. He'd jumped to conclusions without even asking for her side of things. And now he saw it, clear as day: his anger about the photos wasn't the real story. It was a shield, a cheap trick his brain had pulled to avoid what really terrified him: that she might take one hard look and walk away, taking what was left of his heart with him.

The need to find her was like the need for oxygen, full stop. No room for negotiation. He had to understand. To make it right.

Because the thought of not hearing her ramble about light and angles ever again made his chest ache with a rawness he'd been avoiding his whole life.

Fuck, yeah. He was in love with her. Proper, scary, all-in love. The kind that made him want to be better. To try harder. To actually give a damn, every day.

He knew because he'd never felt like that before.

This was it.

And he'd cocked it up spectacularly. Burned down the whole damn bridge without even checking if anyone was still on it.

Maybe she felt the same. Maybe she'd already written him off as another disappointment. But he was going to listen to her. Whatever she wanted to say. Whatever it took.

'Mrs Bellbottom?' The question stuck in his throat like

keys in a rusty lock. 'Could you watch the kids tonight? And tell folks their mail will come late tomorrow?'

Her smile widened. 'Planning a wee late-night road trip, are we?'

'Edinburgh.'

'About time.' She squeezed his arm. 'Go on then; I'll handle things here. It really takes a village, and, lucky for you, you've got one. And I've got your spare keys.'

Jack set off at a run. His boots kicked up loose snow, each step carrying him closer to his car. To her.

If he'd driven all those miles for fucks, he could put on a few more for love.

20

Her Edinburgh flat was like a hotel room. Temporary, sterile, half-lived in. The walls were nondescript Magnolia that wiped out any trace of personality. A generic floor lamp cast a harsh light over the room. In the kitchen corner, the spotless stove made it all look staged, as if it were waiting for the next tenant. Nothing here was Trish's. Merely borrowed space.

Not even twinkly lights on the twenty-third of December.

Outside Trish's small bay window, Edinburgh's New Town stretched out in dark, brooding rows, all those grand Georgian facades looking down their stone noses, polished windows closed up tight as a drum. A snowy drizzle clung to the street, turning the cobblestones slick as mirrors, catching just enough streetlight to make it eerie rather than charming.

Trish sat on the floor, surrounded by half-unpacked boxes. The faint, stale smell of cardboard lingered in the cold air. Her gear lay around her like fallen soldiers. The Leica she'd bought herself as a graduation present. The vintage Polaroid from her dad. The lens Jack had held for her that afternoon in the garden.

Stop it.

Since she wasn't going anywhere, she grabbed another box and ripped off the tape with more force than necessary. Inside, her photography books nestled together like old friends. Cartier-Bresson. Adams. Man Ray. Leibovitz. Masters of their craft who'd never compromised their vision.

Unlike her.

Trish's phone chimed. An email from Seraphina, probably.

'Fuck you and your Highland fantasy bullshit,' Trish muttered, echoing Jack's words. They still burned, even a week later. But he'd been right, hadn't he? That's exactly what *Wanderlust* had wanted – some twee, romanticised version of Scotland. Tartan and snow and shortbread and men in kilts and a sexy postie.

God, she missed him.

His terrible jokes that landed like lead balloons but somehow still triggered her involuntary snort-laugh. How he brought her food when he thought she hadn't eaten. How he'd helped her with her work. The way his bass became an extension of his hands. And that look in his eyes whenever he talked about his kids, a little dazed, like he still couldn't believe how these incredible humans had happened to him. The way his words filled those small cracks of self-doubt she tried to keep hidden.

Emotion packed itself into her windpipe, part sob, part barbed wire.

The next box held her winter clothes. A soft grey jumper tumbled out – the one she'd worn that night at Hazelbrae. It still smelled faintly of wood smoke and spiced punch. Of Jack.

'Get it together, Patricia.'

Trish tucked the jumper back in the box. The next one held old photo albums and small cases of printed photos. She poured them out onto the carpet, unwilling to face the fallout of her decision.

Her laptop sat on the kitchen counter. The *Wanderlust*

email chain glowed on the screen. Seraphina's ultimatum had been clear: either deliver the Highland fantasy they'd commissioned or consider the contract void.

So Trish had done what any self-respecting artist would do.

She'd told them to get fucked.

Well, professionally. With a baroque symphony of words about artistic integrity and authentic representation. But the message had been the same: take the real Scotland she'd captured or nothing at all.

They'd chosen nothing. And made sure everyone in their circle knew about her 'difficult attitude' and 'inability to meet client briefs.'

Her phone had stopped ringing altogether. The industry wasn't kind to photographers who bit the hand that fed them.

Smart career move, that. Really showed them. Two years of building a reputation gone in one principled email. And now, she could barely afford rent. If she didn't land another job soon, she'd be pouring flat whites in a café just to scrape by. But every time she looked at those photos – the real Kilcranach, the real people – Trish knew she couldn't have done it any other way.

She'd rather shoot third-class weddings in Edinburgh for the rest of her life. Even if it meant being right and broke instead of wrong and well-paid.

Now, here she was, still starting over. No big break in sight. She'd torpedoed her career. At least she had principles, right? She couldn't stomach flattening Kilcranach into tourist bait. To turn Jack and the others into Highland caricatures. To package up their lived reality into something fake and marketable.

Her phone quivered against the carpet. Marla's name lit up the screen.

MARL (19:52) How's the flat? Missing you xx

Trish's fingers hovered over the keys. How to explain that Edinburgh felt like a hollow replica? That she kept expecting to hear Gwen's laugh floating up from the pub or smell Mrs Bellbottom's shortbread? That every damn Royal Mail van kept making her heart do this stupid, traitorous little leap?

She typed: 'Flat's fine. Miss you too.'

Delete.

Start over.

Story of her fucking life.

Trish sprawled on her living room floor, photos on her screen. Each one a story. Each one a piece of her heart. Thumbnails cascaded across the screen. She scrolled through them slowly and scanned the images, a small smile playing on her lips.

Then she saw them. The ones she'd forgotten about. The ones Jack had taken of her. Trish's hand froze. She clicked on the first one, her lungs seizing like a spluttering projector as it filled the screen.

It was her, naked, lying on the bed in the castle. Like some Renaissance painting gone rogue, every vulnerability exposed in unapologetic detail. Her first instinct was to slam the laptop shut, pretend none of this existed. But she forced herself to look, to really see. Her eyes traced the curve of her own body, the way her hair spilled across the pillow, the way her lips were slightly parted.

She clicked to the next one. This time, she was grinning, her hand reaching out to him as if to pull him into the frame with her. She remembered that moment, the way he'd made her laugh, the way he'd made her feel so… all-around okay.

Trish kept clicking, each image peeling back another layer of that night. There was a tenderness in these shots that made her throat tight. She saw the happiness in her eyes, the contentment in her smile. She saw a woman who was adored, who was seen, truly seen, by the man behind the camera. A woman who felt safe enough to be herself.

Her body told a different story than the one she'd been telling herself for months.

Trish's heart swelled, a warmth spreading through her chest. She reached out, her fingers skimming the lines of her own body on the screen, as if she could touch the happiness, the beauty, the love that radiated from the image.

How had they lost this? Somehow, they'd ended up here – her in Edinburgh, him in Kilcranach, with nothing but silence between them. Had it happened when she'd talked about maybe staying? The way his face had shuttered for a second? Or when she'd hesitated to tell him about the *Wanderlust* thing? Tears bled the images into watercolour ghosts. She'd had something real, something rare, and she'd let fear poison it. They both had.

Her phone lit up. Not a text, an unannounced call. Like in the Middle Ages.

'I'm staging an intervention,' Marla announced without preamble.

'Hello to you, too.' Trish adjusted her glasses. 'No need. I'm fine.'

'Bullshit.'

'Really, I'm—'

'If you say "fine" one more time, I swear to God...' Marla's voice crackled through the speaker. 'I had a very interesting chat with Niall.'

A stone dropped in Trish's stomach. 'Oh?'

'Yeah, oh. Apparently, Jack's been playing like a tone-deaf orangutan.'

'That's...specific.'

'You're both miserable.' Marla's tone grew soft. 'And you're both too stubborn to admit it.'

'It's complicated.'

'No, quantum physics is complicated. This is just you being a silly cow…ard.'

The truth of it seared along her nerve endings. 'I'm not—'

'Remember what you told me?' Marla cut in. 'When I was too locked in my own damn pride to admit my feelings for Niall?'

Trish's neck prickled with a slow, burning awareness. 'That was different.'

'Was it? Let me quote you: "I'm not your friend only to tell you what you want to hear. Sometimes I have to tell you the things you need to hear. Even if you don't like it".'

'Using my own words against me?'

'Hey, if it works.' Marla paused. 'Talk to me, Trish. What's really going on?'

Trish's fingers traced the edge of a photo on her screen – Jack in his Santa suit, eyes crinkling at the corners. 'I… After Marc…'

'What about Marc?'

'It wasn't just the breakup itself.' The words came slowly, like pulling teeth. 'Ten years of shrinking myself to fit into his narrow view of who I should be. I muted my voice, dulled my ambitions, and avoided anything that might challenge his fragile ego. And the second I finally started to reclaim myself, to shine a little, he walked away. That's what broke me. Not just losing a relationship but having lost myself. The whole thing wrecked my optimism.'

'Oh, love. I know. We're taught to make ourselves small, to be palatable. To apologise for taking up space, for wanting, for being anything more than a supporting character in someone else's narrative. It's a kind of violence, what relationships like that do. They don't just break your heart; they fracture your sense of self. And rebuilding? That takes more courage than most people understand.'

'Yeah. And Jack…saw me.' The syllables wrestled with each other. 'That day at the opening, when everyone else was celebrating or dealing with the chaos, he found me. Or I found him. And he just…got it. No questions, no judgment. Only understanding. We talked and laughed, and it felt like a never-ending hug.'

'So what's the problem?'

A rough laugh clawed its way out. 'The problem is, I'm terrified of messing it up. Of ruining everything – his life, my life, *your* life…'

'My life?' Marla's words bristled with sudden confusion. 'What the hell are you on about?'

'You've built something amazing there, Marl. This community, your business with Hazelbrae. If Jack and I tried and it went wrong…'

'Oh my God.' Marla's laughter burst through the phone. 'You absolute muppet.'

'Excuse me?'

'You think I care about that?' Marla's voice wobbled between laughter and tears. 'Trish, babes, I'd be over the moon if you and Jack got together. Even if you fucked it up spectacularly.'

'But—'

'No buts. I was only worried because Jack's been hurt before. And so have you. Very recently, might I add. That's relationship quicksand. But listen to me. This place? It's built on messy relationships and complicated histories. Small-town life, what can you do? Mrs Bellbottom used to have a secret fling with Hamish's sister. Linda's first husband runs the football club. And don't get me started on the great sheep-farming feud of '98.'

'That's different—'

'It's the same.' Marla's voice turned fierce. 'Being human with other humans is always messy. That's what makes it special. We don't exist in a vacuum. We exist with each other. We fuck up, we make up.'

'I'm panicking,' Trish murmured.

'Good.' Marla's voice softened. 'That means it matters.'

'But what if—'

'Stop. Stop trying to be perfect. Stop hiding behind your camera. Life isn't a magazine spread or a shoot, Trish. It's chaotic and complicated, and sometimes it hurts. But it's worth it.'

Trish blinked hard, but the tears spilled over. 'I think I pushed him away.'

'No, you both pushed each other away. Because you're both afraid of the same thing – being seen and then judged for not being enough. That's a deadlock if ever there was one.' Marla paused. 'In the time I've known Jack, I've never seen him smile like he smiles at you. Now stop being an idiot and talk to him.'

Her advice landed like a stone in a pond, rippling outward.

'I'll think about it.'

'Don't overthink. Love you!'

'Love you, too.'

The call ended, and silence pressed against Trish's skin as she sat surrounded by moments she'd captured but been too afraid to live.

Her laptop stood on the coffee table, cursor blinking on a blank email. She should write to him. Explain everything.

No. She didn't have his e-mail address.

I could ask Marla and Niall... Not tonight.

Trish opened her old punk playlist. If she was going to have an emotional breakdown being eaten alive by her doubts and fears, she might as well have the right soundtrack.

Maybe a simple text...

Hey Jack

Delete.

Hi. What's up?

Delete.

I'm sorry...

Delete.

Hours ticked by. The sky outside her window deepened from dark grey to deep purple. Street lights cast long shadows across her floor as she paced, phone in hand, thumb hovering over his number.

Tomorrow. She'd call him tomorrow. Or the day after. Probably after Christmas.

She lay on the floor amid the scattered photos, letting The Clash fill her flat with raw, honest anger. The music matched her mood, all rebellion and yearning and fear wrapped in electric guitar.

Ten o'clock. Eleven. Midnight crept past.

The cursor kept blinking. The blank email stayed blank. Her courage stayed buried under layers of what-ifs and maybes.

One in the morning found her still there, surrounded by memories captured in print but not lived.

The doorbell rang.

Trish froze. One in the morning. Nothing good ever came from doorbells at one in the morning.

21

The buzzer for Trish's flat bellowed through the Edinburgh night. Jack pressed it again, heart ricocheting up and down his ribcage. His breath fogged in the cold air, joining steam from a nearby grate. The metal button was icy under his trembling finger.

No answer.

He jabbed it a third time, harder than necessary. His stomach churned with every second of silence. What if she'd already left? He was an idiot for coming unannounced. But he couldn't wait. If he did, he'd be back to second-guessing everything.

Come on, Shutterbug. Be home.

Static crackled through the speaker. Then her voice, thick and raw: 'Who's there?'

'Royal Mail.' His weak attempt at humour died in the frigid air. The silence stretched, broken only by distant traffic and his thundering pulse. Each heartbeat felt like judgement.

'Jack?' Her voice cracked on his name. 'What are you—'

'Let me up?' He moved closer to the speaker as if he could will her to say yes. 'Please? I know I don't deserve it, but…please?'

More silence. Then, a sudden metallic chirp that made him jump. The door lock clicked.

Four flights of stairs, no lift. By the time he reached her floor, his thighs were burning and his courage melting. But there she was, silhouetted in her doorway, wearing the Clash t-shirt he'd left in her room and ratty sweat shorts. Ice cream stains dotted the front. Behind glasses, her eyes were swollen and red.

'Have you been crying, Shutterbug?'

She swiped at her nose with her wrist, half-hiding behind the door. 'No.'

'Liar.' The word came out gentle.

'What do you want, Jack?'

Everything. He wanted everything. But the words tangled in his throat. 'I saw the magazine. Or rather, didn't see it.'

'Oh. *That.*'

'Yeah. *That.*' He inched closer, afraid she'd close the door again. Which would be perfectly okay, even if it'd rip his fucking heart to shreds. 'Why aren't our photos in there?'

'Because… I pulled them.' She lifted her chin in defiance. 'All of them.'

'But the job and your career—'

'Fuck the job and the career.' The words burst from her. 'I couldn't… They wanted this sappy fantasy. But you were right. That's biscuit tin bullshit. What Kilcranach is – its people – it's real. Multidimensional and complicated and… I couldn't cheapen that. Thank you for helping me see clearly.'

'I… Can I come in? Please? I want to explain. To apologise. To grovel, honestly. And I couldn't wait until morning.'

'Okay.'

He stepped into her tiny flat, barely bigger than his living room and kitchen. Boxes, books, and camera equipment covered every surface. A half-empty tub of ice cream melted on the coffee table, spoon stuck upright like a flag of surrender.

Who eats half a tub of ice cream?

A mug of tea sat beside her laptop, screensaver cycling through her photos of Kilcranach. His heart clenched at the sight of his kids' faces among them – Beth mid-laugh, Phil concentrating on his cookie decorating, Junior proudly holding up something undefinable green.

'I've been editing.' She cleared her throat. 'Well, trying to. Mostly just staring.'

'About the magazine—'

'Don't.' She hugged herself, his shirt swimming on her frame. 'I made my choice. I won't compromise my vision just because some London twats want picture-postcard Scotland. I should have said that much earlier, but I was so tempted by that job offer.'

'That's what I love about you.' The words broke free before he could catch them. 'You don't settle. You see the real beauty in things. In people.' He swallowed hard. 'Even when they can't see it themselves.'

'Jack. I—'

'No, let me finish.' He paced, boots silent on her worn carpet. 'I've spent most of my life running. From feelings, from commitment, from anything that might hurt. But you...' He gestured helplessly. 'You dive right in. You see something worth capturing, and you go for it. No fear.'

She let out a wry laugh. 'No fear? I'm terrified all the time. Of not being good enough. Of letting people down. Of...' Her voice fractured. 'Of letting myself want things I can't have.'

'Like what?'

'Like...you.' The words hung between them. 'Like this crazy idea that someone who's known me for three months, or weeks, could actually want...' She trailed off, blinking hard.

'Want what?' He closed the distance between them.

'The mess.' She waved a hand at herself. 'The neurotic

photographer who talks too much about f-stops and cries over ice cream. Who's so desperate to prove herself she almost sold out what she believes in.'

'You think that's what I see?' His voice roughened. 'A mess?' He clasped her restless hand, stilling it against his chest. 'I see someone brave enough to walk away from money and a cushy job because it didn't feel right. Someone who makes my weans laugh until milk shoots out their noses. Someone who...' He rested his forehead against hers. 'Someone who terrifies me because she makes me want to be better. And that's a fucking first.'

'I don't want you to be better.' Her fingers latched onto his jumper. 'I want you to be you. The postie who makes terrible puns and plays in a band called the Salmons of Knowledge—'

'Oi, we're a respected local institution.'

'—and somehow makes me feel safe enough to be myself. Even the parts I usually hide.'

He traced the curve of her jaw. 'I'm not good at this. At letting people in. At risking...things.'

'Like what?'

'Everything.' The word came out raw. 'My heart. My kids' hearts. The whole damn village's opinion if this goes tits up because I'm—'

She put her finger on his mouth. 'Stop. You're not a disaster, Jack. You're...real and exactly what I want.'

'I'm sorry.' The confession punched out of him, fast and graceless as tripping up concrete steps. 'I was an arse and a coward.'

'Yes. You were. But I—'

'Shhh, I'm grovelling. Let me grovel, Shutterbug.'

A smile broke through, then vanished. She exhaled slowly, looking away. But then she nodded, arms loosening a little.

'I ran like a wee boy.' His voice trembled at the seams. 'Not from you. From this.' He sliced his hand through the space separating them. 'From how right it felt. Too good to be true for someone like me. Too good to be true after such a short time. But it was true. It is.'

'Jack…'

'I panicked.' He raked both hands through his hair. 'Of how much I wanted this. How right it was. You with the kids, stealing my shirt…'

Her fingers tightened in the fabric. 'I was going to return it. Via mail.'

'It's okay.' He leaned close enough to see the tiny freckle beside her left eye. 'Part of me was hoping you'd take it with you. I'm sorry for freaking out.'

'Yeah, but the thing is… I'm not innocent in all this.' She toyed with the frayed hem of his t-shirt. 'I was hiding behind my profession. Behind what everyone expected. I've been so busy trying to make everything picture-perfect that I forgot how to just…be. How to be me. How to live.'

'You never needed to hide. And I don't want you to.' His fingers found that wild curl by her ear, the one that never stayed put. 'To me, you're perfect when you're real. When you're you. Even with ice cream on your chin and yesterday's mascara under your eyes.'

She smiled. 'Still a smooth talker.'

'I mean it.' He yanked her closer. 'I love how you stick your tongue out when you're concentrating. The fact that you made my kids personalised cookies. Your brilliant brain that knows every photographer who ever lived, but you still laugh at my dumb jokes. You make me want to actually give a damn. And that daunts me, but not as much as the thought of not having you in my life.'

Her eyes turned glassy.

'I know, we've only just met. But it feels like I've known you all my life. And aye, I'm only a postie.' The words scraped his throat. 'I can't give you fancy holidays or posh restaurants. Or any restaurants besides Eddie's chippy. But I can give you film nights and pancakes and three weans who think you hang the moon. I can give you our reality. My heart, if you'll have it.'

Her eyes went wet and shiny, and Christ, he'd rather take a roundhouse kick to the face than watch her cry.

'I don't want fancy—'

'Trish, I'm falling in love with you.' The truth broke free like a dam bursting. 'With the way you see beauty in everything, even a grumpy postie and his fucked-up life. I want that. All of it. I want to watch you chase the perfect light and hear you swear when the shot isn't quite right. I want to carry your tripod or anything else you need me to carry. I want to love you through deadlines or dark rooms or whatever comes our way.'

'But what if I ruin it? I'm neurotic and obsessive and—'

'Perfect's boring.' He guided her hand to his thundering heart. 'You think I don't wake up shitting myself every morning? Worrying that I'm not enough for my kids? That I'll fuck up, and as soon as they're old enough, they'll leave like everyone else? But I love your kindness, your talent, your patience. That you make my kids laugh and my heart race and—'

She kissed the words right off his lips.

Her tongue tasted of salt and chocolate ice cream. His hands found her waist, pulling her closer. She felt like coming home.

They broke apart, foreheads touching. 'I'm falling in love with you too, Postman Pat.'

His thumbs traced circles on her hips. 'Even though I'm a commitment-phobic slacker who drives you mental?'

'I kind of like that about you.' She smiled against his mouth.

'I'll grovel properly.' He kissed her nose, her cheeks, her

tear-stained eyelids. 'For days. Weeks. Years. However long it takes.'

'Good.' She pulled back, eyes bright despite their puffiness. 'About the commitment-phobia—'

'I might not be cut out for relationships, Shutterbug, but I sure as hell am cut out to be with you.'

22

Trish's brain short-circuited. Jack stood in her flat at one in the morning, snow melting in his hair. And here she was, wearing his band shirt she'd snatched, covered in Ben & Jerry's stains. Her legs hadn't seen a razor since last Tuesday when she'd left Kilcranach. Almost a week ago. Her hair was a greasy disaster. She probably smelled like emotional breakdown and cookie dough.

'God, I must look a right state.'

'Shut up.' His eyes were so warm, so sincere. 'You look like everything I've been missing.'

'I haven't showered since yesterday. I think. I've been busy wallowing.'

He stepped closer, and the warm, rugged mix of soap and skin muddled her senses until the room felt off-kilter. He smiled. 'I love how you smell when you're all you.'

'That's disgusting.' But her heart tripped over itself with joy. 'And probably a sign you need therapy.'

'Probably.' His thumb traced her cheek. 'Or just a sign that I'm stupidly in love with you.'

She led him to her tiny couch. The cushions dipped under their weight, pulling them closer until his knee nearly touched against hers. Jack's body was like embers beside her, solid and real.

'I even love how you smell after a looong day of wallowing.' He pressed his face into her neck, inhaling. 'All sleepy and sweaty. It's hot as fuck.'

'You're weird.' But she melted into his side. 'And possibly deranged.'

'Definitely deranged.' His lips found her pulse. 'For you.'

Her heart felt too big for her chest. 'Sure?'

'Extremely.' He pulled back, eyes serious. 'No more running. No more hiding. No more buts.'

'Not more buts.' Trish stared at him, this man who'd driven through the night just to tell her he loved her sweat. Her brain felt fuzzy like she'd had too much wine. Or not enough.

'The kids?' she managed.

'With Mrs Bellbottom.' His fingers drew patterns on her thigh. 'She practically shoved me into the car.'

'And work?'

'Post might be a bit late tomorrow.' He grinned. 'The village will survive.'

Her heart squeezed. 'You drove over three hours just to—'

'Tell you I'm an idiot? Aye.' His thumb found the soft spot behind her knee. 'Worth every mile.'

'And what if we mess this up?'

He pulled her tightly into his arms. 'Better than being perfect alone, isn't it?'

'How'd you get to be this wise-ass person?'

He kissed her temple. 'Maybe I just needed the right person to be wise-ass for.'

She tried to laugh, but it came out more like a sob. 'I haven't even washed my face.'

'I noticed.' He kissed her nose. 'It's adorable.'

'And I'm wearing your ancient shirt.'

'Keep it.' His voice roughened. 'Keep all my shirts. Keep me.'

Her fingers found his jaw, rough with stubble. 'Yeah?'

'Yeah. Come home, Shutterbug.'

The words unlocked something in her chest.

Home.

Not London. Not Edinburgh. But a small Highland village where the postman played bass, her best friend ran a haunted hotel, the former teacher was some sort of lesbian Gandalf, and three kids loved her baking.

'Okay.' She smiled through tears. 'Take me home.'

Trish felt the firm grip of his hands as he pulled her onto his lap, the warmth of his body seeping through the thin fabric of her shirt. Her pulse skated along the edges of her ribs, and gravity pulled her closer. Her lips skimmed his in a kiss that was both a question and an answer, a dialogue of soft bites and searching tongues.

'First, I would like to take…you.' His voice resonated in the hollow of her chest.

'Yes. Yes.' The words slipped out on a relieved sigh.

'Take off your shirt.' His request was a command, but his eyes held a hint of vulnerability.

Trish pulled back an inch. 'I'm stinky, and I'm not wearing a bra,' she warned in a teasing tone.

'Good,' he growled.

'Which one?'

'Both.'

'You're the worst,' Trish laughed against his mouth. 'We should move this to the bedroom.'

'Why?' His hands slipped under her shirt. 'Your couch seems fine.'

'Because my neighbour Mrs Chen is eighty and has excellent hearing paired with light sleep.' She nipped his lower lip. 'And I'd rather not traumatise her more than necessary.'

'Thoughtful.' His fingers traced her spine. 'But I drove

four hours to see you. Don't really care who hears us. Also, I don't think you'll be living here much longer. So…'

'Jack…' She tried to sound stern, but his mouth on her neck scattered her thoughts.

Trish fumbled behind her, setting her glasses carefully on a nearby moving box labelled 'KITCHEN – FRAGILE' in her messy scrawl. The world went soft around the edges, but Jack remained in focus. Maybe because she'd spent so much time memorising every line of his face, or maybe because some things you just felt in your bones. Her heart thundered as his hands slid higher under her shirt, and she decided being able to see was overrated anyway.

Outside, Edinburgh's nightlights twinkled like drunken stars. But Jack only had eyes for her.

Trish's shirt hit the floor. Her breath stuck like a thread on a nail as the cool air caressed her bare skin, sharpening the sizzle radiating from Jack's palms. His hands, roughened by playing bass and years of delivering letters in all weathers, cupped her with a reverence that belied his next move – a playful tweak of her nipple that sparked a fizz of electricity.

'Shit. Jack.' Her back arched instinctively, pressing herself into his touch.

'Aye?'

'Don't you dare stop.' A blaze ran down her spine, each vertebra lighting up.

His laughter was a warm puff against her skin. 'Wasn't planning on it.'

His mouth replaced his fingers, the wet heat of his tongue tracing lazy circles around her nipple before he sucked gently, then not so gently. Trish's hands threaded through his hair, pulling him closer. 'More.'

Trish felt his hard length against her core, even through the layers of their clothes. She couldn't resist rolling her hips, seeking that pressure, and leaned in to kiss his chin. The stubble there prickled against her lips.

Jack's hands bracketed her hips, urgent and absolute. 'Every time I look at you, I'm overwhelmed by how fucking awesome you are.' His voice was husky like he'd been shouting or crying. Maybe both.

Jack captured her mouth in a fierce kiss, his tongue sweeping against hers. That man wielded his tongue so well.

When he pulled back, his eyes were shadowed with hunger. 'I love how you look at me when you're turned on. Like you need me. Like you want to devour me.'

Trish grinned, nipping at his lower lip. 'Maybe I do.'

'Maybe?' He pushed his hips forward, making her gasp. 'Just maybe?'

'Definitely.' She ground against him, the seam of her sweat shorts grazing her most sensitive spot like a teasing fingertip. A shudder ran through her, every nerve singing a filthy, electric hymn.

'I definitely want to devour you.' She nipped at his earlobe again, her hips moving in a slow, torturous rhythm.

Jack groaned, his head falling back against the couch. 'You know just what to do to drive me wild.'

And she did. She knew how to touch him, how to kiss him, how to make him lose control. As if she'd studied and memorised his manual. It was a heady feeling, this power she had over him, his body, his pleasure.

Jack's hands traced the contour of her waist. His touch was hot, possessive. 'You look so precious when you're horny.' His breath seared her ear. 'Your cheeks all flushed, your eyes all bright. Precious.'

His words washed over her like a warm shower. 'Precious?'

'Aye. You're precious to me. So fucking precious.'

She closed the distance between them, her lips finding his in a slow, sensual glide. She breathed him in. Their mouths moved together, tongues stroking and retreating. Silk-soft nibbles dissolving into hungry, consuming claims. Until she couldn't tell where she ended and he began.

God, that man can kiss.

His hand slid up her spine, fingers splaying across her back, holding her flush against him. Trish felt every contour of his body, the hard planes of his chest, the lean strength in his arms. She reached between them, her fingers finding the button of his jeans, and popped them open one by one. His hard ridge strained against his boxers, and she stroked him through the fabric.

Jack groaned, hips jolting. 'Fuck, Trish.'

'Too much?' she teased, stroking him again.

'Jesus, no. Not enough.' He grabbed her wrist, stilling her movements. 'I want your mouth.'

'Good idea.' She slid off Jack's lap, her knees sinking into the worn carpet.

Trish tugged at his jeans and boxers. His cock sprang out, hard and thick. She leaned in, her tongue darting out to steal a taste of the salty bead that glistened at the tip. Her eyes flicked up to meet his, a smirk playing on her lips as she ran her tongue along his shaft, and his hips jerked forward.

She loved his reactions to her, like he couldn't help it.

Jack's hands fisted in her hair. 'Don't be a fucking tease, Trish. Take it all in. I've been dreaming about your lips, and now I want to feel them.'

Trish circled her mouth around him, and he let out a long sigh.

'God, I love the way you suck my cock.'

Trish went molten at his words. She wrapped her hand around him, moving from the base to the head, twisting and revelling in the sounds she elicited from him. She felt every ridge, every vein, as she took his length down her throat.

'Fuck!' Jack's grip on her hair tightened, his breath coming in ragged gasps. 'How *the fuck* are you so good at that?'

She pulled back slightly, her tongue circling his tip.

'Come here, baby.' He slowly pulled her up, his hands gentle but firm on her shoulders. 'If you don't stop, I'll come in your mouth. And that's not an option. Because we still have unfinished business.'

Trish licked her lips, tasting him. 'Oh, yeah?'

'Yeah.' He leaned forward, his lips hot against hers. 'But thank you for sucking my cock so well.'

His voice alone made her pussy clench. 'You're welcome,' she breathed.

His pupils were wide, edged with want. 'Now get naked, Patricia.'

Trish's insides flipped like they were suddenly weightless as she pulled off her shorts and shimmied out of her underwear.

Jack's eyes roamed over her. 'You're unbelievably beautiful, you know that? Naked and ready for me, just the way I want you.' His voice was thick with desire.

Trish had never been this turned on before. Her body was taut, throbbing with need. She was so wet she felt it on her thighs.

Jack took off his jumper and his shirt, then he lifted his hips and pulled his jeans down just enough. The soft glow of the streetlights outside filtered through the window, casting long shadows that danced across his face.

She felt exposed, vulnerable, yet strangely safe under his gaze as she waited for him.

'Come to me, sweetheart.'

Sweetheart.

No one had ever called her that.

His hands found her waist, and he guided her onto him. Slowly, she straddled him again. This time, skin to skin. She felt the solid warmth of him between her legs, the light rasp of his chest hair against her breasts. His breath fanned across her collarbone and made her skin prickle.

Jack's thumb pushed into her lower lip. 'You're strong and brilliant. You don't need anyone to tell you that. But I will.'

His words sank into her, each one a comforting weight settling in her chest. Her pulse quickened, and her body responded to his words with a surge of tingling.

'I've watched you,' Jack said. 'I've seen how you light up when someone appreciates you. When someone sees you for who you are. When *I* do.'

Her breath stuttered, a small, involuntary sound that echoed in the quiet room.

'You deserve to be taken care of,' Jack said lowly. 'And I'm here to do that. Now and every day.'

Fever spread through her, starting in her chest and radiating outwards. It wasn't just his words, but the way he looked at her, the way his touch lingered on her skin.

'When it comes to fucking, I want you to feel free to say what you need. Whatever it is. Okay?'

Trish's pulse thudded unevenly as she scrambled for the right words. Asking for what she wanted had never come naturally; it was a skill she'd never had to develop. Hadn't been a requirement. But with Jack, it felt possible. Like the door she'd always assumed was locked might actually give if she pushed.

'I want to…be the one who makes you feel good.'

The need sparked under her skin as if she were wired straight to the anticipation. The thought of watching him unravel, knowing she'd caused it, set a deep tremor low in her back, unfurling like a drop of ice melting against warm skin.

She craved to see the change in his eyes, to know it was her touch that made his breath catch. 'I…need to hear that I'm doing it just the way you like.'

'I see.' His lips parted hers in a tender kiss, drawing her lower lip between his. 'You know what you could do for me right now, what I would really like?'

It was like he'd reached into her soul and pulled out her deepest desires, laying them bare. Her throat flexed, the sensation thick and hot.

'You could ride me. Make my cock stop aching. What do you say?' His fingers trailed the dip of her hip, the shape of her ass. She shivered under his touch.

'God, y-yes.'

When his hand touched her sex, she let out a moan.

'Jesus. So wet,' he groaned and slid his digits through her folds. 'So fucking beautiful.'

He plunged two fingers inside her.

'OH.'

'God, you feel so tight, so hot…'

His fingers moved faster, and words were like gasoline on the fire burning inside her. Trish let out a low, keening sound.

Jack reached for his wallet, fished out a condom, and tore the packet open. His eyes never left hers as he rolled the latex down. The sight of him, hard and ready, sent a fresh wave of fire coursing through her. She saw the pulse in his neck, the tension in his jaw as he touched himself. It was erotic, intimate, and she couldn't look away.

'Come, baby. Fuck me.' A shadow of a grin tickled his lips. 'You do want to come on my cock, don't you? Because that would make me feel like a king.'

A tight, warm flicker danced low in her belly. 'Yes.' She pressed her palms against his pecs. 'I want to.'

'Then do it. Make me happy.'

She reached down, wrapping her fingers around his steely girth, and guided him to where they both needed him to be. Her face scrunched up as she began to lower herself. It was a delicious burn, a stretch that bordered on pain laced with pleasure.

His eyes glazed over. 'Fuck, Trish. You're so beautiful when you struggle for me.' He lifted his hips ever so slightly, pushing an inch more into her. 'Now come on. Show me how much you deserve this.'

She bit her lip, her body tensing as she pushed down, taking more of him. She wanted this, wanted him. All of him. She took a deep breath. Inch by inch, the burn gave way to a deep, satisfying fullness.

'That's it. You're doing so well, baby.'

She let out a little cry as she finally took all of him, her body trembling with the effort.

'I am so, so proud of you.' His hand held her hips firmly. 'That tight little cunt is so good, so brave.'

His mouth found her nipple, drawing out a low moan from deep within her. Her head lolled back, and he kissed her collarbone, tracing a path down to her breasts. His resting cock pulsed inside her, anchoring.

'Ride me, Trish,' he growled. 'Fuck me as hard or slow as you need.'

She began to move, her hips lifting and falling. It was slow at first, her body adjusting to the feel of him, the sensation of him filling her over and over. Then she found her rhythm.

'God…only you feel so good…' His voice was rough, his breath hot against her skin. 'Yes, keep taking it… Keep going…'

She picked up the pace, her hips rocking, grinding, chasing the pleasure that was building inside her. She took her time, and she felt him, the way he hit that spot deep inside her that no one had ever…

Jack's head rolled back, and he let out a deep groan. 'You know exactly…how to fuck me.'

Her hands gripped his shoulders, her fingers digging into the muscle. She pounded down on him with a ferocity that both stunned and turned her on.

Again. Again. Again.

Trish was floating, her body just a collection of sensations. Her breaths turned shallow, each one tangling with the next, as if her body couldn't keep up as she pushed herself higher, harder.

'Oh, holy fuck…Jack,' she gasped, her thighs shaking. 'I-I'm really…close.'

'I know, baby.' His hands gripped her ass, helping her move. 'I can feel it. Shit. You're squeezing me so fucking tight. Now ride me harder. Slam down on my cock like it's the only thing you need.'

She was losing control, her mind blanking out everything but him inside her. Her body tensed, her climax right there, within reach. She was on the edge, her breath punching out in uneven bursts.

'And now be a good girl and come all over me.'

His hand slipped between them, the heel finding her clit. It was a light push, a small circle, but it was enough to send her spiralling.

'AH! Jack! N-now… Oh my GOD!'

When it finally happened, her orgasm wasn't a gentle wave or a slow burn, it was a fucking explosion, detonating in the pit of her stomach, sending shockwaves of pleasure outwards. All-consuming and unstoppable. She threw her head back, a long, trembling moan tearing from her throat. She was coming, coming, coming so hard she thought she might black out. Her hips ground against his as she rode out the waves of pleasure.

The room seemed to spin, the walls blurring together as her mind was overtaken by pleasure. Tiny stars erupted behind her eyes, illuminating the dark corners of her mind. It was like the universe itself had decided to devour her whole.

Jack met her thrust for thrust, his hips lifting off the couch to drive deeper into her. 'Fuck, Trish…' His body tensed beneath her. 'God. God. Jesus FUCK.'

She felt him come, his heat pulsing inside her. He buried himself against her neck, his lips hot on her skin as he groaned her name one last time. She collapsed against him, her forehead resting on his shoulder.

Her body was boneless, her mind blissfully empty.

The intensity of her orgasm, the closeness she felt with Jack in that moment, nearly overwhelmed her. Her body was shaking. And she was crying with relief and release.

She was home. She was loved. She was his.

Jack's strong arms came around her, holding her close, his lips pressing soft kisses to her chin, cheeks, nose. She clung to him as if afraid he might disappear if she let go.

'You okay, Shutterbug?' Jack asked, his voice soft with concern. He pushed a strand off her forehead. 'Was that too much?'

'No,' she whispered, her voice hoarse. 'That was…amazing. How…did that even happen?'

'I have no idea.' He stroked his hands up and down her back. 'That was all you.'

'It was… It was intense. Like there was an explosion of something inside of me.'

'That's generally called an orgasm.'

'I know, dummy.' She swatted his chest lightly. 'But it was more than that. It was like…like everything just clicked into place.'

'I'm honoured. Truly.' Jack wiped her tears away with the pad of his thumb, his eyes full of love. 'You coming on me is the most beautiful thing I have ever witnessed. Might want to do that again.'

She sighed, basking in this proximity to him, the weight of his strength holding her steady. With Jack's arms around her and his heart beating beneath her ear, Trish knew that she had found her place.

She laughed, a watery sound. 'Guess I've got a thing for when you talk like that,' she admitted.

Jack laughed, and the vibration of his chest seeped into

hers. 'I could tell,' he said, a hint of smugness in his smile. 'We'll explore that together.'

And she was ready to.

'But…' He trailed off, his brows knitted together.

'But what? I thought we said, "no more buts", Jack.' For a second, doubt wanted to creep back in, but she kicked the door shut.

'I know, but… Well…poor Mrs Chen.'

Trish laughed so hard that her chest rattled against Jack's. 'We might've scarred her for life.'

Jack grinned. 'Think it's safe to say she'll have some stories for her knitting circle.'

'Oh God.' Trish buried her face in his shoulder, her giggles muffled by his skin.

They stayed like that for a while, their bodies entwined, their hearts beating as one.

It was messy, it was sweaty, it was real. Complicated. And galaxies away from perfect.

Thank fuck.

Epilogue

One year later…

Trish adjusted her camera settings, capturing Jack Jr.'s epic eye roll as Phil belted out *All I Want for Christmas* for the fifth time that morning. The fairy lights twinkled in the bokeh behind him, creating perfect little stars.

'Da, make him stop,' Jack Jr. groaned, flopping dramatically onto the couch.

'Naw, let the wee man sing,' Jack called from the kitchen, where something smelled suspiciously like burning toast. 'It's Christmas, pal.'

Beth sprawled on her stomach under the tree, arranging and rearranging presents with military precision. 'Trish, you have to open this one first.' She pushed a small lumpy package wrapped toward Trish's feet. 'We all picked it.'

'Even me,' Phil announced, pausing his Mariah Carey tribute.

'Oh, I wonder what it could be.' Trish smiled. She loved the three little mites with all her heart.

Morning light spilled through the windows, catching dust

motes that danced like snow. Trish lowered her camera, settling cross-legged on the floor beside Beth.

Her phone pinged. Another text from her mother, no doubt with more subtle digs about 'wasting her potential'. One year later and she still couldn't let it go.

Her problem.

The previous Christmas message had been a masterpiece of passive-aggressive concern: 'That curator position at the Tate is still open. Simon says they'd love to have you. Much more suitable than…whatever it is you're doing up there.'

Whatever it is. Like five spring weddings already booked wasn't real work. Like her commissions for the *Highland Herald* didn't matter. Like her first exhibition opening next month in Oban was just pretending to be an artist. Small jobs, maybe. Local jobs, definitely. But they let her tell real stories about real people.

And wasn't that what photography was meant to be?

But the messages had lost their power to wound. Hard to care about that when three little voices were leading you in a Christmas morning dance-off to holiday classics.

Trish slid her phone deeper into her pocket, focusing on Beth's excited face as she arranged presents.

The smell of burning toast grew stronger. 'Jack?' Trish called. 'Need a hand there? Should I ring the fire brigade?'

'All under control!' His voice carried over the sound of scraping. 'Mostly.'

'Trish!' Beth tugged her sleeve. 'You're not looking!'

'Sorry, my love.'

The light ignited Beth's hair, turning it into gleaming copper.

'Open it!' Phil bounced on his toes, his small body nearly vibrating with excitement.

'Okay, okay. I'm on it.' Trish peeled back the paper. It revealed a wooden key painted in wobbly rainbow stripes and glittery stars.

'It's a symbol,' Beth explained very seriously. 'Because…' she made a dramatic pause, '…we want you to move in with us! Not just stay over sometimes.'

'Yeah,' Junior added, trying to sound casual. 'Your flat's tiny, and you're always here, anyway.'

'And you make better pancakes than Da,' Phil stated.

'Oi!' Jack appeared in the doorway, bearing slightly charred toast. 'I heard that.'

Something tender pushed against Trish's ribs as she traced the painted key with her finger, feeling each bump and ridge of dried acrylic. Her nail caught on a thick droplet of paint, and something caught in her chest, too.

'You all want this?' The words came out smaller than she'd meant them to, like they'd shrunk under the weight of what this meant. A home, a proper home, with people who chose her. Not because they had to but because they wanted to.

'Duh.' Junior rolled his eyes again. 'We wouldn't have spent three hours painting that thing if we didn't.'

'Even Maw thinks it's a good idea,' Beth said. 'She thinks you're good for Da because you make him do actual adult stuff sometimes.'

During the past year, Trish had watched the custody battlefield transform into neutral ground. Now, Jack and Melissa actually talked instead of trading barbed texts, and the kids bounced between homes without that awful tension. Last week, they'd all managed to sit through a school concert together and even grabbed a fish supper after.

Jack set the toast down and perched on the arm of the couch. 'No pressure, though. If you're not ready—'

'Yes.' The word burst out before he could finish. 'Yes, I want to move in.'

Phil launched himself at her with the force of a small missile. Beth squealed. Even Jack Jr. cracked a genuine smile.

'Thank fuck,' Jack exhaled. 'Because I already cleared out half my closet.'

'Language!' Beth and Trish said in unison, making everyone laugh.

Through her viewfinder, she captured Jack collecting wrapping paper, his Santa hat askew. The morning light framed his profile just right. God, she loved photographing him when he wasn't paying attention. The way his whole face softened around the kids.

Beth was sorting her art supplies by colour while Junior tested his new headphones, already lost in whatever game he was playing. Jack dropped onto the floor beside her, pulling her against his chest.

His breath tickled her ear as he whispered, 'I love you, Patricia Gabriela Velasco-Whitmore.'

Her heart stopped, then expanded to infinity. Those words, in his voice, with her full name – the name she'd spent years trying to shake off, sounded like music.

'I love you too,' she whispered back, meaning it with everything she had.

The truth smacked her square in the chest, hard enough to wind her. She was madly in love with this man – a love so deep it settled in her marrow, unshakeable and permanent. The kind that stitched itself into every future she could imagine. She adored his kids. This wasn't the life she'd planned. Her mother would have an aneurysm if she could see her now, sitting on a floor strewn with toy cars and glitter, watching a postie try to untangle fairy lights while his kids offered increasingly unhelpful advice.

But it felt right. Like finally exhaling after holding her breath for years.

'Da, that bit's wonky,' Beth pointed out.

'Your face is wonky,' Junior fired back, making Phil guffaw.

'Hey, Shutterbug.' Jack's voice pulled her back. 'Stop

thinking so loud, and help me with this technological nightmare.'

'You're a Scottish postie, not a Victorian time traveller,' she teased, setting her camera aside. 'They're just fairy lights.'

Their fingers brushed as she took the lights, sending sparks up her arm. Ridiculous, really – they'd done far more than touch hands, but he still made her feel like a teenager with her first crush.

'See?' She untangled the strand with practised ease.

'Show-off.' But his smile was so bright it put the star on top of the tree to shame.

This was it, she realised. This was what Marc could never give her, what her parents would never understand. Not just love – but freedom. Freedom to be completely herself and be loved for it.

Phil demolished his second mince pie, scattering crumbs across his Batman pyjamas. Her camera sat idle in her lap. The painted key dug into her palm, each glob of glitter telling its own story. Beth's careful planning, Junior's pretend-casual contribution, Phil's enthusiasm spilling outside the lines. A family effort.

Her family now. The thought still hit her out of nowhere sometimes.

'Da, you've got jam in your beard.' Beth reached up to swipe at Jack's face with her sleeve.

'Leave it,' Jack grinned. 'I'm saving it for later.'

Trish's chest filled with a warm, steady certainty. She gave Beth a kiss on the cheek and hugged Phil tight, breathing in his little boy smell of sleep and sugar. Her camera sat forgotten beside her, but for once, she didn't mind missing the shot. Some moments were better lived than captured.

– THE END –

Want to read all about how Jack took Trish home to the Highlands? Read the FREE bonus scene here: beatricebradshaw.com/christmas-village

Love in the Scottish Christmas Village is the fifth book in the 'Escape to Scotland'-series of standalone romances:

Book 1: *Love in the Scottish Winter Highlands*
Book 2: *Love on the Scottish Spring Isle*
Book 3: *Love on the Scottish Summer Coast*
Book 4: *Love in the Scottish Fall Forest*

Thank you so, so much for reading. If you enjoyed Trish and Jack's story, **please take a minute to leave a review on Amazon or Goodreads**. It doesn't need to be epic. Just two sentences can help the book a lot, and I'd be grateful. <3

Read on for a sample of book 1, *Love in the Scottish Winter Highlands* – the story that started it all.

Keep reading… >>>

Love in the Scottish Winter Highlands

CHAPTER 1

Pale morning light pierced through the clouds. The cold air smelled like peat fire and rain, like smoke, like frost, like everything that she loved about winter. The hills around this small town were almost as chalky as the sky. From a distance, they looked like folds of a wool blanket. It was still early. Marla flipped up the collar of her peacoat and walked along the cobblestoned street. Despite the November chill, her face was glowing.

This place, half-snuggled in a valley, was a far cry from the busy, tiring city of London she had called home for fourteen years and left behind yesterday morning.

Yet here she was. In Scotland.

Marla swallowed, unsure of what lay ahead. The past few weeks had been a whirlwind. A swirl of conflicting emotions surged in her chest. There was a rush of anticipation, yes, but also a warning that nagged at her mind, reminding her of the risks. It was the glimmer of possibility, too hard to ignore, that made her cheeks flush.

I'm really doing this, aren't I?

As she sauntered to her appointment with the solicitor, she took in the sights and sounds of Kilcranach's old core. Side roads led up the hill and wound their way through the village like a gemstone necklace that someone had carelessly dropped. In contrast, the high street was built in a straight line and flanked by quaint shops with whitewashed facades. With their slate roofs and pointed gables, the houses looked like they had been there since the time of Mary, Queen of Scots. Or at least since some enlightened, eighteenth-century landowner had stuffed his crofters into efficient lodgings so they could collect kelp while sheep grazed on what used to be their land. The sea, as the screeching chorus of gulls in the background announced, wasn't very far away.

Behind a bend, Marla noticed the small castle looming in the distance. A structure with blonde sandstone walls, over-grown with ivy. Even from afar, it appeared as sad as in the photos. And calling it a castle was a stretch. It looked more defeated than defensive. Although it must once have been an inviting eighteenth-century country house. Marla imagined glamorous balls and hunting parties with people wearing tweed.

In truth, she had no concept of what the Scottish nobility used to do in their extensive spare time two hundred years ago. Even two years ago, for that matter.

Today, the former grand house was a neglected three-storey building with dull panes in its many large mullion windows. It seemed tired, forgotten, and lonely. This house had the weight of well over two hundred years pressing down on it – and it appeared as if it was done pushing back.

Her house now. Her weight.

Marla snorted in disbelief, and a frosty cloud of breath formed in front of her nose. What the hell had happened? Four weeks ago, she had been living her life in London, working as an oncology nurse for the National Health Service NHS. Mostly reading books while curled up on her couch. Completely unspectacular and utterly intentional. After everything, Marla had designed her life to be as stable and safe as possible. A solid wooden drawer with cosy velvet lining.

Until one phone call changed it all.

She had just returned from running errands when her mobile rang. At first, she thought it was a prank. Who wouldn't?

'Good afternoon! Marla Wilson? You will not have heard of me, but I have something important to tell you,' said the male voice on the other end.

'Not at all a bizarre thing to say. Bye.'

'Wait! There is something you must know,' the unknown caller cut in.

'Oh, really? Must I?' Marla's day off had been unpleasant so far. She was in a *mood*. 'Let me guess: you're calling in the name of Prince Harry and need cash for a charity? Or better still, you're a Nigerian prince and need my help with wiring four million dollars to my account? Guess what, I don't believe in princes and—'

'Miss Wilson, there seems to be a misunderstanding. My name is William Collins. I work with Arniston Solicitors, and the reason I'm calling you today is to inform you of an inheritance.'

'Ha! I knew it. No thanks,' she scoffed.

'Does the name Gordon Wilson ring a bell?'

Marla gasped. That was her grandda's name.

How does he... What...?

Anger welled up inside her. 'What do you know of my grandfather? Is this a cruel joke? My grandda died two years ago. Don't you feel ashamed using dead people's names in a scam?'

'No, no! Of course not, Miss Wilson. It is just... How do I put this delicately? It seems that in his youth, Gordon Wilson had made an acquaintance of some...emotional significance. Let us leave it at that.'

'Pardon me?' She noticed a trace of shrillness in her voice.

'I would much prefer to discuss the details with you in person. But as far as we know, he knew the young Lady Hamilton, and it appears that Gordon Wilson...made a lasting impression on her.'

'Lady who?'

'Lady Helena Cecilia Hamilton,' he said.

'Never heard of her.'

'I see. Well, that is not at all surprising. She lived a secluded life. Lady Hamilton passed away six months ago.'

'I don't know what to say. Eh...I'm sorry for your loss?'

'Thank you for your sympathy,' Mr Collins said.

Something in his voice resonated with Marla. She recognised the incorruptible truth of grief. He must have held that lady in great esteem. Marla paced up and down her hallway, the shopping bags still by the door.

'She was our client for many decades,' he continued. 'A good person, an amiable woman. One of a kind. She died without an heir, but her will – here the entire affair becomes more than a little unorthodox – unmistakably states that in these circumstances, the castle and estate should pass to the living descendants of Gordon Wilson.'

'What? Okay. That's...mental. My grandfather mentioned no lady. Ever. And I'm sure my gran wouldn't have approved of other women in his life. If you know what I mean.'

'Certainly, Miss Wilson. I did not intend to insinuate—'

'Right. So, wait. You're telling me that a complete stranger left a castle – an entire castle – to my grandda and his offspring? You can't be serious.'

'I assure you, this is not a joke to me, Miss Wilson.'

'Oh, I don't think this is funny either. And I have a lot of questions. Like why didn't he tell anyone about any of this? Ever? What on earth is going on?' Her voice rose. 'How am I supposed to even know who my grandda was dating in his youth? That's wrong,' she huffed. 'And who in their right mind doesn't give their godforsaken castle to the National Trust instead of leaving it to a stranger? Doesn't that sound suspiciously wrong to you?'

'To you.'

'Who?'

'To you. She left Hazelbrae House to you. We have done some digging, you see. Since he passed two years ago and your mother in 1992, you are the only living blood relative of Gordon Wilson. Unless you have children, of course, but we could not find any records,' he explained. 'Hence, it follows – according to Lady Hamilton's will – that it is you who inherits her estate.'

Marla flopped onto a chair, ungracefully landing on the cupcake she had bought herself as a treat and placed there when her phone rang. She didn't notice it. All she noticed was a tingling numbness ascending from her legs, along with an uncomfortable ringing in her ears. After a pause, she said, 'No siblings. No children. Neither existent nor planned.'

'I apologise if this sounds intrusive. But you certainly see that we—'

'Estate,' Marla mumbled. 'What does that even mean?'

'I would much rather discuss everything in person. But for now, I can tell you that the inheritance encompasses a large, listed house with a few acres here in Scotland. Although the building is in a state, most unfortunately, and the land is a fraction of what it once used to be.'

'Sorry, I have to ask, for the record – are you for real? Do you have any proof of whatever you're saying, like…right now?' Not that any serious, self-respecting scammer would answer that question with anything close to the truth. Nonetheless, she had to ask.

'I guarantee that this is a most serious and lawful matter.'

She let out a breath. 'You understand that I can't simply believe everything a random stranger tells me on the phone? That's one thing my grandda taught me,' Marla said, mostly to herself, feeling the comforting weight of Gordon's small knife in the side pocket of her jeans. Along with the all-too-familiar twinge of loss.

'Yes, Miss Wilson. That is sensible. I would expect nothing less. I can send you all the relevant information and preliminary legal documents, the title, photographs, et cetera. And then, if you're interested, Arniston Solicitors would love to welcome you to Kilcranach.'

That had been one month ago. The town hall clock towered above Marla. Its long, thin hands showed a quarter past nine. Almost time for her meeting with William Collins to finalise the particulars of this odd inheritance. She was a few minutes early. But her mind was racing, and she couldn't sit in the car for one more second.

I can't believe it. What if it's too much for me?

Initially, she'd been less than thrilled at the thought of inheriting a castle from a stranger – everybody knew those houses were bottomless money pits – let alone the mystery surrounding her grandda's dubious ex-lady-friend or whatever position Helena *Whatshername* Hamilton had once held in his life.

It was Marla's pal Trish who had encouraged her to take the leap of faith, stuff her car with her favourite clothes and books, and move to Kilcranach to take on her inheritance – a property she hadn't even set foot in.

'Marl, what are you talking about? A flipping castle in Scotland, for fuck's sake. That's an amazing opportunity.

Think what you could do with that!' Trish had squealed from beneath her cloud of brown curls. 'That's how all those Mills & Boon novels start! And if it's shit, you can sell it for a few million pounds to a Danish billionaire and bam! No more worrying about pensions or any of that. That's you, sorted for life!'

Marla couldn't help but smile at the memory of Trish's innate enthusiasm and unwavering faith in the world. Most of the time, it was unfounded. But it somehow still made things better. Inexplicably. Or maybe even magically.

She moved past the bookshop. A narrow, three-storey, timber-framed building with a small café on the ground floor. A few people were grabbing a coffee to go. There was a pair of American tourists in trainers, hunched over their phones.

Probably a lot fewer of them in the Highlands in November than during summer.

The faint aroma of roasted beans and the scent of yellowed books wafted into the cold air. A young woman wearing a pointy hat and a black coat was peering into a shop window. Her long, emerald-green hair was fashioned into a braid and flowing down her shoulders on top of a woollen tartan shawl. She looked like a witch. Maybe this tiny town had more edge than Marla had imagined.

Whatever her doubts, and there were plenty, she was here now. After having drained a reassuring bottle of Bordeaux with Trish, Marla had made a promise to herself. Come rain or shine – and considering that this was Scotland, rain was the much more likely scenario – she would find a way to make it work.

This wasn't just an unexpected inheritance. It was a once-in-a-lifetime opportunity to give back to her colleagues in the NHS, who worked so hard to save their patients' lives. Create a retreat for tired doctors and nurses. Like herself. Like the ones that tried to save her mum twenty-five years ago or the ones who took care of her grandparents at the end. Renovating Hazelbrae was also a way to be connected to her grandda. To honour his memory, to find out who he had really been and where he was from.

And to start over after all the loss and sorrow.

The solicitor's office was in one of the historic buildings just off the town square. The heavy door creaked as Marla opened it, revealing a claustrophobically small lobby. It wasn't even large enough to contain a gathering of five people. Two timeworn oak chairs and an equally ancient wooden reception desk testified to the age of the office. The darkly panelled walls were adorned with antique paintings of ships conquering raging waves. It smelled of dust and varnish, with a slight salty tang. The entire room seemed like the wooden sea chest of a nineteenth-century naval officer.

Behind the panelled desk sat a woman with white streaks in her red bob, knitting what looked like a Fair Isle jumper. She didn't so much as lift her head when the door creaked.

'Hi. Good morning.' Marla plastered on a polite smile.

Now the woman looked up. She gave a nod and put down her needles. 'Morning. Welcome to Arniston Solicitors. How can I help you?'

Marla explained who she was and why she was there. The receptionist nodded again. This time, with squinted eyes. As if she couldn't believe it. Neither could Marla.

'Of course. Mr Collins is expecting you, Miss Wilson.' She rose from her chair. 'Please follow me. And watch your step. It's a wee bit uneven.'

Marla walked behind her up a narrow spiral staircase with ornate cast iron steps and rails that were cold and coarse under her fingers.

'Ah, Miss Wilson,' Mr Collins called from the back room. 'Welcome to Arniston Solicitors! Glad you made it. How was the journey? Not entirely unpleasant, I hope?' Mr Collins emerged from his office wearing a tweed suit with a waistcoat and a pocket watch, round glasses perched at the end of his pointed nose. He looked like an obscure side character in an unpublished Sherlock Holmes story, scholarly and anachronistic to the point of eccentricity. Much more interesting in person than on the phone. Marla liked him right away.

Mr Collins ushered her into his tiny office, where several stacks of documents were scattered around the room. The slope of the roof was low and crooked, Marla could hardly stand upright. A square window let in a few resilient rays of winter morning sunlight, illuminating several shelves of books lined up like soldiers at attention.

Over a cup of tea, Mr Collins explained the legal details of the inheritance. There was no family dispute, since this was a minor branch of the Hamiltons without relatives. The property had been surveyed and valued, the inventory and other forms completed, taxes and debts paid. So was the basic upkeep for a year, excluding insurance. Now was the time for the title transfer.

Marla understood all of it, or so she hoped. Dealing with small print had never been her core strength. She would inherit Hazelbrae House with about ten acres of surrounding land. Apparently, Helena Hamilton had declared that the house was not to be turned into a museum. 'Hazelbrae is neither a shrine nor a zoo, it is a home,' were her words, as related by Mr Collins. Miraculously, there was no remaining debt on the estate, but there had been no renovations since the 1980s. Good bones, neglected state. The estimated renovation and conservation costs were... Astronomical didn't even begin to describe it.

And yet... Marla had felt drawn to Hazelbrae since she had first seen the pictures in Mr Collins' e-mail.

It was still baffling, though. 'What about their relationship? Were they...' Marla trailed off.

'Lady Hamilton and your grandfather?'

'Yes, those two. Who else would I be talking about?' She narrowed her eyes.

'Sadly, there is not much more that I can tell you.' Mr Collins adjusted his glasses. 'She changed her will shortly before her serious health problems started, and I never had the opportunity to ask her personally. It is all a mystery. Or simply private.'

He dug out a document and followed the lines with his index finger. 'According to Lady Hamilton's will, in which she bequeathed her estate to his family, Gordon Wilson was, and I quote, "the truest, dearest friend I ever had. I owe him my life and more than I could ever repay." End of quote.'

'What's that supposed to mean? Did he give her a kidney or something?'

'I could not tell you. Lady Hamilton was a private and fascinating woman.' Shifting his glasses again, he continued. 'My guess? Since your grandfather was from this area and moved away when he was twenty, if our research is correct, they most likely knew each other in their youth. Mr Wilson must have been a friend or confidant to Lady Hamilton. Class difference aside.'

Mr Collins leaned back in his squeaking swivel chair and folded his hands in his lap. 'We could try to investigate further. Although I have not the slightest idea how. We looked at her correspondence, but it didn't include any significant private letters or documents, unfortunately.'

Marla shrugged. 'I'm just so curious. I mean, who wouldn't be? There must be more to this story, but it seems we're not getting anywhere right now. So be it.' She straightened her shoulders. 'All right then, Mr Solicitor. Let's do this.'

With the legal details outlined, explained, and mostly understood, Marla picked up Mr Collins' pen in her right hand, her left hand on the document. She felt the tight weave of the paper fibres under her fingertips. The pen had an old-fashioned shape and a black, lacquered finish that had been worn smooth by generations of signers. Marla took a deep breath.

A few circles and scratches later, Mr Collins announced, 'Congratulations, Miss Wilson. You are now the proud owner of Hazelbrae House. Good luck.'

Marla left the solicitor's office exhilarated, bordering on terrified. To calm her jittery limbs, she decided to walk from the village to the castle and explore the area. It was eleven. Plenty of time in the day.

Time to make plans.

Marla would restore Hazelbrae House, find a new purpose and her roots here. It dawned on her how much she had been longing for a new beginning.

There was no way back. She had rented out her tiny flat in London and quit her job. A half-ruined castle in this remote Scottish village was her home now, which left only one possible conclusion: she must be insane.

Chapter 2

Niall trudged along the churned-up dirt path through the forest on his inspection rounds, his boots squelching in patches of moss and mud. Winter had stripped the trees of their foliage, leaving behind brittle branches outlined against the hazy sky, like a charcoal sketch.

A heaviness crept into the air. He knew the Highland weather and these woods like the back of his hand. This was his land, after all. It had been his father's and his grandfather's before that. But Niall didn't feel a sense of connection. Not anymore. Only obligation, to an extent.

Besides his own forestry, he had been an estate manager

on the Hamilton land for thirteen years now. Close to a third of his life. It was a job that needed to be done, and he happened to be the one doing it. There was nothing more to it.

'Barclay? Barclay!' Niall called out for his dog. He paused and listened. Nothing but the long, rolling sigh of the breeze as it rustled through the branches. Niall turned around to survey the territory, to reassure himself that everything here was fine, that nothing was out of place. There were only familiar sights, like the old, gnarled ash tree with its branches twisted into shapes resembling faces. He called again, and this time he heard a bark in the distance.

That silly bugger can't help himself, he thought affectionately.

Thirty seconds later, the black and white border collie came shooting out of the thicket towards him. Niall smiled and scratched Barclay behind his ears. 'You sure love to run off on your own, don't you, boy?' At this time of year, there was nothing to be wary of on this part of the estate, and he allowed his faithful companion these independent excursions.

At least Barclay always returned to him, no matter how far he had run off. It was some comfort that there was one thing he could always rely on – the unconditional love of his dog. 'Let's get going, eh?' And the two of them plodded along the same trail they always followed, Barclay alongside his owner and friend. It was in fleeting moments like these when Niall was almost at peace.

Almost.

As they walked, Niall noticed the ambassadors of winter, like a stray snowflake settling on his shoulder, the chill in the air, the flurries of fallen leaves being tousled by the breeze. Out here, in the middle of the forest behind Hazelbrae House, there was always an air of peace, a serene atmosphere that he had come to cherish.

Hazelbrae.

It had been over half a year since old Lady Hamilton had

died in the care home where she had spent the last months of her life. A heart attack, they said. Niall still didn't know what was going to happen to that place. That unsettled him. He didn't like loose ends.

But, more importantly, it had brought his plans to an indefinite halt.

He had mulled over it for much longer than anybody in Kilcranach would ever have suspected, but when the developer had approached him with an offer to buy his land about a year and a half ago, Niall had been ripe and ready to make a deal. He wanted to move on. There was no spark of excitement or new beginning about it. This wasn't about opening a new chapter.

No. It was about finally closing an old one.

Because, more often than not, Niall felt trapped – like a solitary wanderer in the frame of a gloomy landscape painting. Forever doomed to roam the moors.

Or forest, in his case.

With the money from selling his acreage, he would likely never have to work again. At least if he lived sensibly. He could buy a boat and live on it. Go sailing. It used to be his favourite hobby when he was a student, his soul unbent, his heart unbroken, his light undimmed.

Before…everything.

He hadn't done it in ages. But he rather wanted to be at the mercy of the elements than at the mercy of the memories that surrounded him here at every turn.

Niall stopped and zipped up his lined wax jacket. He emitted a cloud of white breath and resumed the walk while his thoughts wandered in their own direction. He couldn't say that he had been pleased with the plans the developer had for the area – a huge luxury hunting, shooting, and fishing billionaire playground with a spa for clients with helicopters and such – but it could bring a few jobs to Kilcranach. To people who needed it. Frankly, he cared little about the details. Times were changing. That was a fact. Better to change with them and make the most of it. He had been looking forward to it.

But just when he had started to feel something akin to hope, Niall had learned that Hazelbrae, sitting in the middle of it all, was a crucial part of the deal. They wanted the entire bloody thing. Not just his land. No, the crumbling mansion on the hill was the cherry on top of their billionaire-property cake.

Niall had tried to convince them otherwise. In vain. He had also made several attempts to persuade old Lady Hamilton to sell. To no avail.

A part of him knew she would never be willing to cut ties to her home of over seventy years, the place where she had been born.

Still, he had to try.

Not that he didn't understand her. Hazelbrae was her home, the place where her family's memories lived. Their presence was tangible in every nook of the house, starting with the faded pictures and paintings that spoke volumes about family roots that ran generations deep within this forgotten corner of the world.

No matter how eloquently Niall argued when they discussed estate matters, neither facts nor feelings made any difference. Lady Hamilton's friendly but firm response was always the same.

'My dear, dear boy,' she would say in her commanding voice, only a little frail. 'Don't you know that all of Hazelbrae is part of me? And I wouldn't sell my own arm now, would I? And what would your father think of that?' she had asked, patting his hand and shaking her head.

How am I supposed to know? It's not like you can phone people in the afterlife.

The last time they had spoken about it was a month before

she suffered a second stroke and had to move away into care. A good six months before her death.

She had finally left this place for good. He was still stuck here.

Niall had even tried to sell his land discreetly to other candidates. Unsuccessfully. Unless it was an absurdly large acreage with a romantic castle, a potential nature reserve, or one of those tiny symbolic bits of land with a fantasy title, no one seemed prepared to buy land in the Scottish Highlands.

The canopy of wiry branches parted to reveal the decaying grandeur of Hazelbrae in the distance, a splendid house in a state of forgotten glory. Grass, moss, and birch saplings sprouting from the black rain gutters. All giving silent testament to its neglect.

Only a few harsh winters away from falling into utter disrepair, Niall reckoned.

Astonishingly, the roof still held up, withstanding the years, the wind, and the intense rain here in the West. He hadn't set foot inside of Hazelbrae since… not in a long time. There was a quick sting of pain and loss. A feeling as familiar to him as these ancient woodlands. Relentless murmurs of his unforgivable mistake. Niall shook his head in an attempt to shake off his memories.

He didn't know how Lady Hamilton had spent her last time there or what the inside of Hazelbrae might look like. All he knew was this half-ruined grand house stood between him and his ticket out of Kilcranach. Between him and his hope of lifting the crushing weight that had been suffocating him for six years. Whether he liked it or not, Hazelbrae was the key to his freedom and peace.

Barclay dashed towards a babbling brook beneath a small slope. Following the path to the left would lead them past the gates of the grand old house.

Och, why the heck not? Let's see how deep those cracks really are.

He whistled. Barclay obeyed and came back as fast as an arrow. Niall and his dog walked side by side through the woods.

Suddenly, he heard a voice from somewhere in the nearer distance.

'You treacherous damn shitty shit tree!'

Barclay pricked up his ears. Niall frowned.

What the…

'I hate you! I hate you from the bottom of my heart! Stupid fucking tree!'

Yes, that sounded like a woman. An *angry* woman. The only problem was that her voice seemed to come from…above?

Barclay jolted towards a mature oak tree and barked.

'Well, hello there! Awww, look at you. Such a good boy,' the voice said to Barclay, all anger vanished. Niall took a few steps closer to the tree. He squinted in disbelief as he peered up at the top.

A woman in a dark blue pea coat was clinging to one of the oak's branches. Her jeans were splattered with mud, and her complexion was bright red. She stared at him with a mix of surprise and suspicion. Niall blinked in bewilderment. He had no inkling who this woman was or what she was doing here.

In a tree, no less.

One of his trees, by the way.

'Hi,' she called out. 'Hello! Oh, thank God. Do you think you could help me down? I can't seem to do it on my own. Not that I would normally admit that to anyone.' She laughed nervously.

The warm sound of her voice tingled in his ears. Niall furrowed his eyebrows in puzzlement. Why would a normal grown-up person climb a tree? He scoured his brain for explanations, but there were none that made any sense to him.

'What are you doing up there, if you don't mind me asking?'

'Major Tom to ground control: might I suggest I tell the tale once I've returned to Planet Earth?'

'I'm afraid I sold any spaceships or flying tin cans to the charity shop ages ago anyway,' Niall replied.

'Ah, so you're a funny one. But I'm about ten seconds away from a proper panic attack, so if you don't mind.'

'*You* started with Major Tom.' Niall noticed he was smiling. Barclay wagged his tail in excitement. That there on the tree was not the usual squirrel.

'Get me down. Now!' she insisted. 'I mean…please?'

'All right, all right. Let's see.' Niall examined the situation. It seemed that the crucial branch about halfway down had broken, preventing her from descending the same way she must have got up. He would have been irked by the sight of damage done to the trees under his care and supervision. But he knew the inhabitants of his forest well. This particular tree was a bit of a troublemaker that had been worrying him for a while. 'Can you turn around?' he asked.

'Are you joking?' She sounded slightly angry again.

'You know, I could continue my walk and pretend this never happened.' He was oddly enjoying this bizarre encounter.

'You would not.'

'Try me.'

'Okay, I guess I could make a quarter turn.'

'Brave girl,' Niall said. 'If you turn and slowly try to sit down on the branch that you're standing on right now, you could jump.'

'And break my ankle? Not a fat chance,' she said resolutely.

'I could catch you, you know.'

'You? But you're a stranger! How do I know you won't take a step to the side and let me land face-first in the mud?'

'Guess you won't know for sure until you try.'

'Honestly.' She looked dispirited. 'This is not a good way to encourage someone with trust issues.'

He folded his arms. 'Sometimes you have to take a leap of faith.'

'Really? Okay, as soon as I'm on firm ground again, we'll go into town and get matching "Live, Laugh, Love" tattoos.'

And Niall laughed. A sound so rare that Barclay barked twice in confusion.

The woman in the tree shifted her feet awkwardly, still clinging to the higher branch. Gradually, and with wobbly knees, she lowered herself into a sitting position, while holding onto the bark of the thick tree trunk.

'Okay, I'm sitting.' She looked relieved.

'I can see that.'

'And now I jump?'

Niall positioned himself underneath her. It was less than six feet, not too terrible. He spread his arms out. 'And now you jump.'

She landed on him like a hundred sacks of flour. The momentum pushed Niall backwards, staggering. She wasn't a fairy, this was a woman of substance. He lost his balance, and with a thud, they both landed on the mossy, leafy forest ground.

Barclay ran circles around them, while Niall lay flat on his back. Judging by the pain, his coccyx must have hit a thick pinecone or something.

'Ouch.'

'Sorry,' she replied, sitting astride him.

Niall stared into a pair of grey eyes with a silver glint under long, dark lashes. Tiny beads of sweat had formed a tiara at her hairline. There was a dab of dirt on the tip of her nose.

She bit her lower lip. 'I'm Marla, by the way. Thank you for being my mattress, Major Tom.'

Barclay licked her cheek and she let out a low, contented giggle.

Deep inside, Niall had always suspected that there must be some magical creatures living in these woods.

He just never thought they would be so…gorgeous.

Escape to Scotland right now and get *Love in the Scottish Winter Highlands*!

Glossary

- Awright = alright
- Bampot = a fool, a mad person
- Baws = balls aka testicles
- Braw day = a beautiful day
- Bevvy = drink
- Ceilidh = Scottish country dance in groups and pairs
- Da = dad
- Daft = silly, foolish, stupid
- Dinnae = don't
- Eejit = idiot
- Fae = from
- Faffin' aboot = wasting time, messing about
- Gie = give
- Gie's a break = give us a break, stop bothering me
- Haud yer wheesht = hold your tongue/ shut up and listen
- Hogmanay = New Year's Eve
- Isnae = isn't
- Ken = know
- Maw = mum

- Nae/naw = no
- Numpty = idiot
- Ootside = outside
- Pish = piss
- Steamin' = very drunk
- Weans = children

Resource: Dictionary of the Scottish Language https://dsl.ac.uk/

Author's note

Dearest Reader,

This book was written in a rather short time. Honestly, I didn't even know if I'd finish it. Yet here we are. Jack would probably say it's because of sheer grit, but I like to think a little magic helped me along the way.

I can hardly believe we've reached the end of the 'Escape to Scotland'-series. When I first began this journey with *Love in the Scottish Winter Highlands*, I never imagined how much life, love, and chaos this little village of Kilcranach would come to hold. Not just for my characters, but for me, too.

I always knew I wanted the series to end where it began: in Kilcranach, our favourite little fictional Highland village, somewhere near Oban on Scotland's west coast.

What I didn't know, at least not right away, was that this would be Jack and Trish's story. Looking back now, it feels inevitable.

From the beginning of book one, *Love in the Scottish Winter Highlands*, Trish has been there as Marla's best friend. After everything Marla had been through, I wanted her to have someone kind and fun by her side. And then Jack turned up out of nowhere – striding across the village square in his postie uniform with his cheeky grin while I was writing. I knew I wanted him to be a single dad and a loving co-parent, to show a kind and caring father.

I'll admit, I didn't see their story coming at first. But when I wrote the novella *Kilts, Kisses & Chaos*, they met in the middle of Hazelbrae's grand opening. And when they sneaked into that linen closet, I realised I wasn't in charge anymore. Jack and Trish had found each other, and there was no turning back.

It had always been them.

I was just the last to know.

Spending time in Kilcranach again was such a joy, and writing this book felt like a reunion with old friends. Gwen with her pointy hat and her parents, Mrs Bellbottom and her leopard coat, Niall and Marla, Barclay and Muffin, Bert and Fiona, William Collins – solicitor by day and dancing devil by night… Thinking about saying goodbye to them, and closing Hazelbrae's doors for the last time, genuinely makes me emotional.

If I've done my job, this quirky little small-town community has become your group of friends, too. Kilcranach will always be a place you can revisit, where the kettle is on and the fire's warm. It's been an honour to share this journey, and I'm endlessly grateful for your support. As you turn the final page, know that a piece of Kilcranach (and my heart) goes with you. And I hope that whenever you pick up this book – or book one – it feels like coming home. To Scotland.

With love, gratitude, and a wistful tear,

About the Author

Beatrice Bradshaw writes spicy and cosy small-town contemporary romances set in Scotland. Because life can be both.

Photo: Kristy Ashton

Scottish Historian and German journalist/ translator by day and romance author by night, she has escaped from Berlin to Scotland in 2018. And not looked back once.

Beatrice Bradshaw is the pen name/ pseudonym of Jessica Beatrice Wagener – chosen so as not to have German narrative non-fiction confused with her (English) romance books.

She enjoys sharing her love for her adopted home country with others, bringing a sprinkle of the real Scotland into her books.

When she isn't glued to her desk in Glasgow, surrounded by baked goods and coffee, she can be found wandering around in Scottish castles and landscapes, finding peace and stories on cemeteries and in old buildings, or binge-watching romance series online.

Love in the Scottish Christmas Village is her fifth romance novel, the next idea is already in the making and will be published in 2025.

Connect with Beatrice here:
instagram.com/beatricebradshawauthor
facebook.com/beatricebradshawauthor
www.beatricebradshaw.com

Love in the Scottish Christmas Village
By Beatrice Bradshaw

First published in the UK by Jessica B. Wagener under the pen name Beatrice Bradshaw in 2024.

Copyright © Jessica B. Wagener as Beatrice Bradshaw, 2024

Suite 624
Claymore House
145-149 Kilmarnock Road
Glasgow, G41 3JA

Proof reads: Micki McNie

Cover design: Jessica B. Wagener

Print ISBN: 978-1-0685768-3-6
Ebook Edition © November 2024
ISBN: 978-1-0685768-0-5
Version: 2025-11-02

www.ingramcontent.com/pod-product-compliance
Lightning Source LLC
Chambersburg PA
CBHW031258120726
47906CB00003B/805